Books by Betty King
Published by The House of Ulverscroft:

WE ARE TOMORROW'S PAST
THE FRENCH COUNTESS
THE ROSE BOTH RED AND WHITE
MARGARET OF ANJOU
THE LADY MARGARET

○THE CAPTIVE JAMES○

While seeking sanctuary from the ruthless uncle who threatened to deprive him of his future throne as King of Scotland, James Stewart was captured by pirates in the North Sea and delivered to Henry IV of England. Henry was quick to see the advantage of retaining his illustrious prisoner. As the years dragged on — with first Henry V and then his infant son becoming King of England — James grew ever more desperate to return to Scotland. It was not until he had been held prisoner for seventeen years that he found a woman who could uplift him from his sad plight.

First published in Great Britain in 1967

First Large Print Edition
published 2001
by arrangement with
Robert Hale Limited
London

British Library CIP Data

King, Betty, *1919 –*
The captive James.—Large print ed.—
Ulverscroft large print series: romance
1. Love stories
2. Large type books
I. Title
823.9'14 [F]

ISBN 0–7089–4347–0

Published by
F. A. Thorpe (Publishing)
Anstey, Leicestershire

Set by Words & Graphics Ltd.
Anstey, Leicestershire
Printed and bound in Great Britain by
T. J. International Ltd., Padstow, Cornwall

This book is printed on acid-free paper

BETTY KING

THE CAPTIVE JAMES

Complete and Unabridged

ULVERSCROFT
Leicester

Acknowledgments

For the historical accuracy of this book I am deeply indebted to the works of E. W. M. Balfour-Melville, *James I, King of Scots*, Sir James Ramsay, *York and Lancaster*, E. F. Jacob, *The Fifteenth Century*.

My gratitude is extended to the staffs of the Enfield Public Library, the British Museum Reading Room, Windsor Castle Library and the Public Records Office of Scotland.

I should also like to thank Colonel R. O. Dennys, O.B.E., F.C.A.; Rouge Croix Pursuivant; Colonel J. R. B. Walker, M.V.O., M.C.; Lancaster Herald, and Mrs. I. Braun for their help and ask my family to accept this novel as a small tribute for their continuing encouragement.

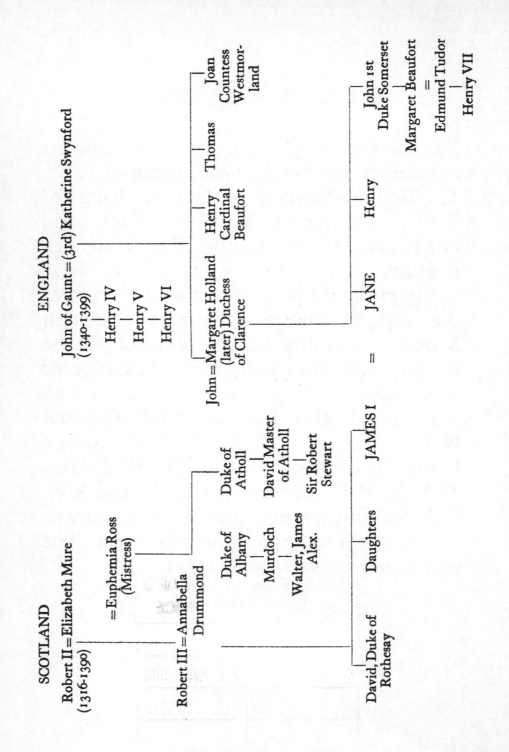

SCOTLAND

Robert II = Elizabeth Mure
(1316-1390)

= Euphemia Ross
(Mistress)

Robert III = Annabella Drummond

Duke of Albany

Murdoch

Walter, James
Alex.

Duke of Atholl

David Master
of Atholl

Sir Robert
Stewart

David, Duke of Rothesay

Daughters

JAMES I

=

ENGLAND

John of Gaunt = (3rd) Katherine Swynford
(1340-1399)

Henry IV
Henry V
Henry VI

John = Margaret Holland
(later) Duchess
of Clarence

Henry
Cardinal
Beaufort

Thomas

Joan
Countess
Westmor-
land

Henry

JANE

John 1st
Duke Somerset

Margaret Beaufort
=
Edmund Tudor

Henry VII

1

James stood at the small window looking, without seeing, as the great waves pounded on the rocks beneath the castle walls. The roar of the blustering January wind filled the chamber but it had not prevented him from hearing the news his tutor, Bishop Wardlaw, had just broken to him.

He gripped the sill and fought manfully to check the pain in his throat which threatened to turn into a sob. He longed for the warm comfort of his mother's arms. As the youngest of the seven children of Robert III of Scotland and Annabella Drummond he had received an abundant share of her affection and at first, when on her death four years before, he had been sent to the austere discipline of the house of the Bishop of St. Andrews, the lack of womanly understanding had proved almost too much for him. A stern self control, however, had helped him face the future and until this moment he had believed the raw places had healed. Without turning he lifted his head.

'Why does my Lord father think it necessary for me to go to France?'

'He thinks you will learn your lessons with more peace at the French Court and at the same time come to speak the language as a native.'

James did not reply at once and Bishop Wardlaw knew that in his logical way he was assessing the meaning of the despatch which Sir David Fleming of Cumbernauld, the King's most trusted friend, had ridden through pouring rain to deliver not an hour since. He realised that the King's desire that his only remaining son and heir should be sent by the earliest possible vessel to the care of the French King was not without precedent. Such a move by an ailing and infirm King could only mean that he considered his heir's life in danger. Danger in this instance could be applied with justification to the Duke of Albany, the King's brother and James' uncle.

The Bishop regarded the stocky twelve year old as he came from the window and stood in front of him. The lock of hair which would fall across his high forehead no matter how often James pushed it back gave his grave face a pathetic appeal and the man spoke more gently than was his custom.

'France boasts a cultured heritage and the climate is warm and sunny. There is much to be said in favour of going there for a short time. You will make new friends and have the opportunity of finding out other countries and people at first hand.'

'It will mean leaving Scotland, which is my home and suits me well enough,' James said slowly. 'I have found no lack of learning in your house, sir; besides, I shall not have Henry with me.'

'Your father does not state that he wishes you to go for ever!' Bishop Wardlaw said with a brightness he was far from feeling.

When the balding Sir David Fleming had managed to retain sufficient breath in his stout frame he had not spared his words as he confided to the Bishop that there was a serious decline in the King's health and that his mind was becoming as sick as his body was feeble. In the opinion of Sir David and many others who had accompanied him to St. Andrews it was obvious that Robert III was failing and that it might be only a question of months before James would be called upon to take his place.

'Go and find Henry and tell him your news; he will more than likely be envious of your going across the sea.'

The thought of sharing the coming departure with his friend, Henry Percy, grandson and heir of the rebellious Earl of Northumberland, seemed to lift James'

3

spirits. He went from the comparative warmth of the sparsely furnished chamber into the icy passages which led to the quarters they shared.

As he closed the door behind him the down draught brought a billow of damp, smoky air from the open hearth and the Bishop called for his page to bring dry faggots and a cup of spiced wine. Comforted by the more cheerful blaze and warmed by the drink he sat in the only chair and huddled his thick robes around his feet.

Although he had known James for little more than a year when he had been sent to Wardlaw, as the newly created Bishop of St. Andrews, to receive his education, he was fond of the boy. James had a lively and reasoning mind, which given proper training, would develop into an outstanding intellect. This intelligence James had inherited from his mother, Annabella Drummond, for his father the King, although a pleasant amiable man when young, had had the misfortune to be kicked by a horse before he was thirty years old and this accident had impaired his health and his zest for life. It was as a direct result of this tragic occurrence that the old King Robert II had entrusted the government of Scotland to his second son, the Duke of Albany, leaving Robert titular heir only.

Albany was something of an enigma to Wardlaw. The duke was a large bluff man with a ruddy complexion and a mass of fair hair. His manner was almost too friendly and the bonhomie which he extended to his fellow nobles was bordering on the ingratiating. He had a careless open handed generosity to his cronies which the Bishop mistrusted; it was as if the man had something to hide and sought to cover it by buying popularity. The Bishop could not feel at ease in his company but he thought it unlikely that the King had had suspicions of his brother and, indeed, admired him for his rude strength, contrasting so markedly with his own sickly state.

Unfortunately for Robert before the old king died he had seen enough of his heir's eldest son, David, Duke of Rothesay, to cause him anxiety for the future of Scotland should the boy ever succeed to the throne. As a safeguard against Rothesay proving unworthy he had invested the ambitious Albany with stronger powers.

When the old king died Rothesay, brash and eager for self glory, supported by his mother's brothers the Douglasses, not unnaturally resented his uncle Albany's aspirations and lost no time in influencing his enfeebled father sufficiently to have the Wardenship of Scotland taken from the older man and granted to himself.

It was not long, however, before even Rothesay's own supporters realised that the old King had had good measure of the heir's weakness and that they had entrusted the government to one who was utterly incapable of the responsibility. His vices were whispered behind the closed doors of every castle in Scotland although, while his mother was still alive he apparently made an effort to conceal the lascivious life in which he indulged, with her burial he interred the last scruples of conscience and gave himself up to the pursuit of his selfish pleasures. It was said that no woman was safe from his amorous advances and that he took delight in sadistic and cruel practices.

Resisting for as long as possible his Counsellors advice to marry he dealt the last blow to his crumbling support when he jilted the daughters of Sir William Lindsay and the Earl of March in quick succession.

Sir William retired from Court but the Earl of March was not the kind of man to take this cursory treatment lying down and immediately allied himself to the English who were always ready, truce or no truce, for a show of arms in the North. The Scots could be grateful that Owen Glendower chose this moment to raise rebellion in Wales and

Douglas was able to push back at Cocksburnpath the combined forces of March and the Percies — still at this time loyal to Henry of England.

King Robert III could no longer blind himself to the very obvious shortcomings of his heir and after much deliberation recalled his brother Albany to take up again the government of the country. Heart heavy, the sick king gave orders for Rothesay to be temporarily installed in some well guarded stronghold while the older man took up the reins of state.

Rothesay, having wind of this plan, took horse on a night of driving wind and thunderstorms intending to seek refuge at St. Andrews. Between Nydie and Strathtyrum he was overtaken by a combined force of Douglas and Albany and although he struggled violently he was overcome and bundled unceremoniously into a cart and driven to the grim fortress of Falkland.

He arrived drenched to the skin and shivering with the ague and possibly weakened by the dissolute life he had been living, died very suddenly of dysentery.

Bishop Wardlaw moved restlessly in his chair as he recalled the torrents of rumours which now poured through Scotland. The kindest of these reported Rothesay had died from the effects of being thrown still damp into a dismal cell lacking even the most primitive comforts where he had been fed on a diet of coarse bread and brackish water while the most gruesome told of the heir to the Scottish throne being reduced to eating his own fingers to stave off the terrible pangs of enforced starvation. Whatever the truth of the matter those who had removed the body for burial had hardly been able to recognise the emaciated wreck as Rothesay.

It was not difficult to see why the King thought his remaining son would be safer if removed from the suspicious influence of Albany. More so as Albany had from the time of Rothesay's death gathered about him a larger following than ever, consisting of the most ambitious and unscrupulous men in the kingdom. This had been very necessary for although the Estates declared the young man had died from natural causes there was still a belief among the merchant class and the lesser nobles that he had been murdered by his father's brother.

A general undercurrent of rival factions was making itself felt throughout the land.

As this seethed and threatened to erupt the English returned to their border raiding and the Scots were forced to amass an illequipped army to combat the menace to their

8

Lowlands. Their first efforts met with success and the invaders were pushed south as far as Newcastle but the victory proved short lived for on the return to Scotland the army was overtaken by a vastly superior English host who put them to rout.

In the disastrous engagement seven Scottish nobles were killed and twenty eight taken prisoner. Among these was James' uncle the Douglas and Albany's heir Murdoch.

Bishop Wardlaw thought as he leant forward to stir the reluctant wood that a future ruler of Scotland could not have chosen a more uneasy time to spend his boyhood. There was no peace at home or abroad while his very life was menaced by unspoken threats.

It would have helped him had he the strong hand of a healthy and competent father to guide him or the loving solace of a gentle mother but he was denied these birthrights and had to tackle his future within the limits of his own powers.

Shaking his head over the tribulations of his pupil the Bishop called for his page to light him to his bedchamber and rose stiffly from his chair.

2

Henry Percy was curled up on his narrow pallet bed covered chin high with blankets as he talked sleepily with James' squire, William Giffard, who, crouched by the brazier in the corner of the room, was waiting to help his young master to bed.

Henry grunted a greeting as James came quickly into the chamber, pulling off tunic and belt as he did so; he could hardly wait to tell Henry the news the Bishop had just passed on to him but wanted to test his reactions without the squire present to curb Henry's response. William would hear in good time from the Bishop that he would be embarking for France within the week; he proffered a bowl of warm water and James dipped his fingers and wiped them on the coarse towel. He grinned at the young man and ushered him to the door.

'You are in a great hurry to get to your bed this evening,' Henry said.

'What would you think of being told that you were about to leave for the French court?' James asked him.

The blankets slipped away from Henry's

bare shoulders as he sat up and whistled with excitement.

'When do we leave?' he asked.

Cursing himself for his impetuosity James replied:

'Unfortunately it is only I that am to leave. Would that it was the two of us.'

Henry fell back, disappointed, but quickly propped himself on his elbow and regarded James.

'Oh, well, that was too good to be true, I suppose. But it will not be for ever and you will soon be back with me.'

'That's what the Bishop told me and he said that I should enjoy learning from the French tutors.'

'Of course you will.' Henry's practical North Country nature was now reasserting itself. 'Why are you going now, just when I thought we were doing quite well with Bishop Wardlaw?'

'He did not tell me the exact reason, but Sir David Fleming brought news from my father which makes it necessary for me to set out in the very near future. You and I have talked many times of the death of my brother David, and it seems likely that the rumours that he was murdered by some unknown hand have convinced my father that it would be wiser to have his heir out of the country for the moment.' Involuntarily James shivered. Not even to Henry had he admitted that he was afraid of sudden kidnap and imprisonment and the lurking terror that it might be his uncle Albany who desired his death. Wardlaw had imposed the strictest reticence on James' retinue and the castle servants but it had been inevitable that an intelligent boy over hearing whispered conversations and sensing the meaning of the sidelong looks he received should reach a conclusion nearing the truth. He had spent many hours in the eerie darkness of night going over and over in his mind the ramifications of his brother's death. He had hardly known Rothesay, for the young man had rarely been at the family home since James could remember. His impressions of his flying visits had been bound up with his mother's strained face and tears which, as a small child, he had felt on his cheek when he nestled close to her face. He had had no especial affection for Rothesay but he had been his elder brother and he had cared for his mother's hurt.

Now, James almost brought himself to confide his fears to his friend but decided against it when he realised that he could not form words to condemn his own uncle, even to Henry. Also he could never forget that

Henry's father had died in revolt against his sovereign, which made the complex situation touchy indeed.

'The French have always been good allies of the Scots, haven't they?' Henry was saying. 'King Robert is well advised to trust you to them because it will help to strengthen the bonds that unite your two countries.'

Turning his mind from the distressing subject of the reason for his journey to Paris James concentrated on what Henry had said.

'Yes, it is as well to be secure with one's known wellwishers. For my part I do not see why we cannot live amiably with your people. After all Border raids have been carried out since the kingdoms were made and the English are not above fighting among themselves are they?' He smiled at Henry to take the sting out of his remark and went on. 'You and I are friends enough to prove it is not impossible. It seems that your Kings make the mistake of pressing their overlordship. We Scots are too proud to bend the knee because we are afraid that having once admitted English sovereignty we shall become nothing more than a vassal state.'

'There doesn't seem much fear of that!' Henry laughed. 'The Scots are not slow to fight for what they believe in!'

'You are an exile from your home.' James

went on. 'Do you not want to return to your estates?'

'What there is left of them,' Henry said ruefully. 'Since my grandfather came with me to Scotland and stays in Berwick King Henry has confiscated most of his lands and divided them between his Queen and his sons. His throne is still too insecure to risk trusting a Percy or receiving him at his court. I must admit that now you are for France it will be dull here and I would rather be at home — wherever that is!'

Seeing the look on James' face he hurried to talk of how James was to make the crossing and who was to accompany him.

'You are bound to have a retinue; it will not be at all like being at school here,' he said. Then as a new thought came to him. 'There might even be some girls at the French Court!'

James grimaced.

'I've almost forgotten what they look like,' he answered. 'It seems years since I was surrounded by my sisters all talking at once, full of secrets and the men in their lives. At the time I longed to escape from their chattering and the never ending dressing up and moods but it's odd that since we've come here I've realised that there is more to them than their giggles and fripperies. Anyway, I'll

14

write and tell you how they conduct themselves at King Charles' court. I believe they — the Court, that is — have their differences and by what Bishop Wardlaw tells me they are divided about who should be the real Pope.'

'Oh well,' Henry said hastily, 'I'm too sleepy to start talking about that old business now. Come to think of it I don't grudge you the crossing at this time of year, whatever pleasures are stored up for you in France. Perhaps there is compensation in staying here after all.' He yawned and turned on his side.

James envied him his undisturbed sleep. He lay awake for a long time watching the glow from the brazier become dimmer as the chamber grew cooler. When he closed his eyes his brain was still wide awake and teeming with the prospect of the journey that he was to make into the unknown land. He drew vague comfort from the mention Henry had made of his retinue and realised that at least he would not be alone and friendless with the strangers. He had been brought to St. Andrews by an escort and whoever was chosen to accompany him to France would have the seal of his father's choice and would be as trustworthy as was possible. Unable to encompass the thought of it being otherwise he pulled the blankets over his ears and at last drifted into sleep.

Bishop Wardlaw and Sir David Fleming spent much of the next week making plans for James to leave the castle and begin his journey to the French Court.

The King had made it known he would prefer that James visited him first at his castle of Rothesay and leave from the port of Dumbarton on the Clyde which he thought would be a safer route. After much discussion however his advisors had decided that it would be quicker and give less opportunity for surprise attack if the Prince were despatched from the Firth of Forth. Bishop Wardlaw was inclined to favour the King's wish but was overruled when he realised that the larger volume of traffic down the Firth would serve as effective cover for the ship that carried James. A suggestion from one of Sir David's companions that it would be far simpler to ask Henry IV for a safe conduct through his Kingdom to the short sea route of the Channel via Dover was dismissed as being the pipe dream of a young man who had not fully grasped the delicacy of the situation existing between the Scots and the English throne. Truce or no truce it would be asking too much of the King of England to allow the Scottish heir to pass through his territory when his father refused to pay him the feudal homage he asked.

It was agreed at last that Sir David and his company should escort James to the Bass Rock, a bleak small island at the mouth of the Forth, where he would await a suitable ship. The route was to be by way of Kirkcaldy and Rosyth to Stirling, Falkirk and Edinburgh, travelling with as much speed as was possible without tiring the boy.

William Giffard, at the Bishop's request, made an inspection of James' scanty wardrobe and reported to Wardlaw that the boy did not have one suitable garment in which to present himself to the French King and that his existing clothes were worn and almost outgrown. His spare doublet and hose were quickly despatched to a woman in the town for patching and darning while a plea to the men accompanying Sir David was made on James' behalf: one of the younger men parted, not too reluctantly, with a velvet tabbard while Henry gave his friend a pair of hose that matched tolerably well. These had been a recent gift from his mother who shared her father-in-law's enforced exile, and although Henry felt a pang of regret at his generosity he thought it was worth it when he saw James' pleasure as he tried on his new outfit. He could not help thinking that it was

17

odd that the King of Scotland's heir should have to attend the French court in borrowed finery but accepted the fact when he remembered that the Scots lived in an austere fashion which would not be acceptable to his autocratic family.

Bishop Wardlaw despaired also for although King Robert had sent jewels and plate, which the Bishop realised had strained the exchequer, to cover the cost of the journey, it did not need much judgement to assess that there was perilously little margin when the lodging and ship had been settled to give James even a pittance as an allowance.

As the time approached for him to leave Henry he became reconciled to the separation, which he hoped would not be for long, and began to look forward to the adventure ahead of him.

Sir David had told him of the route they would take through Fife and the Lothians to North Berwick where they would arrange for a rowing boat to carry them to the Bass. James was glad when he heard this piece of information that the sea had lost the ferociousness of the January gales and settled with a quietness he hoped would last. His only experience of journeying by water had been fishing in the loch at Linlithgow from a small coble and he realised that this did not fit him for a voyage on seas such as had stormed against the castle rock on the night Sir David brought the news of his departure.

When the party set out in the early days of February it was tranquil enough, frost touched the hedges and the grasses and the air was clear and cold. James took Henry by the arm as Henry gruffly wished him Godspeed and a safe journey into France. He leapt abruptly into the saddle of a pony which a groom held waiting for him and did not look back as they cantered away from the Castle onto the Leven road. Although a strict silence had been enforced a small band stood at the gateway to wave them off and a few curious townspeople stopped to watch them ride by. Sir David, with the safety and secrecy of his mission paramount in his mind, glanced uneasily from side to side, seeing in every bystander a possible Albany spy. He knew that he also had his enemies but they became as nothing when the sole heir of his friend was entrusted to his care; he would give his life rather than harm should befall James.

Leaving the cobbled streets behind with a sense of relief he fell back to where the boy was riding between William Giffard and the groom. He did not talk to him at first for

James was subdued and the older man, in his kind way, knew that he was thinking about the friend he had left and the future that awaited him. Sir David was glad when a flock of lapwings rose up as they passed and James turned in the saddle to watch them circle and settle down again.

'They tell me that Bass abounds with many strange seabirds and that seals are quite common,' Sir David said.

'Perhaps we shall see some,' James said and turned eagerly to William. 'Did you hear that?'

'Yes, I did,' William replied. 'But you had better not be too excited in case we are not there long enough for you to do any exploring!'

'That is true,' said James. 'Do you know when the ship is to call for us, Sir David?'

'Not as yet, but I am expecting to receive word when we arrive at Leith and meet up with the messenger your father is sending.'

'You will not be accompanying us, will you?' James asked.

Sir David shook his head.

'No, my party and I have to return to your father.' James was sorry that he was not to have the support of the genial knight who had spared time while he had been at St. Andrews to talk to him about his father and recount

20

some of the adventures they had had together as young men.

'Whom do you think my father will send?'

'It was not finally decided when I left Rothesay but it is most probable that the Earl of Orkney, a tried and trusted friend of the King's, will be in command and it is likely that Sir Archibald Edmonstone will support him.'

Making for the small hospice at Kinghorn the cavalcade passed through rolling countryside, brown and bare with winter. Now and again they caught long vistas of treeless wastes sweeping down towards the Tay and the distant Sidlaws. The crisp air brought the blood to James' cheeks and he glowed with the exercise. He was quite content, however, to fall somewhat sleepily from the saddle when they halted for the night to eat a hasty meal and tumble into the truckle bed made up for him close by William and Sir David.

When he awoke the next morning he was glad that the party had no further to travel than to the Cistercian Abbey at Culross for he was stiff and sore from the unusually long time he had spent in the saddle on the previous day. Feeling that, with the strenuous exercise he had taken in the curriculum at St. Andrews, he should be more fitted to stand the strain of the long ride he declined

William's offer of some rubbing oils. Before the party was through the woods between Burntisland and Aberdour he bitterly regretted his stoic pride for the track was uneven and jolted him unmercifully. He envied the stout Sir David who jogged easily, if a trifle heavily, throughout the day showing no obvious signs of any discomfort. It would have been easier if the company had been in better spirits. Scouts travelled in advance and to the flank of them and speed was the preoccupation of every man. James, concentrating on keeping himself upright without flinching, was in no mood for conversation either. The Firth glinting through the pines caught his eye now and again but it was not until Sir David pointed out to him the sacred island of Incholm about a mile from the shore at Aberdour that he was able to forget for a moment his pain. Sir David told him that as well as a monastery there was a minute hermit's cell on the isle. At any other time James would have requested that they stop and row across the Forth and explore but he contented himself with the knowledge that the Bass was an island and they should be there before too long.

Culross with its narrow streets and hospitable Abbey was reached with silent gratitude by James. He was certain that another quarter of an hour in the saddle would have been his undoing. He was somewhat surprised to discover that the inside of his thighs were still recognisable as such and had not disintegrated into raw, pulped flesh. However, he asked William for some warmed water and took himself off to the garde robe to bathe his aching limbs. Without comment William brought soft linen towels for drying and a pot of sheep's grease mixed with a distillation of herbs which miraculously eased the pain.

By the time James and his escort had gained the hospice of the Abbey of Cambuskenneth on the following evening he was becoming accustomed to the unceasing motion of the sturdy pony and had begun to enjoy himself. Sir David had chosen the houses of the monks rather than the castles along the route, for it was unlikely that informers would be harboured in them. At the same time it was easier to keep James unrecognised as the heir to the throne in the company of men whose minds were supposedly on the spiritual rather than the worldly plane.

He made an exception to this rule at Linlithgow, Robert's own Palace and one that had been a favourite of Queen Annabella's. James understood that Sir David could not have foreseen that the empty halls and silent chambers would have dismayed him as they did. At each remembered stairhead and doorway he could see the loved figure of his mother and he was jolted back into the days when the world seemed an endless delight of homely comfort. When he was not observed, he went quietly to her own apartments and wandered round running his fingers over the heavy furniture, now covered in thick dust. He leant his cheek on a tapestry which was hung against a wall and closed his eyes. He recalled, as if it were yesterday, the hours he had spent here, sitting crossed legged in front of the fire while she stitched at this or some other canvas. He could almost hear the sweet cadences of the songs she had taught him. Sir David had told him that there was no time for him to visit Rothesay to receive his father's blessing and he knew as he went slowly out of the solar that he had made his farewells.

Passing close to where the Queen Margaret ferry crossed the Firth Sir David explained that he had considered this too hazardous a journey with so many men with horses and baggage and had chosen the long way round as being safer and quicker. Edinburgh was skirted by the northern roads but James could see in the distance the high crag on which the Castle was built as it glowed in the rosy light of the dying sun. He felt no urge to stay and walk through the streets and wynds or join in the bustling life of a great city. Now that Linlithgow was behind him he had caught Sir David's desire for haste and wanted to lose no time in making the severance from his native land.

A brief halt at Leigh was made while Sir David went to the quays of the fishing port to try and establish contact with the agents who were arranging the ship that was to carry James and his escort from the Bass. When he called at a sailloft not far from the water's edge he was relieved to be told by the man who had been used as the go-between that the choice had fallen on a Dantiz merchant ship called the Maryenknyght, whose Master was Henry Bereholt. The vessel was lying at anchor not far from Leith and she was expected in within the next day or two to take on a cargo of hides and sheepskins. As soon as she was laden she would make for her rendezvous at the Bass Rock.

This information Sir David passed on with pleasure to James in the morning. The elderly man seemed to relax a little in the knowledge that he could see his charge safely installed at the Bass knowing that the chosen ship would be coming as swiftly as possible to take him on board with his escort.

Leaving the port they entered the woods screening them from Seton Castle and providing welcome protection from the biting wind which, in exposed places, had borne down on them all along this southern shore of the Firth. The tiny fishing communities of Prestopans and Aberlady were little more than a huddle of crudely erected turf huts but most of the party would have gladly exchanged an hour in the saddle for shelter under their low roofs. Sir David did not agree with these sentiments. With the end of his mission in sight he was possessed with an even more urgent desire for speed. He ordered that food should be taken in the saddle and looked with disfavour on any man who requested permission to dismount to relieve himself. By common consent spurs were put to horses' flanks and the Law behind North Berwick came into view as the sun was setting in a cloudless pale sky. Never had the weary men so gratefully slipped from their saddles and led their beasts to oats and water. Later the company gathered round the hearth of the Abbey while their mugs were filled time and again with ale. Only a handful of men at arms would be required to accompany James and Sir David to the Bass and only William and two servants from his retinue would wait with him for the

Maryenknyght; this seemed as good a time as any to celebrate the success of their mission as protector of the King's heir.

With the first light Sir David and several of the soldiers were rowed out to the Bass to inspect the shelter and check the possibility of lurking enemies or hidden beaches where unsuspected landings might be made. Satisfying himself that the bleak island was deserted he gave instructions for the small stone fortress to be made as weatherproof as possible and went back to the abbey where he had left James and William. Messengers were awaiting him from the Earl of Orkney to announce that he had been chosen as the leader of the Prince's escort and that he and his company would be with James within the week. He sent word to Sir David that once James was safely on the Rock the King was desirous of his presence at Rothesay to hear news of his son.

On the following morning the boy was accordingly rowed out with William and his servants while Sir David followed in another boat. He stayed long enough to make a tour of inspection of the island with James and gave William his final instructions for the few days that must go by before the arrival of the Earl of Orkney and the Maryenknyght. At last he felt satisfied that he had carried out his instructions to the very best of his ability and told James that he must be on the mainland before nightfall so that he could start for Rothesay on the West Coast, at dawn the next day. James with William and the two servants, stood at the shingle slipway while they wished each other Godspeed and then helped him step awkwardly into the boat. James waved to him until he was out of sight on the grey waters of the Forth, sorry to be parted from the kindly old man who had watched over him with such devotion. With darkness falling they returned to the fort and made preparations to settle as comfortably as possible for the short time they were to spend on the isle.

At first the Bass proved an interesting and fascinating change from the long journey the boy had made. It was fun to be away from the discipline of St. Andrews although the enjoyment would have been doubled had Henry been there to share in the new found delights. William did his best to take his place but he was not over keen on scrambling up sheer rock face to explore ledges and crannies for the eggs of guillemots and razorbills. This, after he had assured James that although the birds were to be seen soaring over the island it was as yet too early in the year for them to leave their winter quarters far out at sea and start nesting, was especially trying, but he found lying hazardously on narrow shelves high above the sea just watching the constantly moving water even more irksome. He did not confide his unwillingness to James but brought out from his baggage his bow and fashioned a target from a stock of sea grasses. It did not take long to interest the boy and they passed many of the short daylight hours shooting. William noticed that, as with anything James attempted, he worked at it until he became highly proficient. At this time James was indifferent to any of the few books that Bishop Wardlaw had included in his scanty belongings. William made him sit at them for an hour each day but he saw that the boy could not concentrate and would spend most of the time staring out of the open doorway or gazing into the fire.

They had been on the island for almost a week without any news except for that which the servants gleaned when they went ashore for extra food. When on the sixth morning of their stay they saw a small boat approaching the Bass William told James to wait in the back cell of the fort while he and the servants went down to await the arrival of the stranger. It proved to be a messenger of the Earl of Orkney who had arrived in North Berwick the previous evening and sent word to say that he was awaiting Sir Archibald Edmonstone and the accompanying Bishop who had been in Wales at the court of Owen Glendower. As soon as his party was complete he would be with James. William Giffard looked round the meagre quarters and hoped that the party would not be cooped up for too long under such conditions. He asked the messenger if he had news of the ship they were awaiting but the man shook his head.

'I have other news,' he said slowly.

'What is that?' William asked sharply.

'It concerns Sir David Fleming.'

'What of him?'

William had feared some ill had befallen the King and although he felt relief that this was not the case he was saddened that it concerned Sir David. James came down to meet them at this point. He had realised that the stranger was friendly as he had heard no sounds of dissention and was eager for news.

'What of Sir David?' he repeated.

'He has been ambushed and murdered,' the man answered.

'Murdered!' James and William said together.

'Yes, the knight and his party were on their way to rejoin the King, your father, my lord,

30

when they were ambushed at Langherdsman-
ston by a small army under the command of
James Douglas of Balvany and Alexander
Seton of Gordon. The battle was short and
bloody and the poor old man was dragged
from his horse and most foully done to
death.'

James turned away, saying nothing. He
found it impossible to believe that the large
kindly man who had taken such care of him
was now dead.

'Why?' William was asking. 'Who could
possibly have wished such a thing?'

He put his hand on James' shoulder.

'He was an old man. Take comfort from
that.'

'He did not deserve to die in such a
manner.'

William turned his mind to the problem of
the approaching visit of the escort and
impressed it on the messenger as he and
James went with him to the boat that they
must bring bedding and firewood. This last
was becoming an urgent need as the barren
island had few trees and the supply was low.
The exposed position of the Bass meant that
it was buffeted by the wind from all directions
and the cold weather showed no signs of
relenting. When the messenger had gone
William set James as well as the servant

searching for driftwood. He knew that the boy was suffering under the blow of the tragic news which they had just heard and wished that he might have been spared the knowledge of the murder until they were safely installed in France.

On the following morning they awoke to leaden skies and a heavy stillness. Before the short day was over snow fell in great feathery flakes, blanketing the earth and melting silently on the seas surface. James was able to forget his sadness in a running snowfight with William and the servants. When they came in, glowing and exhilarated William broached the small keg of wine which the Earl of Orkney had sent them and they sat round the hearth where the driftwood steamed and warmed their frozen fingers. Heartened by the wine they hummed a few choruses and went to bed happier than they had all been since they left St. Andrews.

But it was not until the beginning of the third week that several long boats brought the expected escort. James stood at the slipway to greet them. The Earl of Orkney and Sir Archibald Edmonstone, wrapped to the eyes in hodden grey cloaks against the cold, bowed over James' extended hand. The Bishop was half carried ashore for it appeared that the short journey had been too much for his delicate stomach. After making a perfunctory greeting he was led towards the stone House.

With the coming of the escort, who had no fresh news of the Maryenknyght other than that she had completed taking on her cargo, the free and easy life on the island came to an end. The tranquil existence became a continuous bustle of preparation and fuss. It was soon obvious that what sufficed for the heir of Scotland was in no way good enough for his retinue and a chain of messengers plied back and forth to the mainland for extra comforts. James would find a spot sheltered from the wind and watch the huge, graceful seabirds as they glided downwards or plummeted into the sea for fish. He took comfort from their perpetual movement and found them more companiable than the men, kind as they tried to be, who were to accompany him to France. When he was with them at the seemingly endless meals he forced himself to a polite attention. The only time he had been really interested in what they were saying was when they were discussing the murder of Sir David. The Earl of Orkney advanced the theory that apart from a private family quarrel, the only reason that he could think of for the attack was that the Douglasses were jealous of advancement made to Sir David by the King at their expense and they made much of the Earl of Northumberland's disappearance into Wales just at the moment when there appeared to be a chance of exchanging him for the Earl of Douglas. Although there was no proof that Sir David had sent warning to Northumberland the Douglasses had thought there was sufficient evidence to murder the man who had thus prevented the return of their lord.

James said nothing, glad at least that Henry's grandfather was safe. William made a mental note to redouble his prayers for the speedy arrival of the Maryenknyght for it proved to him that it was imperative that the Prince should be removed as rapidly and as far as possible from the seething discontent within his father's realm.

In this his prayers were answered for just after the middle of March the ship was sighted. She came on the leeside of the island and dropped anchor while she waited for James and his escort to come aboard.

Sir David's speed in reaching the island as quickly as the ground could be covered had been wasted, for what was hoped to be a brief stay on the Bass had become a marathon of endurance. James, with William and the two servants had been there for almost a month.

3

It took some time to get the company aboard, for the sea was rough and several journeys had to be made back and forth with the ships boats to pick up the countless bundles and chests, heavily secured with iron clasps, that made up the baggage of the entourage. James' own small wooden box and a canvas bag looked very meagre against it.

He had been put on board first and had enjoyed pulling himself, hand over hand, up the rope ladder which curved inwards against the hull. The ship was about eighty feet in length with a single stepped mast and one huge sail flapping as the Maryenknyght lay head into wind. There was a roughly constructed shelter at the stern but no other housing on deck.

The Master, Henry Bereholt, greeted James courteously but without servility. He told the boy that he was a native of Danzig and James was fascinated with his gutteral accent. William guessed that he had been chosen for the mission as he would have no particular leaning towards any Scottish faction. He took them below to a hold which was communal to the party and the cargo. This it was not difficult to discover, consisted of wool, hides and woolfells smelling strongly of the byre and sheep fold. Their main advantage was the padding they provided against the cold. William lost no time in taking over a corner for James and himself.

'I hate to think,' James said softly to him, 'What my lord of Orkney will say to the accommodation provided for him.'

'So do I, but he will survive, my lord, and let us hope that this time we shall not be delayed. With fair winds we should be at sea less than a week.'

'That is fortunate,' James said with a grin. 'For this movement is enough to turn my stomach.'

'It will be easier when we are under way and the sail takes up the force of the wind,' William replied.

It took most of the remaining hours of daylight to put the party in satisfactory quarters and the master and crew had weighed anchor and set sail long before the Earl and his retinue were settled. Food was prepared and when it was eaten James gladly took himself to his corner and slept.

It was not necessary for him to go on deck in the morning to realise that now they had gained the open sea and were standing well off the coast the weather had deteriorated and a gale sprung up. The Bishop was blanched with the heaving motion of the ship while Orkney and Sir Archibald had been on deck since the first light, unable to stand the cramped evil smelling hold. William hastened James aloft and they found a clear piece of deck where it was possible to wedge themselves against being blown or washed overboard. With admiration they watched the crew in burly sheepskin jackets go about their business of keeping the Maryenknyght as close hauled as possible. William noticed that the sail was well shortened and kept an anxious watch on the seas which he was certain were becoming increasingly rough. Now and again the bow of the ship buffeted into a wave which broke the cascades over the foredeck.

It was obvious by the third day, when most of the entourage were listlessly sitting or lying around that the gale was increasing rather than abating and that the sturdy ship was no longer bowing to the occasional larger wave but wallowing from the crest of one huge wall of water to the lowest depth of the next. The timbers groaned as she shuddered upwards and crashed down with frightening force. It was impossible for any but the crew, who were secured to the mast with rope lashing, to remain above deck. The conditions in the dimly lit hold became hourly more intolerable as the stench of vomit mixed with the other smells. James, manfully propped against a bale of sheepskins, fought a nausea which floated with the ship's lurching from his stomach to his head. He averted his eyes from the rest of the party who, in the main, had succumbed to seasickness and shook his head when William offered him food.

About midday the hatch was pushed back with great difficulty and the Master, in a flurry of crashing water, came below. He pulled the hatch to behind him and staggered to the Earl of Orkney. He told the Earl that he had held his course as long as he was able and stood off the coast as had been agreed but that, in the opinion of himself and the crew, if they did not at once run for shelter of the land the ship would founder and they would all be lost. It did not take the Earl more than a moment to give his consent to this alteration of plans; he looked briefly round at his companions who nodded their agreement. Anything was preferable to the torment of being thrown helplessly on an angry sea. Fears of wreckers or boarders were forgotten in the face of the present ordeal.

Henry Bereholt pulled himself up the short companionway and banged on the hatch feet grabbing dirks and swords as the clash of steel mingled with the noise above. The first man had reached the foot of the ladder as the hatch was pushed back and a large face appeared. This was quickly followed by another, weather-beaten and magnificently bearded.

'Well, Hugh!' the man cried. Then he called over his shoulder. 'Come on you lot. There's more prizes here than hides and woolfells!'

Before the startled Earl or his company could do more than raise their sword arms five or six enormous men had pushed their way into the hold, filling the confined space with their bulk. As quickly as they had entered they stripped the escort of their daggers and other weapons, unhesitatingly lashing out with fists at any resistance. Two of the Earl's men went down on the deck, staggering under blows which left them senseless. The Earl, holding a blanket around himself to hide his disarray, pushed with difficulty to the front, while William as unobtrusively as possible, kept James hidden behind him. The boy, after the first surprise, was almost enjoying the situation. He felt no alarm for about him were the men his father had sent to guard him and that was sufficient. This would indeed be something to tell Henry.

which was opened sufficiently wide enough for him to drag himself on deck. His voice, roaring orders to the men, was lost in the scream of the wind through the rigging.

As the Maryenknyght bore off on the starboard tack there was a frightening minute as the gale caught her beam and she heeled over almost into the waves but with all the crew grappling with the tiller she righted herself and lurched forward.

There was very little improvement in conditions below deck and those who were lying on the starboard side were forced to drag themselves towards the keel of the ship to avoid the water from the bilge now slopping above the planking. As the prospect of survival increased so did the grumbling and James was never to forget that in the face of fear it is possible to see courage or its lack in many guises. Watching William's calm behaviour he had pushed his own terror away from him, drawing comfort from the fact that William did not appear to be unduly concerned and that therefore all would be well. Now that the ship settled gradually to a heeling motion the squire acted as though before very long it would be calmer and James caught his mood and was surprised to find that he was drowsy. William covered him with blankets and when he saw that the boy slept, lay down beside him and closed his eyes.

Gradually as night fell the sea moderated and the approaching land gave shelter from the wind, but it was not until dawn that Henry Bereholt had the hatches thrown back and permitted the bedraggled escort to come up for air. Low scudding clouds and driving rain obscured the coast and the Master said that as near as he could judge they were off the Holy Isle to the North of the Tyne. He explained to the Earl that he would come in as close as he dared to take advantage of the quieter water and believed that the gales which were expected at this time of the vernal equinox would keep ashore those who made their living from piracy. This was the season when the wreckers hoped to get rich, for any ship that thankfully beached on an isolated shore to avoid shipwreck ran the very real risk of losing its crew by murder at the hands of the unscrupulous men who lay in wait for such an eventuality. The wreckers were aided by the law of the land which allowed salvage only when a vessel had foundered with all hands.

During the day some of the party were able to eat a little food and James had a few sips of wine and a piece of dried meat. By the evening all the party were sufficiently

recovered to take some supper. Although most of the faces in the dimly lit hold were still pale, the strain was eased and an air of gaiety was apparent. The younger men talked of the fabled beauty of the women at the French court and told James that they envied him the prospect of a prolonged stay with them; more than one of them regretted that they would have to return to Scotland once they had safely delivered the young prince to Paris. James, whose limited experience of women confined him to memories of his mother, nurse and sisters, felt slightly uncomfortable when the discussion became freer as the wine went to the men's already unsteady heads. He smiled when they asked him if he did not consider himself most fortunate and thought privately that he would rather return to St. Andrews to Henry's companionship than go to France whatever the extent of French hospitality. It was in this mood of relaxed relief that the party settled down for the night.

They were awakened, in the grey light of morning, by a jolting crash that jarred the Maryenknyght from stem to stern. This was followed by the rattle of chains and loud thuds on the deck above them accompanied by cries of anger and shrieks of pain. James' escort, rubbing at their eyes stumbled to their

At this moment the whole party fell sideways as the ship heeled over onto the port tack. It was then that the Earl found his voice.

'Who the devil are you? And what is the meaning of this outrage?' As he went towards the man called Hugh, the other man with the beard detained him with one hand.

'We are merchants from Yarmouth and Clay in Norfolk.'

'Merchants,' the Earl snorted. 'Pirates more likely. Where is the Master and his crew?'

'Those that are still alive have been put on board our vessel and the others . . . ' he broke off and leered round the hold. 'They are where any of you will be if we have any trouble.'

'Trouble!' Sir Archibald echoed. 'We demand that you recall our crew and put us on our way as quickly as possible.'

'Demand,' said the bearded one. 'Ye're in no position to demand anything. We've captured you and by the look of you there should be a pretty ransom to be had.'

'There'll be no ransom, this is a time of truce.'

'There's no truce that I know of,' Hugh retorted. He turned and looked up to the hatch where another man had appeared.

'What is it Will Oxeney?'

43

'We've got some richer cargo than we reckoned on. What do you make of this pennant I've just found in some baggage at the stern?'

Hugh grabbed the sodden piece of bunting and held it up. Suddenly he whistled through his teeth.

'John,' he cried turning to the man with the beard. 'This is a lion; a Royal lion, if I'm not mistaken.' For a second his voice faltered.

'That's not the Standard of England,' said the man called John. 'Don't fret, our Henry's not at sea in this weather, nor would he allow any of his offspring either.' He put his hand up to scratch under his fur hat. 'But it is a royal badge, all right and no mistake,' he went on slowly.

Suddenly Hugh shouted.

'I have it!'

The hold had become very still and the air was charged with something other than fear.

'This badge is the badge of Scotland.'

No one moved.

'Which one of you is the King of Scotland?' Hugh demanded. 'Sit down, all of ye, with your backs against the woolfells while we take a proper look at ye.'

Aided with unceremonious shoves and kicks the escort sank down. Hugh and John, now joined by the third man, William

Oxeney, went from one recumbent figure to the next roughly turning their faces to the small quantity of light which came from above. They rejected the men at arms as being beneath their notice and lingered longest over Sir Archibald and the Earl of Orkney. They talked in low whispers over the still figure of the Bishop who was lying, completely shocked, in the dimmest corner. One of the men caught sight of the huge ring on his finger and hastily crossed himself.

'That's not him,' he cried. 'He's a churchman.' They turned hastily away and as they did so Hugh saw for the first time the sturdy boy who sat quietly at William's side. James looked back at him unblinking, as the man stared at him, although his heart was racing and he was becoming afraid.

'Of course!' Hugh shouted. 'This is what we are seeking.'

'That's only a boy,' Will Oxeney said doubtfully.

'Only a boy maybe, but hasn't the King of Scotland a young son and isn't it possible that things are not too healthy for royal heirs in their own country.'

'Yes,' said Oxeney slowly. 'There was some talk about one of them being murdered.'

James winced and moved involuntary

closer to William, who longed to comfort him but knew better than to show, at this moment, any signs of emotion.

The three pirates leant over James and pulled him to his feet. They took him under the hatch.

'Look up,' they commanded.

James turned his face to the sky, which he was surprised to notice had cleared.

'Are you the son of the King of Scotland?'

'Yes,' James replied bravely.

To his amazement the men slapped each other on the back and threw back their heads in uproarious laughter. He watched them in consternation. Breaking off their merriment to look down on him they saw the expression on his face.

'There's nothing to worry about, my lord, we wish you no harm.'

William stood by James now and the boy turned round to him.

'What do they want then, if they do not wish my life?' he asked in perplexity.

'Ye're much more good to us alive, my lord, than feeding the fishes; we are just making merry at the thought of the reward we shall get from King Henry when we deliver you to him.'

Orkney was on his feet at this.

'We are taking the boy to France and we

46

cannot allow you to deliver him to King Henry.'

'There is no question of you allowing anything,' Hugh said. 'We shall put into Yarmouth and John Hacon and I shall take the King's son to London, while William Oxeney and Nicholas Steward, who is at the tiller, will accompany your party. It is no good resisting for we are burgesses of the town and have the support of the townsfolk.' With a swell of pride he added, 'I was mayor the year before last and we are an important town of the Staple.'

The Earl raised his eyebrows but said nothing. James during this conversation was trying to realise the overwhelming change that had come about in his life within the short space of an hour. He had known that he was to leave his native country for an indefinite period but to be delivered to King Henry meant to be prisoner and deprived of his freedom. With a sense of shock he saw that he would be in the same position as Murdoch, his cousin, Albany's son, who had been confined in England since the battle of Homildon four years ago. Four years was a lifetime and he had thought the possibility of spending one at the French court long enough. The full realisation of his predicament hit him like a blow, while for a moment it seemed as if the walls of the ship moved in closer until he was suffocating. He stood still, showing no sign of the consternation he felt, while he fought down his fear. Hugh was speaking again and he dragged his dazed mind to concentrate on what he was saying.

'Well, now that's all settled we don't want to be at odds with each other. Have ye eaten?'

He looked round and noted those who shook their heads and shouted up aloft for a sack of victuals. As it was handed down he ordered some of Orkney's men to open it and share out the food. Prodded by the pirates the men at arms took out bread and some cold fowls.

'That's better food that ye'll have had for some time, I'll warrant,' Hugh said on a gust of laughter. 'Set to and enjoy it while we go above and see how your ship is progressing; ye'll feel better when you have eaten.'

The hold was quiet until the bulky Yarmouth raiders had heaved themselves up the short ladder to the deck when everyone spoke at once. James took the leg of the bird that William gave him with a piece of coarse bread and a mug of wine. He alone seemed unable to talk and through the welter of his own thoughts heard only dimly the excited chatter of his companions. The general opinion of the Earl and the others was that it was futile to attempt any counter measures while they remained on board. Apart from being in a weak position generally none of them was capable of handling the Maryen-knyght, especially if they were to encounter seas such as they had experienced after leaving the Bass. It did not take very long to decide that they would accept the captivity while they remained at sea but that once they had regained the land each would try to escape. William, sitting silently beside James, had already been turning over in his mind the problem of rescuing his young master. As he examined each possibility he was confronted with apparently insuperable difficulties. He guessed that the first things the pirates had confiscated had been the small chests of money and plate which had been hidden in Henry Bereholt's quarters and without these it was unlikely that they could come by a horse unless they stole it. There was the added hazard of travelling through an unknown, hostile country. This could be difficult enough but with the inevitable pursuers fast on their trail it was almost hopeless to evade them and cover the many hundreds of miles which would separate them from their own country. William decided that he would make every effort to send word to King Robert as soon as he was able and trust that something could be done to help James in his peril.

He looked up to see James making for the ladder to go above and unnoticed they climbed to the deck. They were greeted with curious looks from the pirates but were allowed to walk unhindered to a space forward of the mast.

James gulped down the sharp thin air, filling his lungs gratefully. Once free of the stifling hold the panic which had threatened to overcome him began to subside and looking up he watched the graceful gulls as they circled and wheeled around the ship. William drew his attention to the long low coastlines showing on their starboard bow and told him it was England. James, with difficulty, studied the land which was the country of the men who had captured him and was surprised to discover that it did not appear so very different from his own. For a fleeting moment he almost laughed as he wondered if he had been expecting some dreadful and awe inspiring shore encompassing the portals of nightmare.

They came into Yarmouth at nightfall on the day after the boarding and the Scottish party were kept below decks while the merchants made arrangements to transport them to Westminster. Hugh with William

Oxeney and the others had changed their minds and decided that they would travel as one party rather than split into two groups, thus retaining their complete strength. William Giffard regarded this as the final blow to their chances of escape and before the escort settled down to try and sleep he took aside one of the Bishop's servants. He told the man that he thought that of all the Scots the Bishop had the greatest opportunity to give the Yarmouth merchants the slip and the churchman's poor health would serve as a ready excuse for lying up in some friendly abbey. Having left his master safely housed and cared for the Bishop's servant would then be free to travel as swiftly as possible to Rothesay Castle to inform the King of what had befallen his son and his retinue. William was not quite sure of the outcome of the King of Scotland receiving this momentous news but he felt that it was the only course open to them. To his relief the servant readily agreed to look for the earliest opportunity to part company from the band as it made towards London.

In an almost dreamlike state James climbed into the saddle of the pony that was allotted to him on the following morning. He was oblivious of the frankly curious and excited crowd of townspeople, who despite the early hour and the cold, had gathered to watch the party leave the Maryenknyght and make ready to leave. Once astride the horse he thought the beast was swaying in the wind until he realised that he had not lost the sensation of movement from the ship. This added to the phantasy of the situation and needed all his concentration to keep upright. Had he been able to look about him he would have discovered that he was the object of most of the attention and it was largely sympathetic. As it was, he was glad when Hugh gave the order to move off. At once, John Hacon and Nicholas Steward took up their position at his side. William Giffard, watching him, saw the straight set of the shoulders and mouth, but he saw also the unusual pallor of the face and the eyes which watched, pupils dilated, the way ahead.

They spent four nights on the road, passing through Norwich, Wymondham and Thetford on their way to Royston, Waltham Cross and Westminster. The party stayed at ale houses which were a far cry from the hospices that had sheltered James on his journey round the Firth but were at least a little better than the hold of the Maryenknyght.

William saw at once on the second morning that the Bishop and his servant did not muster with them as they set off and realised with a surge of relief that the gap was unnoticed by Hugh or the other pirates. As the day wore on he guessed that the churchman had probably made for Ely where he could be certain of a welcome while his man continued on to meet up with the great North road at Stamford. William could only surmise that Hugh and the others were so besotted with the prospect of delivering James to their sovereign that they had overlooked the simple precaution of counting the number of their captives. The Bishop's escape had been aided by the cold, blustery weather which necessitated everyone muffling up to the eyebrows.

The loss was discovered, however, when the company halted for the night and a sharp altercation ensued. It died down as the merchants decided that the Bishop was no great loss, but, they watched the rest of the Scots with redoubled attention from this time on. Fortuitously they did not appear to be aware that the Bishop had had a personal servant who had vanished as well.

The winds lessened as the band came to Enfield and Highgate and James had his first glimpse of London through a clear, rain-washed air. For the first time since he had left the Bass his spirits lifted a little and he turned to William Giffard and smiled.

4

Westminster was so different from any Scottish castle that James had ever seen that he found it difficult to believe that this was a residence of a single monarch.

The party of Scots were kept waiting in an anteroom while Hugh, William and the other two Norfolk merchants begged an interview with the Secretary to Bishop Arundel, Archbishop of Canterbury and Lord Chancellor. They had not long to wait for once the reason for their prayer was fully grasped the Chancellor lost no time in sending word to the King.

James had an opportunity to look round his escort as they waited and even in his present detached frame of mind he had to admit that none of them showed up too well against the splendour of their surroundings. All of them from Orkney downwards looked illkempt and travel stained and were ill at ease to a man. It was not an envious position, to await, with the prince whose protection they had provided, the pleasure of a hostile sovereign. If Henry had once been lenient with the citizens of Edinburgh on his father's account there was no especial reason why he should look with favour on the son or the retinue of the man who had, more than once, refused to pay him homage. James saw well dressed courtiers pass through the room eyeing his company with curiosity mingled with humour. It was probably the first time so many Scots had been present at Westminster and James was sorry they did not make a better showing. He looked down ruefully at his crumpled and worn doublet and hose.

He was led with Orkney and Sir Archibald and William Giffard in attendance to the King's chamber. Kingship being synonymous in his mind with old age and frailty he thought at first that they had been brought into the presence of the King's son, for the man that awaited them was not yet forty years of age and was handsome and well proportioned. Led by the Secretary to bow over the outstretched hand proffered to him he realised that this was indeed the King of England. He thought, too, before he lowered his head he had detected a faint twinkle in the king's eyes. So engrossed was he in the conflicting impressions of this self made monarch that he missed the welcome he extended to James and his party.

'Why were you going to France, my lord?' King Henry was asking him from what seemed a long way off. James concentrated sufficiently to be able to reply.

'To learn the language, Your Grace.'

'If the Scots were grateful they would have sent you to me to be taught, for I too know the language,' Henry said laughingly.

James relaxed a little, for these were not the words of a heartless tyrant.

'What shall we do with you, my lord? and with my lord of Orkney and Sir Archibald? I think it would be better if you stayed here, as my guests, until we decide. Looking at you, clean clothing and rest would not go amiss!'

James blushed but as the words echoed his own private thoughts, he knew they were kindly meant.

'Do you take these gentlemen to the private chambers and see to their comfort,' Henry said to the Secretary. 'And My Lord Chancellor will you be as good as to have the merchants of Yarmouth and Clay sent to me.'

Orkney and Edmonstone exchanged glances at this description of their captors, realising that they were to be summoned to hear the extent of the reward for the rich prize they had brought to the King. Their heir of Scotland was a most useful bargaining weapon to have in hand against his royal father and the Governor of Scotland.

James' party had not long to wait before

William Giffard was able to bring them the information that the pirates had been requited with the Maryenknyght and her entire cargo. There was one stipulation, however, and this was that the ship and her contents were to be properly valued before being handed over. All agreed that this seemed the action of a just man.

The rooms allotted to James were rich in panelling and had fine ceilings ornately carved and painted in bright colours picked out in gold. He was amazed at the luxurious covering and curtains for the bed and the quantity of solid furniture. It was a far cry from the castle at St. Andrews and for that matter any of his father's homes.

Hot water was brought and poured into a tub in the garde robe while William handed James' linen to one of the many servants who hovered near. It was apparent that the heir of the Scots and his party had aroused much interest in the palace and all were eager to have sight and first hand knowledge of the strangers.

James fell into his bed, wholesome and pleasantly drowsy. The turn of events which had snatched him from a ship at sea and driven him in a headlong ride through East Anglia had temporarily thrown his usual reasoning mind into a state of confusion. At this moment he could quite easily push thoughts of his cousin Murdoch and his long captivity away from him as a fate that could not befall him. He was, after all, the heir of the King of Scotland and he clung to the belief that King Henry would acquaint his father with the circumstances of his capture and that Robert would thereupon insist upon his repatriation. That there would undoubtedly be the question of a huge ransom and the unfortunate truth that his uncle, Albany, wielded the power in his father's kingdom, he refused to dwell upon at this stage. These thoughts brought the knowledge that Albany had not been successful in securing the release of his own son, James hastily shied from the whole subject.

As he was drifting off to sleep he let his imagination dwell on the difference that his friend Henry Percy would have made had he been with him to share the unreal happenings of the last ten days. With him he would have been able to enjoy the tree covered flatness of Norfolk and the gentle beauty of Suffolk; as it was he had found it impossible to confide in the attentive William and had experienced a devastating loneliness of spirit. He had wished that he had paid more attention to Bishop Wardlaw when he had spoken to them of the comfort of the Holy Ghost for he had felt a real need for aid outside human capabilities.

Now, warm and comfortable in a soft bed the melancholy dissipated and he slept. Tomorrow would be soon here to take up the travail once more.

William busied himself during the next days, on James' behalf, making as many acquaintances as was possible under the constrained circumstances of their virtual confinement. None of the party had been to the King again, neither had anyone been allowed outside their allotted quarters. The Earl of Orkney and Sir Archibald spent hours in deep discussion, punctuated with much head shaking and shrugging of shoulders. They still had an intangible air of guilt for what had befallen their royal charge and they avoided him as much as was possible, treating him, when they met at mealtime, with courtesy that was at once sheepish and well meant.

It was largely due to William's efforts that James roused from his apathy and sat for a short while each day at his Latin and French exercises. The latter he approached with a rueful grimace.

It was William who asked Orkney to pray for permission to use a little courtyard which backed on to their apartments and here he and James practised wrestling and hand ball.

Coming in from exercising one morning early in April James forced himself to ask William if word had been sent to his father; William had been in two minds about telling the boy of the Bishop's messenger who had parted from them during the journey to Westminster but had decided against it when he realised that the news might raise false hopes. He had forestalled James' curiosity about the man's disappearance by telling him that the Bishop had pleaded infirmity to the innkeeper where the party had spent the night. This man, impressed by the cleric's habit, had smuggled him and his servant to the local priest's house to await friends from Bury St. Edmunds Abbey.

Now, faced by a direct question, William told the prince that he hoped word would have reached the King by this time. He judged that the man, making all haste to Rothesay would have arrived there and plans to aid James would already be in motion. William did not hold out much hope of a speedy release of the Scottish heir for he well understood that James was a most valuable asset to the English King, beset as he was with touchy nobles in his own country as well as rebellions in Wales and Scotland. William had not had to reside at Westminster for very long before he realised Henry's election to the throne had been almost too successful and that, as well as the Percies, he had other powerful enemies. His Chancellor, Arundel, was unpopular, and it was whispered that some people looked towards the King's son, young Henry of Monmouth, as a possible successor. As Prince of Wales he was well supported by his father's half-brothers, the Beauforts, but was absent from court most of the time, for although only nineteen years of age he was chief commander of the armies lined up against the Welsh in the Marches.

James' face lit up as he heard William had tried to send word to his father. It was a crumb of comfort that the king would know his whereabouts and that they would be able to communicate. Wondering why he had not thought of it before he asked William for some parchment and a quill. William found some with difficulty. Giving them to James he admitted to himself that Henry might not give permission for letters to pass between father and son and it also came to him the English King had probably sent messengers to the Castle at Rothesay. William hoped they would not clash.

It was now Holy Week and the court was fasting but ample quantities of fish were sent in to the Scot's apartments and Orkney commented that he was certain the exchequer clerks would be kept busy recording on the rolls the cost of feeding their party. Each day they spent in England added to the amount which would be needed to ransom them.

James attended the private chapel in the Palace and on Easter Sunday went with his party, at the King's invitation, to hear mass in the Abbey Church.

He had had one further interview with Henry and had been presented to a monk who came thereafter each morning to give him tutelage. Henry had told him he regretted that his young family were at Kenilworth and that he would have to take his instruction alone. On this occasion James had met Henry's second wife, Joan, daughter of Charles, King of Navarre. James judged that she was considerably younger than Henry and supposed that the family the king spoke about were hers. He was surprised when William told him later that although Henry and the Queen had been married three years they were childless and the six young people of the Royal family were all mothered by Mary de Bohun who had died some years before Henry became King.

Against his conscience James envied the four sons and two daughters this strong, virile father, but was consoled when he learnt from William that the crusader and hero of the tournament as Henry undoubtedly had been he was now subject to bouts of a distressing illness which were becoming more frequent as he became older.

This disability was a factor in the growing popularity of the Prince of Wales for there were periods when Henry was incapable of governing. The parallel between the King's case and his own father's touched James' sympathy and he felt drawn to the King against his will. He had at the same time a certain resentment against Henry of Monmouth although they had not met.

Henry did not send for James again and William heard it rumoured the King was undecided as to the best course of action for the young heir.

April 12th was a day of showers and bright cold sunshine. When it was dark the Scots were glad to have a fire lit for them and a meal of fat capon and stewed onions. James was sitting with them as usual a little apart and withdrawn, when a page came in and requested the Earl of Orkney to present himself with William Giffard immediately in the King's private solar. James looked up with surprise as his squire rose and followed Orkney, for it was late for an audience. He dismissed the hope that word had come from his father and decided that Henry had spent the day hunting and was only now dealing with the business of the day. It was possible that he had made up his mind about the future of James and his entourage.

Orkney and William Giffard knew, as soon as they entered the king's chambers and saw the men who stood with him, that they were to hear momentous news. For the men were Scots and they had the look of bearers of ill tidings. They were also, to a man, of the household of the King of Scotland at Rothesay.

Henry wasted no time in coming to the reason for calling Orkney and William. He greeted them gravely and told them the messengers, who had arrived in Westminster after days of hard riding, brought the unhappy news that King Robert of Scotland on hearing the news of the capture of his son and heir had been unable to bear this further tragedy and had died of shock.

Henry looked fearlessly at the Scots as he spoke although his hands were clenched at his side. It was William and the Earl of Orkney who were unable to meet his eyes. William felt a sensation of hopeless finality as he heard the words which told him that he had most probably been instrumental in causing his sovereign's death. With this uneasy realisation came the knowledge James was King of Scotland.

It was about this that Henry was speaking.

'So therefore, I very much regret that it will be necessary for me to have the boy and you, my lord Orkney, with Sir Archibald and Giffard removed to the Tower in order that a closer watch may be kept on him.'

Orkney opened his mouth but said nothing.

'You will leave in the morning,' Henry continued. 'Would you have me tell the boy of his father's death?'

'If it please your Grace,' Orkney said quickly. Henry looked at William.

'May I bring him to you?' William asked. 'It would help if that were possible.'

'Very well,' Henry said and motioned the Scottish messengers to leave with Orkney and William. Once outside they vied with each other to tell the story of how the sickly King received the news from the Bishop's messenger of his son's capture.

Robert had been sitting at supper on Palm Sunday and on hearing the news had turned ashen white and slumped back in his chair. He had taken to his bed later that night and from then on had lain with his face to the wall refusing to speak or take any nourishment.

Three days later those watching over him had heard him give a groan as of great despair and on rushing to his side had found him dead.

Orkney seated the messengers in their chambers and sent pages for food for them. William braced himself to bring James to the King. The boy looked up at him swiftly as he asked him to accompany him and followed him without a word. He had seen enough to know that he was once again to face unhappy news.

Henry came forward to meet him and raised him quickly as he bent to him. Quietly, sparing the details, he told the boy that his father was dead. James stared at him, his eyes widened with pain. Although he heard what the King was saying he could grasp but half of it. He only understood he was now an orphan and that for some reason Henry thought it advisable to commit him to the Tower.

Dully he tried to bring his overtaxed brain to fathom the reason for this decision but it was not until he heard Henry say something about the late King of the Scots that the truth came to him. Heat burned in him from his toes up through his body to his head and he broke out in a sweat of dismay as he suddenly saw very clearly that Henry had no other course of action open to him. He, James, was now King of Scotland.

5

In the early morning of the following day James, Orkney, Edmonstone and William Giffard were taken by barge from the steps of the landing stage at Westminster to the Tower.

It was a bright cold morning with a sharp breeze ruffling the dark river. James, still numbed with the news from Rothesay, was glad of the thick cloak William had insisted upon him wearing. Despite the misery that seemed to dog him, coupled with the uncertainty of his future, he felt a stirring of pleasure as he saw the faint bloom of new leaf on the trees and heard the shrill call of birdsong.

He watched the boatmen as they pulled the heavy craft safely through the narrow passage under London Bridge, amazed at the swiftness of the tide as it fell. He admired the well tended gardens sweeping down to the water's edge and at any other time would have asked to whom the great houses belonged. The skyline was cut with the steeples of churches on both banks and he guessed the largest on the north bank to be the St. Paul's of which he had heard.

Coming round the sweep of river he saw the Tower, square and impregnable since the days of the Conqueror. He took great breaths of the air which smelt of the sea and braced himself for what lay ahead.

The gate clanged behind them as they were met by the Constable, Sir Thomas de Rempston. Orkney and the others exchanged glances as they were led through St. Thomas's Tower to the stone walled rooms they had been allotted in the Beauchamp Tower. Each chamber was simply furnished with low beds, plain hangings and a table with two chairs.

James sat quietly in a corner while William was overseeing the stowing away of their meagre possessions and the Earl and Sir Archibald settled into the new quarters with a good deal of officious bother.

James and William had talked deep into the previous night and he felt happier as a result of their discussions. He had experienced difficulty in bringing himself to unburden himself of the perplexing misfortunes which had come to him in such a short time, but William had helped him by a quick understanding which had been sympathetic but at the same time astringent. James found himself wishing that he had not been so reticent before.

William had assured him that he would

urge Orkney to seek speedy repatriation of their new King. He told James that he was certain they had nothing more to fear from King Henry than imprisonment. All the Scots were agreed, and William's enquiries at Westminster bore them out, that he was not cruel or vindictive. William comforted his young master by advising him to make the best of the inevitable waiting he would have to endure by applying himself to his lessons. Henry would doubtless send tutors to the Tower and it was not difficult for James to realise that he would require much wisdom when he returned to claim his throne.

He was thinking over all that had been said and he determined to shake off the melancholy which had lately been gaining a hold on him. It was the future that mattered. The past was over and the present could be endured; his one regret was that he had no young companion to share in this challenge. While Orkney had Sir Archibald and William the other squires, he was alone. He wished for the hundredth time that Henry had been with him.

James looked up as the Constable came in, almost in answer to his thoughts bringing with him a slim, dark youth of about fifteen whom he presented to James as Griffith, son

of Owen Glendower. Sir Thomas de Rempston had had him brought from another part
of the Beauchamp Tower because he thought
each might lighten the other's captivity.

Although they were secretly delighted they
regarded one another with the wary assess-
ment of pugilists. The pleasure of the
encounter quickly broke down their reserves,
however, and before long they were talking
without restraint.

In the days that followed each recognised
the other's worth. Griffiths stood in no awe of
the King of Scots for he was older than he
and more than a head taller. He also thought
of himself as the true heir of the mighty
Glendower which made him the equal of any
ruler in the land. It did not take him long to
find out that James, although shorter and
heavier in build, was a strong and courageous
athlete, while in the classroom despite his age
he was so far ahead of him to make
competition useless. Griffith had thought at
first that his new friend's sad eyes marked
him as a dreamer but he was to discover this
was true only on the rare occasions when
James thought of the future.

James, in his turn, admired the Welsh boy
for his graceful courtesy to the older men of
the party and the ease with which he would
entertain them with stories from his country's

70

legends. His voice had a compelling quality enhanced by the way he spoke English and he sang in a melodious tenor matching James' as yet unbroken treble.

One of the first favours he begged on James' behalf was a visit to the menagerie close by the Middle Tower which they reached by the bridge over the moat. They enjoyed watching the lions and leopards as they paced restlessly to and fro in the compound, feeling a bond of sympathy for the beasts who had lost their freedom as they had done. Griffith had been imprisoned in the Tower since his father's defeat at Carmarthen and by silent agreement the boys did not speak of time as a factor in their captivity.

If the boys did not talk much on the subject, Orkney and Edmonstone spoke of little else. William would not allow James' illusion that the Earl was mainly concerned with his King's release to be shattered but he was under no misapprehension himself that the letters despatched by the Earl to such people as Sir John Forrester of Corstorphine begging for money for ransom purposes were in Orkney's own interests.

So too were the earnest conversations he had with the Earl of Douglas, James' uncle, who although still a prisoner of Henry's seemed to be a hostage with privileges for he was living in a house he owned and was free to come and go among the merchants and shopkeepers of the City.

Douglas had come quickly to visit James when he had first arrived in the Tower and although he had been sympathetic and promised to do all he could to hasten the boy's release William was convinced his prime objective was to return to Scotland himself where he could resume his personal struggle with Albany.

Another visitor of James had been Murdoch, heir of Albany. He had made no haste to come to the Beauchamp Tower and once there James found it difficult to be natural with him. He had expected to receive much advice and perhaps some comfort from his cousin, who was eight years his senior, but he found the older man had deteriorated sadly during his years of captivity and thought little but of drinking and gambling with his fellow prisoners.

'So you are now King of the Scots since my lamented Uncle passed away,' he drawled as he leant against the wall and pared his nails with a pocket knife. 'It was fortunate indeed when my father proclaimed this fact to the Three Estates when they met in Perth he was able to comfort them with the knowledge that he would look to their government during your absence.'

James flushed, recognising the barb but refusing to let it hurt him.

'It was well indeed,' he agreed mildly. 'Let us hope he will not have to bear the responsibility too long alone.'

'Exactly so. We all wish to return home and my father presses continually for my release.'

'How fares your wife?' James interrupted quickly.

'Well enough, I believe,' Murdoch said. 'With a quiver full of sons to keep her busy.'

James was glad his cousin did not seek him out often and that his own days were filled with the daily coaching Henry had provided for Griffith and himself.

He enjoyed the lessons in Latin, mathematics and Canon Law but the young Welshman found them tedious and longed to be outside in the summer air.

He had recently formed an attachment for the daughter of the washerwoman who came once a week to take their linen. James watched with interest as it was his first experience of anyone in the throes of calf love. He thought Griffith was acting the languishing lover but found he was mistaken and that his new friend was pining in truth.

They took their daily exercise by walking

on the narrow parapet and one warm evening, heady with the scent of the roses in the walled garden below them, they stopped and leant on the brickwork gazing out towards the City.

'If she does not let me kiss her before Midsummer's Eve I shall throw myself into the moat or leap in with the lions,' Griffith blurted out to James.

'That would be a waste!' James answered.

'Waste?' Griffith echoed. 'Why, she is the most fascinating girl I have seen in an age!'

'Is she?' James asked and added slowly. 'She seems a trifle thin and pale to me.'

'That only makes her the more interesting,' Griffith said. 'That's where she lives,' he said pointing towards the City now bathed in the rosy light of the setting sun.

'How do you know?' James asked.

'She told me herself that she and her mother have a room in a street close to the Fleet.'

Griffith was quiet a long time then he turned to James and said in a drawn out sigh, 'Do you not miss girl's company?'

James regarded his friend in the dying day.

'Well,' he said slowly. 'My sisters were good enough friends when I was at home with them. At St. Andrews there was only Henry. Of course we used to talk about girls,' he

74

added hastily, not wishing Griffith to think him completely naïve.

'Oh, did you,' Griffith said with quickened interest. 'And what did you say about them?'

'Oh,' James replied rapidly searching for an answer that would not show up too readily the discrepancy in their ages. 'Whom we should like to marry and that sort of thing.'

'Marry!' Griffith interrupted laughing. 'I wasn't thinking about that yet awhile. There's plenty of time for that when we are released from here — if we ever are,' he added suddenly gloomy. 'No, I had in mind a little pleasant dalliance to distract us from our unhappy lot.'

James was at a loss for he knew what Griffith implied and was well aware of the number of women, some of them wearing the scarlet hood of the harlot, who were secreted into the Tower for the pleasure of the prisoners. He decided he would rather have Griffith think him wooden headed than a prude.

'Girls are all right at the loom and in the still room but they are not a lot of use with the bow or at the tilt.'

Now that he had said it the words seemed a little thin even to his own ears but to his relief and somewhat to his surprise Griffith threw back his head and shouted with laughter.

'Let's walk again,' he said indulgently. 'I was forgetting you are so much younger than I!'

James accepted this disparaging remark gratefully and they continued their stroll in the warm dusk.

For the first time in his life James thought about women as an object of desire. He found his mind baulked at the idea of wanton behaviour between the sexes, vaguely connecting overheard stories of his brother Rothesay and their mother's tear stained face.

Suddenly he found himself thinking of the deep comfort of being embraced by a woman and he had a momentary vision of a golden girl, softly curved and welcoming. He sighed, almost as deeply as Griffith had done as a pleasant warmth rushed through his veins.

'Beat you to the gate!' he said to Griffith, somewhat breathlessly.

He must escape from this magic evening and his own new thoughts before they overcame him.

Not long after this he found half formed sentences and phrases jostling in his brain as he sat at a Latin exercise. Forgetting completely that he was supposed to be transcribing Caesar's Occupation of Britain he scribbled down some of the lines and to his delight discovered they scanned and took on the pattern of poetry. He was altering a word here and there when he was abruptly recalled by the tutor asking, apparently not for the first time, if he had completed the translation.

He mumbled that it was not quite finished and hastily pushed the verses aside. He stood up and made as good an effort as he was able from a hurried glance at the text, hesitating so many times that Griffith looked at him in mock dismay and the monk dismissed them obviously thinking that on this occasion the summer weather was proving too tempting for both his pupils.

His new found interest proved absorbing and sustaining. James sat in the shade of a wall with paper and ink rather than shoot or wrestle with Griffith.

It was fortunate that he was so occupied, for an embassy that came from Scotland with high hopes of obtaining his release arrived in July and left without it, taking with them the impression that Henry had listened most courteously to their demands and had even agreed with their reasons for making them but had no intention of granting them.

It sustained him also when Orkney and Douglas, the latter promising never again to war against Henry, were granted temporary permission to go to Scotland to discuss the ransom and the possibility of a perpetual truce with England. They returned with the news that a larger embassy were to come to Westminster at Christmas on James' behalf.

In November William reported that he had heard on good authority that Leicester King at Arms had gone north bearing Letters from Henry to Albany. When James asked him if he considered this was a favourable move, coupled as it was with Orkney's and Douglas' visit, he could not commit himself to an optimism he could not honestly feel. He had had much conversation with the Scots who had been granted safe conducts during the Summer, and they had all told him that Albany might pay lip-service to the cause of James' release but his main concern was obtaining the repatriation of his own son Murdoch. William, listening to them felt a hopeless fury against the fates which had so played into Albany's hands and sent James a prisoner to England. With Douglas and most of the supporters of the old King Robert also in the Tower a speedy return to Scotland seemed impossible. Surprisingly, Albany did not appear to be very successful in the matter of freeing Murdoch and when the embassy from Scotland, very much smaller and less important than the previous one, returned after Christmas accomplishing nothing William felt a grudging admiration for Henry. If he were not strictly against Albany he was most certainly not for him either.

James had other worries to contend with for Griffith received the unhappy news that yet another of his brothers had been killed fighting in Wales. The young man was sullen with grief and bitter against Henry of Monmouth and it took all the patience James possessed to coax him back to a happier state of mind.

With the Spring Orkney managed to raise the three hundred gold nobles needed for his ransom and he returned to Scotland, promising his urgent support for James' cause, but no word had reached the boy in the Tower when he and Griffith with William Giffard were removed to Nottingham Castle.

This precaution was to protect them from the plague which they knew was raging in the narrow streets of the City, where refuse was allowed to rot and open sewers carried waste unchecked close to water conduits and food stalls.

The visits of the laundress and her daughter had been stopped and Griffiths did not feel this as keenly as he might have done during the summer that was past for he confessed to James that he had managed to separate the girl from her mother on several occasions and had found the swift tumble in a secluded corner satisfying enough but so well flavoured with onions to be most repulsive. James resisted the obvious retort for Griffith's spirits were still not wholly predictable.

The prospect of a move cheered them both and they took leave of the Constable gaily enough. With a large escort they were hurried through the streets of the city and took the road North.

The countryside had never looked more inviting to them than it did on this day. The trees were in full leaf and the commons and meadows thick with bright green grass, while the birds sang unceasingly as they darted from hedgerow to branch.

James was now fourteen years of age and he had added patience to his other qualities. It had not been necessary for William to tell him of the beliefs of the embassies who came to Westminster. It was too obvious as the weeks dragged into months that it was not only Henry who kept him as a prisoner. He could not really believe that he had ever thought it would be otherwise. This had not prevented him writing to Albany as Governor pressing him to give his urgent attention to the question of his sovereign's return. This request had been couched in most polite terms and Albany's reply had been as courteous and evasive as James' letter had been pointed. The sole consolation that James had was that Murdoch was still in the Tower.

It was rumoured that Henry would be at Nottingham during the summer and James wondered if any of his family would accompany him, for he would like to have sight of the young man Griffith contemptuously dismissed as 'that bloody usurper', but who, nevertheless, furnished much of the conversation of those who had resided in the Tower. James had heard him described as wild and a wastrel who frequented bawdy-houses, although it was grudgingly admitted, when Griffith was out of earshot, that he was absolutely fearless and a general of no mean ability. Apart from this doubtful praise Henry of Monmouth seemed an exact counterpart of Rothesay and James hated the very mention of his name.

Nottingham proved to be a formidable fortress, high above the town. Its governor, Lord Grey of Codnor had recently been appointed Constable of the Castle for services in the King's cause against the Scots and the Welsh. Although he had been a great fighter he showed no particular hostility towards his two young captives and they were given fairly comfortable quarters close to

William Giffard's. The Castle was smaller than the Tower but commanded sweeping views of the surrounding fields and woodlands.

Griffith learnt from the Bailiff's daughter, with whom he lost no time in establishing friendly relations, that Henry was expected at Nottingham in the early part of August when a great tournament was to take place. The boys were given permission to practise at the butts and in the tiltyard and were allowed also to visit the open space where already the wooden stands were being erected for the lists.

After preparations taking up most of the last weeks of July Henry arrived at the castle with a large company which included three of his young sons. Henry of Monmouth was not among them but he was expected in time for the tournament. When he had rested Henry sent for James and Griffith.

James was struck by the King's haggard appearance and the stoop of the once proud frame. Henry had aged ten years since they had last met, for although his position on the throne was stronger than it had been at any time since he had claimed it he had had much to make him sad during the past twelve months. His elder daughter Blanche, who after much negotiation, had married Lewis, eldest son of Rupert, Count Palatine of the Rhine and Duke of Bavaria, died suddenly, while her sister Phillipa, though only thirteen years of age had gone to Sweden to marry its new King.

His sons, fast growing to manhood, had become involved in the inevitable controversy between their father's Chancellor and his half-brothers, the Beauforts. The Beauforts, John, Earl of Somerset and High Chamberlain, Henry, Bishop of Winchester and Sir Thomas, were influential and wealthy men, possessing a large degree of ambition. They were the sons of John of Gaunt and the Lady Swynford and had been legitimised by an Act of Richard II recently confirmed by their half-brother. They had always been strong and enthusiastic supporters of Henry but it was common knowledge that their willingness had waned a little of late.

Due to the enormous pressure of work which Henry was reluctant to relegate, he had not much time to devote to his young family and had left most of their education and upbringing to the Beauforts. Henry Beaufort had been Henry of Monmouth's tutor at Oxford and there was a strong bond of friendship between them. It was therefore to be expected that the boys were guided by the Beauforts and reflected their beliefs and persuasions and that when, despite the amity which existed between their father and the Beauforts, he favoured Arundel at their expense, they should take their half-uncles part. This suited the Beauforts for in Henry's sons lay the future power of England.

Coupled with this intangible but ever present situation was the unhappy truth that the King's second marriage was resented by his children, who saw his alliance with the widowed Joanna as an unnecessary complication to their lives. Even after four years she was accepted only by courtesy.

None of this underlying sentiment was apparent when Henry presented his three young sons to James and Griffith. He was obviously proud of their good looks and bearing which made James conscious of his sturdy body and unfashionable clothes. Thomas, Humphrey and John talked with him unaffectedly and without condescension but it was not until a competition at the butts was organised that he was accepted as other than a stranger from a distant and usually troublesome country. As his arrows found their target more often than those of any one else he was surrounded with honest congratulations and enjoyed himself more than he could remember.

On the day of the Tournament he was

presented to Henry of Monmouth and was grateful to William for his foresight in approaching Lord Grey for an extra allowance to provide him with a new doublet.

For Henry of Monmouth was in no way the effete pleasure seeker that he had imagined in a mental picture. He was good looking and above average height, carrying himself in the graceful fashion of his family, and although lightly built gave every appearance of strength. His hair was brown and thick and his complexion clear with the open air in which he lived. His most arresting features were his bright hazel eyes and the deep cleft in his chin. He gave James a smile and a look which seemed to James to understand only too well what he was thinking. The boy had difficulty in preserving a cold politeness, for he would not be won over by the charming manner of the young prince.

Blotting out the handsome figure in front of him he concentrated on the image of the whore monger he had expected. It was quite difficult all the same to see Henry of Monmouth wallowing in the debauchery that Rothesay had enjoyed although the mouth above the cleft chin looked as if it could enjoy the open sweetness of a woman's lips. James gave his attention to what Henry was saying and his resentment stiffened as he realised that there was pity underlying what he heard. This was almost more than he could stand for it hit him in the darkness of his secret, hidden longing to return to Scotland and be with his own folk.

Thankfully he saw Griffith beckon to him that William was waiting to show them to their places in the stand and he made his curt respects to the Prince and fled.

As he walked up the steps of the wooden platform he was unaware that he and Griffith were the focal point of dozens of pairs of feminine eyes. He could hear nothing but the kindly words of the young man who waited to step into his inheritance while he was prevented from going to Scotland to claim his. It was some time before the excitement around him brought him back to his surroundings and he noticed the silk covered stand and the women in their bright gowns. He was dazzled and fascinated by the gauze veils fluttering in the sunlight and the extraordinary shapes of the headdresses. This was the first time that he had been in the companionship of the ladies of a court since he had been a child at Linlithgow and he was overcome with shyness. Griffith did not share his embarrassment and was quickly at ease with those around him, recounting in his lilting voice some anecdotes of their stay in the Tower. It all sounded highly amusing and James envied him his gift of turning the most trivial episode into entertainment. While the women were listening to Griffith he covertly watched their faces, seeking he knew not what. The older ladies were well powdered and rouged and were surprisingly without too many wrinkles while the young girls were vivacious and handsome, flaunting their bared shoulders and widely cut bodices. Sometimes he encountered an answering look to which he could not bring himself to respond, lowering his eyes too quickly to catch the interest they betrayed.

All the chattering ceased as the herald approached the King, who was sitting on a raised dais on the right of them, and announced the first two contestants. This was to be a joust in full armour and the tilts were already in position. James saw with a small shock the banner fluttering from the lance of the first knight was Scottish. He turned quickly to Griffith to ask the man's name.

'It sounded like the Earl of Mar to me,' Griffith said. 'Why, do you know him?'

'He is a cousin of mine,' James said slowly. 'But I do not know him well. Do you think we shall be allowed to meet?'

'We shall see,' Griffith answered and gave

his attention to the knights as they took up positions on either side of the barrier especially erected to protect the horses from rushing headlong into one another. As the joust progressed the precaution seemed unnecessary for it proved to be a well staged courtly affair acting as a preliminary to the real business of the day, a contest with daggers between two Bordelais subjects of the King, one of whom had accused the other of treason.

There was polite hand clapping as the Earl of Mar was proclaimed victorious and rode over to the ladies to claim his prize. James looked down into the half-remembered face of his uncle's kinsman but could not know if Mar had recognised him. It was certain that he would be aware of James' being at Nottingham but it was possible that Henry would not grant permission for them to meet. Even if they did it was no foregone conclusion that he meant well towards his sovereign.

The boy's thoughts were interrupted by a particularly blatant clash of trumpets followed by the arrival of the Bordelais who bowed low in front of the King. They were naked to the waist and well past their first youth. With daggers held aloft they awaited the signal to begin.

There was nothing elderly about the men as, at the given signal they faced inwards and took stock of one another. Crouching almost at the same moment they raised their shields and moved sideways, their eyes never leaving the other's face. Then with swift lunges that made the crowd gasp they met shield to shield. Almost as quickly they were apart and the sun glinted on daggers as they rose and were swiftly turned from finding a mark. The men's bodies were shining with sweat as blow after blow was parried and it looked as if the contest would continue indefinitely until suddenly one man slipped and in regaining his balance dropped his shield. Quick as thought the other raised his dagger high above his head to strike at the bare arm of his opponent, who realising his danger kicked out at his shins. In that moment the defenceless one wrenched away the attacker's shield and with daggers only they faced one another. As they leapt into the fight again the trumpets blared across the arena and the King's herald called to them to stop and present themselves before the King.

Henry rose as they approached him.

'We have seen enough,' he said. 'There is to be no more fighting between you. You have proved that you are both true, loyal subjects and you are pardoned forthwith.'

The crowd broke out into loud cheering as the men bowed a little stiffly to Henry and to each other and went off amiably together.

Later, as they were sleepily discussing the events of the day and Griffith was calling James' attention to the varied attractions of the court ladies, James remembered his cousin the Earl of Mar and wondered if Henry would summon him for an interview.

Henry did indeed send for him in the course of the next few days but it was not to have speech with Mar but to inform the boy that he had granted safe conduct to Hector Makgillan, nephew of the Lord of the Isles, who was coming south to have discussions with Henry and with his own liege lord.

As the Lord of the Isles was well known to be an enemy of Albany James took fresh hope. Somebody was at last having the courage to make a move on his behalf.

6

But James was to be disappointed again for although Makgillan came and had protracted discussions with Henry and long talks with James he only succeeded in forming an alliance with Henry and was unable to further the cause of his King's return to Scotland.

That he had this cause at heart was in no doubt for he had made allegiance plain and promised on his return to ask Donald, Lord of the Isles, to send John Lyon, a priest, to be chaplain to James.

The following years until James was eighteen were ones of rising hopes and subsequent disillusion but he did not waste them. Henry left nothing undone to further the education of his royal prisoner and James took full advantage of the opportunities given him. His tutors pronounced him easy to teach with a rational and nimble brain.

A form of truce between the Scots and English had been established and Albany did everything in his power to obtain the release of his son and further his own interest. It was rumoured that he had had the temerity to offer the hand of one of his daughters to Henry for Prince John. While it became increasingly obvious that he did not intend to make one move to reinstate Scotland's rightful King, Henry became equally obstinate and clung tenaciously to Murdoch.

As he matured James came to admire Henry and to realise the prolonged captivity in which the King of England kept him had far outrun his original intentions. Henry would have been happy to see James go back to Scotland and fill England's coffers with the enormous ransom his release would command.

Henry had sufficient trouble on his hands with the factions who were eager to see the young Henry of Monmouth on the throne in his place. As his health grew markedly worse he suffered several fits and it was rumoured he had been smitten with a form of leprosy.

At one stage the King became so ill that it was necessary to set up a Council, headed by the young Henry, to govern for him. The young man lost no time in bringing in Beaufort to act as Chancellor and for some while it seemed as if Henry would lose his throne.

James, hearing from Griffith stories about the wild behaviour of the King's eldest son who was not above becoming embroiled in affrays and brawls in the narrow streets of London, felt sorry for the sick man who had done so much to help him during the tedium of his imprisonment. It was useless for Giffard to speak in the young Henry's defence for James had shut his mind to the parfait gentil knight he had met at Nottingham and preferred to think of the prince as a womanising trouble maker.

Other illusions were in danger of vanishing also as Douglas went home to plead with Albany to assist in releasing James and broke his promise to Henry to return.

John Lyon, the newly appointed chaplain, brought a bundle of letters for James when he came to take up his appointment.

'It is obvious, dear nephew,' Douglas wrote, 'That your other Uncle, the Regent, is not prepared at this time to further your interests and obtain your release. His main concern is to obtain the restoration of his son Murdoch. This is because he feels, as you may well understand, his son has been confined even longer than you have and he wishes to be reunited with him. Even so, rest assured Orkney and I shall not let the matter end there. I trust you are in good health.'

James turned, with something approaching despair, to another letter which he discovered with pleasure was from Henry Percy at St.

Andrews. It was brief and told James that the old Earl of Northumberland had been killed in a skirmish with King Henry's troops at Bramham Moor and that he had now entered into his grandfather's inheritance.

'Not that it is very much, for most of it has been confiscated to furnish the coffers of the King's family. I must rouse myself and see what is to be done about restoring myself to the King's grace. It grows more tedious here as time passes and what was comparatively easy to bear at twelve years of age becomes almost impossible at eighteen. How is it with you? I think often of the days we spent together here. Is it true a large delegation has come South to negotiate your release on behalf of the Three Estates? Speed the day when we may meet.'

James put down the letter and looked up at Lyon mystified.

'Did a deputation come with you?' he asked.

'No, my lord. Lancaster Herald and I travelled alone.'

James looked so despondent the chaplain did not have the heart to tell him Lancaster had indeed brought a number of safe conducts for the Scots delegates but that it had been common knowledge Albany had taken them and put them on one side for consideration in the future.

'Surely your best plan is to become your own advocate in the matter. Personal appeal should be more effective than employing outside petitioners,' Lyon told him.

James needed no second bidding and when Sir William Cockburn and Sir Archibald Edmonstone came to pay him their respects he entrusted them with a letter to take to the Estates on their return to Scotland. He also gave them a letter for Albany realising as he did so it was a waste of effort but necessary to observe the protocol of the situation.

'You've grown a fine young man, my lord,' Sir Archibald told him. 'It seems a sad age since we were cooped up on the Bass there waiting for the ship to carry us to France.'

'It does indeed,' James agreed. 'How different our fortunes might have been had we arrived safely at our destination.'

He was a little surprised at the nostalgia the sight of Sir Archibald invoked. The years had faded the remembrance of minor irritations and what remained was the memory of dangers and hardships shared. They talked deep into the night with Lyon, Giffard and Sir William.

James saw them depart with high hopes for his plea to the Estates. Neither Lyon or Giffard shared his optimism and they watched as the lengthening days brought a nagging anxiety which turned into the most helpless frustration James had known since he had first been captured.

The chaplain prayed for guidance and was rewarded with a visit from the Bishop of Southwell to the Constable of Nottingham Castle. In conversation with Lyon he spoke of the college attached to the Minster and was very willing to send a clerk to further the studies of the King of Scotland.

The tall, aesthetic monk arrived at an opportune moment for Griffith was suddenly taken back to the Tower and James was left very much to his own devices.

The monk was well informed in the political aspects of the Church but his main source of interest to James was a deep belief in the mystical powers latent in the world. He suggested the reading of philosophers who opened up a new vista for the young man. The poet in James responded to beauties and beliefs hitherto unsuspected.

The monk brought some of the Minster's own illuminated manuscripts and James was fascinated by the intricate workmanship of the ornate lettering. It was but a short step to take up the craft himself and the clerk told Lyon he had never taught a more apt pupil. Designs and patterns flowed from the quills and pigments he provided for James.

If the chaplain and the monk noticed the gold besprinkled capitals were as often used to start a poem of the King's own composition as a prayer for a missal they said nothing and were only happy to see him occupied. They privately thanked God James was steered from the pit of despair which most certainly by this time, would have claimed many less staunch characters.

This strength of will was never more necessary than during the weeks which turned into months after Sir Archibald left to take the messages to the Estates.

No reply of any kind came to Nottingham and Lyon was of the opinion that the Regent would most certainly have been informed of the content of the letter and realising his nephew was becoming a power in his own right would have taken every step to thwart James' plea.

Stalemate seemed to be the keyword of James' existence until quite suddenly the King recovered from his illness and was able to govern without the assistance of his son and Beaufort. Arundel was restored to the Chancellorship and one of Henry's first acts was to send for James to spend Christmas with the court at Stratford.

James found himself in the company of

women again. He discovered a shyness he had never suspected before and was secretly a little shocked at the open advances made to him by some of the bejewelled and married ladies of the court. He was persuaded, reluctantly, to stand up with them in several dances and found his face growing red and his hands damp with sweat as they leaned their almost naked bosoms towards him.

Afterwards when he returned to his solitary confinement he blamed himself for not taking advantage of the favours they offered, for the passionate longings he poured into his poetry could not be for ever bottled inside him.

William, he knew, was enjoying the charms of a magnificent redhead whose husband was conveniently absent in the garrison at Calais but when he could tear himself away from her he had much to tell James about the events which followed the King's restoration to health.

The Prince was not present at Stratford although the breach between himself and his father was now healed. The court still spoke in hushed whispers of the reconciliation which had taken place in Westminster when the young Henry had dramatically appeared in the King's apartments dressed in a doublet of blue damask hung all over with needles.

This the King accepted as a sign of his son's penitence although his advisers begged him to be on guard for a plot of patricide. They refused to withdraw and leave father and son alone and their fears looked more than justified when the young man drew his dagger and held it aloft. The Prince with a sideways glance at the statesmen knelt to the King and proffered him the dagger with the point facing towards his own breast. With tears in his eyes the father begged his son to rise and drawing him towards him kissed him on the brow.

William told James the court was certain the pair would not fall out again and a happier atmosphere prevailed than for a long time.

James was glad this was the case but he reserved his judgement about what he regarded as a fortuitous change of heart on the part of the heir apparent.

Before he left Stratford to stay at the Manor House at Croydon an army had been equipped and sent into France to support the Orleanists and a situation arose which caused embarrassment to both Charles, King of France and the Burgundians. Thomas, newly created Duke of Clarence and Henry of Monmouth were both with the force and admitted themselves at a loss to know what was their next move. Henry returned to England to seek the advice of the Council and his father.

He was distressed to discover the King's health had once more deteriorated and he sent messages to his brother counselling him to pursue the campaign on which they had embarked with caution as he remained in England to support his father.

James arrived in Croydon to discover Murdoch had been removed from the Tower and was to share his captivity. His cousin looked more dissolute than when they had last met and greeted James with a patronising air the young man found irritating.

'William,' he said when they had been shown to the chambers they were to occupy. 'I intend to use every spare moment I have to write to Scotland and press somebody, anyone, to help me obtain my release. It is more than I can bear to be cooped up with that dissipated cousin of mine.'

'Would you like me to go and see what I can do?' William asked him quietly.

James looked at him quickly.

'There could be no one better able to plead my cause,' he said. 'But I do not think permission would be granted for you to go.'

'Probably not,' William answered. 'Perhaps you might ask John Lyon to go.'

John Lyon willingly agreed to go and put James' case.

'I shall miss you,' James told him. 'I have few enough loyal and faithful friends about me.'

'But if I can accomplish something I shall be rendering you a better service than remaining here.'

He set out for Scotland with many carefully worded letters to deliver to the Estates and the Douglasses. Within a few months the Earl of Douglas and two kinsmen were granted safe conducts to pass through England on their way to sign a treaty with the Duke of Burgundy. They called in at the Manor on their way and by the time they left again James felt the first stirring of hope that release might be faintly possible.

'It was worth sparing you from my side,' he said to Lyon who had journeyed south with the Scots. 'I feel certain something will be accomplished because of it.'

'The only thing that gives me cause for doubt,' Lyon told him carefully, 'Is that Murdoch is still as firmly entrenched here as before. It is for his father to give the final word in both your cases and with his son still a prisoner — ' His voice trailed off.

'But Henry would be sure to support my return,' James said eagerly.

Lyon turned away so that the young man should not see the doubt he could not hide.

James was buoyed with hope throughout the summer and Autumn and went to Eltham for Christmas in a complacent mood, was sadly shaken when he saw the acute suffering of the King.

The festivities were a mere shadow of the gaiety which had prevailed during the previous year although all the royal princes were present.

By the following February it was obvious the King was a dying man. Before he returned to his Palace at Westminster he called James to him.

He lay propped up in a canopied bed, frail and surrounded with an aura of illness. His queen and several nurses hovered around him.

James found it difficult to speak what was in his mind. During the last month he had experienced such a revival of hope that he had come to regard Henry with a strange affection. Forgotten were the dreary years he had spent in captivity at his hands while he could only feel gratitude for Henry's scrupulous fairness and generous gift of an education he would never have received elsewhere.

He was not ashamed his eyes pricked with

tears as he bent over the emaciated hand the King held out to him.

A month later Henry was dead, struck down by a violent fit while he was at his devotions in the Abbey Church. His attendants carried him to the Jerusalem Chamber where his eldest son hastened to comfort him.

As the first daffodils shook in the uncertain winds of March James mourned the King's passing and wondered what would be his own position on the new King's accession.

He did not have to wait long to find out. Within the week he and William Giffard were committed to the Tower.

7

The spring weather mocked him as he looked through the slits in the deep embrasures of the White Tower where he was lodged with William. He was almost twenty years of age and full of an urge to live. Since he had received the peremptory summons to return to the fortress that lowered over London he had slipped back into the melancholy that had assailed him as a child. But the cold, chill hopelessness threatening to extinguish him was completely adult. It would have been easier had he not felt in those days at Croydon that there was hope of release for it made this setback doubly difficult to endure.

Although William saw it as a good sign that Murdoch accompanied them to the Tower he refused to be comforted by the knowledge and saw good reason for his pessimism when they were joined by twenty four other Scots, among whom was John Lyon.

James' festering hatred of Henry of Monmouth fed on the hurt which he now suffered at his hand. It was useless for the newcomers to talk of the long vigils Henry had spent at the altar in the Abbey Church and the quiet dignity he had acquired. James told them with bitterness that this was a facade and the new King's true character would emerge when his father was laid to his last rest. William Giffard and John Lyon exchanged glances for it was unlike the generous breadth of James' nature to be so unkind. Later William told Lyon that James had always had uneasy memories of his elder brother and he could only offer the explanation that the young King drew a comparison between the late Rothesay and Henry.

William asked the Constable as soon as they arrived at the Tower if it were possible to arrange a meeting between James and Griffith only to be told the Welsh nobleman had been returned to Wales at the request of the people. When James asked him later in the day if Griffith were still at the Tower he was able to say that he had been removed to another place the whereabouts of which were uncertain. James seemed satisfied with the reply and the small spark of interest that had been apparent died away and apathy returned.

In the days that followed he sat apart from the others and strummed moodily on his lute or held a book open on his knee. John Lyon pointed out to him gently that this was not the way to keep the support of his fellow countrymen and James, making a considerable effort, forced himself to talk with them and even laugh at their sallies. Later he was glad that he had done this for as suddenly as they had arrived the twenty four Scots were released. Reluctantly John Lyon went with them. James insisted that he should go for he was of more use to their cause outside the Tower than within.

The coronation of Henry of Monmouth was to take place on the ninth day of April and the newly arrived Spring was rudely battered with a day of driving snow flurries and hail storms.

The superstitious read omens in the sudden, freakish change of weather and the unhappy James, receiving no share in the amnesty which he heard pardoned certain partakers in plots and offences against the Crown, found himself hoping the signs boded ill for the new King.

James did not see Henry when he rode in from Kingston to spend the eve of the coronation at the Tower. Murdoch however lost no time in trying to petition the King and waited for several hours outside the chapel of St. Peter and Vincula while Henry kept solitary vigil. When the young King emerged, pale and withdrawn his attendants brushed the importuning Murdoch aside and forbade him to disturb their lord. The only satisfaction Murdoch could obtain from them was a promise that they would present to Henry any letter he wrote. William who had witnessed the incident from an embrasure within the White Tower, told James he had no doubt that any letter would be a long string of moans as Murdoch had not ceased talking of the conditions under which they were living which he complained were of a lower standard than during their previous confinement. He had thrown out his blankets claiming they were threadbare and dirty and had demanded from the Governor a regular supply of washed linen. To James, bodily comfort was a minor pinprick compared with the longing he felt to be free and he allowed himself a wry smile at his cousin's pettiness.

James did not permit himself to go to the battlements with William to watch the Coronation procession move off towards Cheapside on the morning of Passion Sunday but Giffard reported that the brilliant velvets and emblazoned tabards showed up bravely in the snow, Henry sat his horse with smiling ease. While the banquet which followed in Westminster Hall, although not as elaborate as the feast which had marked the crowning of Henry's father, was a gourmet's delight.

When he heard this James looked down

sourly at his shabby doublet and pecked at the dull fare which was his daily diet. He refused to think of the succulent roast pig that had been sent up to him on the day of the coronation and which he had sent churlishly away complaining of a queasy stomach.

He awoke a few days later and heard through his reluctantly returning consciousness the wild sweet song of a thrush calling his mate. He listened to the falling cadences until the sounds pierced his defensive armour of apathy and cursing the bird he leapt from his bed and doused his head with cold water from the basin. Splashing as much as possible he was able to drown the song which clutched at his heart. Dressing hurriedly he shouted for William who came quickly as he feared something was amiss.

'William, I beg of you, send to the Constable and ask him if a member of the Inner Temple can be found who would be willing to give me some instruction in the English Law. I shall surely go mad if I do not have something with which to occupy my brain.'

Only too willingly Giffard went to the Constable and returned with the news that a messenger would be sent without delay to the Master who would be certain to know of some struggling young lawyer eager to eke out his existence by teaching such an illustrious student. William gave silent thanks to God for this sign of renewed interest for he knew James had wanted to approach the old King about receiving instruction in jurisprudence when they had been at Croydon but had hesitated to ask for further favours when Henry IV had been failing visibly.

Later James sat alone in his dark chamber, his senses quivering with the return of feeling. He took up his neglected lute and picked out chords at once melodious and of a queer stirring quality reaching down into the depths of his smothered longings. In almost physical pain he struck savagely at the lute sending discords crashing round the cheerless room. He did not hear the door open but as he threw the instrument down on to the bed his eye caught the movement of a skirt and he looked up, startled, into a pair of slanting green eyes.

'I am sorry, Sir, if I frighted you.'

'Who are you?' James demanded brusquely, disconcerted by the nearness of the first desirable woman he had seen for months.

'I am the daughter of the woman who sweeps your room for you, but she is sick and sent me instead.'

'Well, go about your task then,' James

growled ungraciously. Her husky voice was disturbing and he went into the garderobe where he walked to and fro in an increasing state of agitation. He stayed there long enough to give the girl plenty of time to finish the sweeping and go but when he returned, slowly, she was still there. He went quickly to the narrow slit in the wall and bent down to look out. The bright sunlight made him blink and all London seemed wreathed in pale yellow gauze. After a few moments he stood up with his back to the wall unable to see. As his eyes cleared he watched the girl as she moved from hearth to table. He tried to look away but he was fascinated by the graceful movements of her arms and the swing of her hips.

'If ye'll help me we'll move your bed,' she said. 'There's bound to be a mass of dust under it.'

James knew this to be true for he had put an idle hand down between the wall and the truckle only yesterday and recoiled with revulsion as he thought he had put his hand on a dead mouse. Closer inspection had revealed a ball of fluff and dirt.

He went to the bed and she leant over to take the weight on her side. James caught a faint drift of the warmth of her body and a glimpse of the exposed curve of her bosom.

He quickly dropped the bed and returned to the embrasure. Did he see her smile or did he imagine it? Unable to help himself he watched her sweep the stone floor and then, effortlessly, push the truckle back into its original position. James felt a tide of feverish heat rush through him. The girl was taunting him and every fibre of his body was responding. Without a backward glance she took her broom and busied herself in the garderobe. James almost followed her but restrained himself.

As she came back, the thrush, forgotten since it had woken him in the morning, took up its delirious mating call and James put out his hand and touched the girl on her shoulder. With an alacrity which amazed him she came close to him, pushing her dress off her shoulder as she did so. Swept by an overwhelming awareness of her sensuality James smothered her face and neck with kisses, clumsy and hurtful in his need. She held his head to her breast fiercely arching her back and thrusting herself against him. In an ecstasy of aroused passion they fell on the narrow bed and with tembling fingers James clutched at the fastenings on her coarse woollen dress. Her eager hands assisted him while her mouth sought his.

With her bosom bared James fumbled to

lift her skirt. The girl twisted herself beneath him and pulled him with strong arms towards her. Suddenly James was filled with revulsion and pushed her away, covering his eyes to blot out the sight of her wanton nakedness. He stumbled to his feet and staggered into the garderobe where he was violently sick.

He was prepared for tears and perhaps shrieking abuse but he was shocked into returning to his chamber by peals of mirth. The girl, fastening her dress, had her head thrown back and was laughing almost gaily. Resentment flared in James but died down as she put out a hand to him.

'There, there, deary! Was I too much for your sensibility then? I'll warrant you're a virgin and need leading more gentle like. Don't you fret, Sir, I'll not be talking about your shortcomings. It's not the first time it happened to a young gentleman and it'll not be the last!'

Blowing him a flippant kiss she was gone as suddenly as she had come stooping with magnificent grace to pick up her broom.

James was left mollified but strangely at peace. He could not sleep for several nights after this encounter and found himself brooding a great deal about his desire for a woman and the act of gratification. He knew, without doubt, that he had desired the girl with every fibre of his being but in the moment of consummation he had realised her lack.

She was, in physical appearance, everything he had dreamed of in a woman; the tawny hair and the golden skin. At first he could not understand the sudden change of feeling which had made him recoil from her but in the long, quiet hours of the night he came to realise that he asked more from a woman than the swift vortex of coupling. His passionate nature, held so long in check needed more than the sensation of skin on burning skin and the thrust of heaving bodies. He asked for an understanding linked with desire. This knowledge, with the seemingly impossible chance of its gratification in his endless captivity, filled him with unquiet. However, slowly the recognition of his need brought him its own peace and he knew he could wait until eye meeting eye told him he had met his heart's love.

When the young lawyer, gowned and gaunt with lack of sufficient food to line his stomach, came to the Tower he found his pupil more than ready to begin his tutelage.

Later in the year John Lyon was granted permission to visit James regularly and James heard with surprise that Henry was opening discussions with Albany. In August Lyon reported Henry, despite strengthening his defences in the Marches, had concluded a truce to last from this month until the following June. To quell any false hopes his King might have that this inferred Henry was about to return James to Scotland Lyon hastened to point out that several commissioners had come from Scotland and returned without satisfaction. James could only be relieved Murdoch was still in the Tower.

At about this time the plague returned once more to London. The weather was sultry and oppressive and in the airless streets citizens, in increasing numbers, succumbed to the dread disease. It was not unusual to see a sufferer suddenly gripped with a pain that sent him staggering until he fell headlong. Passersby would hastily draw away until one, braver than the rest, dragged the inert figure into the nearest shade and scuttled off.

Word came from Westminster that James was to be removed to Windsor to lessen the threat of him contracting the plague and as before when he went to Nottingham with Griffith he left the grim fortress with a lighter heart and rode into the Berkshire countryside with pleasure.

He could see the rounded keep at Windsor, silver stoned in the clear air, long before they came up to it and it appeared to him to be the most welcoming place he had come to since he departed from Scotland. His small escort halted on the bridge as they left Eton village and crossed the Thames. The river, flowing smoothly on its way to London, seemed very different from the sullen waters which had twice borne him into imprisonment. He felt a happiness for which he could offer no explanation and clattered across the drawbridge with an expectancy amounting almost to joy.

Once established in a pleasant chamber overlooking the chase that swept south from the castle he found again his skill at writing verse and begged for writing materials with which to express his pent up longings. He was glad of this outlet for he had regretted leaving the young lawyer with whom he had spent several hours each day in the Tower. He had learnt much and found real pleasure in the discussions they had had on every aspect of English law. James was determined when he regained his own Kingdom to put into practise many of the statutory laws that helped to govern England smoothly and were, he knew from Lyon and other of his visitors, badly needed in Scotland.

He had not been more than a few days at Windsor when Henry arrived with his court.

James lost a little of his new found peace of mind when William came to tell him he was summoned to pay his respects to the English king. It was the first time he had done so since Henry of Monmouth had come to the throne and James dreaded the meeting.

He bowed himself into Henry's presence, seeing for a fleeting moment the remembered figure. As he straightened from kissing the King's outstretched hand he was struck by the young man's grave demeanour and his appearance of controlled strength. The hazel eyes regarded James levelly and were bright with interest.

James was disconcerted by the King's sympathetic enquiries for his well being and listened almost unbelievingly to the information that Henry had granted permission to several further delegations from Scotland to come south on his behalf. He had built up in his mind a picture of a careless, pleasure seeking youth who squandered his precious freedom in riotous living and he now found this incompatible with the man before him. He was invited to accompany Henry on a hunting expedition in the surrounding forest later in the week and during this time he had further opportunity to assess the new monarch. It was most obvious that Henry had matured rapidly and it was impossible to ignore the impression he gave of a man who gained spiritual well being through self discipline. Henry had earned the respect of his courtiers and servants who hastened to do his bidding. All in all James envied him and not least his tall, graceful figure, for he, James, although grown broader and immensely strong, was still only of average height. They had not been at Windsor for a week together before James admitted reluctantly he was drawn to the new King in the same way he had been to his father.

With the cooler Autumn weather came the news of further outbreaks of trouble from the Lollards and a message from Archbishop Beaufort stated that he regretted Henry found it necessary for James to be returned to the Tower.

James, although not wishing to leave the place where he had been happier than for a long time, fully understood Henry could not have within easy access of Oxford a figurehead the troublemakers could make their own. He went back to London with renewed vitality and a faint hope of one of the emissaries from Scotland meeting with success in beginning some negotiations for his release.

Coupled with his slight optimism was his growing interest in the University at St.

Andrews for which a Papal Bull had been issued for the granting of a Charter. John Lyon had brought back from Scotland the letters which had mooted the idea during the last year and now Bishop Wardlaw was enlisting his absent King's support for the project. James entered into the plans with enthusiasm for he saw education as a strong defence for his country's future. The advantages of having a university in Scotland were obvious and would save much of the inherent dangers of sending receptive young scholars to be impregnated with the diversive idealogies of Oxford or the Sorbonne.

It was as well James had this absorbing interest for during the next year his growing expectation of release was hopelessly squashed when Albany unscrupulously used the money granted him by the Pope towards the ransom of James and Murdoch to obtain the freedom of his son only.

James heard with burning resentment of the preparations made for the departure of the Regent's son for Scotland. There could be no further doubt of who kept the rightful King of Scotland a prisoner in England and although he had no means of knowing at this time how Albany had secured the large sum required to free Murdoch James was sure in his own mind that it had not been obtained honestly.

He was slightly mollified to learn that one of the conditions of the release of Murdoch was the repatriation of James' young companion at St. Andrews, the Earl of Northumberland. Henry needed this youthful nobleman to help him strengthen his Borders while he drew off his other captains and troops to fight in France. It had appeared during the last year as if a lasting peace between England and France was possible but at the beginning of 1415 Henry was preparing to send aid to the Burgundians at their request. This act did nothing to soothe relationships with Scotland who were already sending support to the Orleanists. With despair James saw his chances of going home reduced to nothing.

8

Henry took his army to France and after establishing a base at Harfleur led them to a resounding victory.

Agincourt became a magic name which breathed the true spirit of England. The people were united as they had not been for years behind a man who recalled for them the warrior Edward III and the glories he had bestowed upon them.

Henry was showered with praise and given a triumphant welcome when he returned to London in November. The streets were lined with rejoicing citizens while pageants greeted him at every turn of the road. Hidden massed choirs sang Te Deums with transcending joy and wine ran freely in the water conduits. Henry received the acclamations with quiet dignity.

When this fact was reported to James he was not particularly surprised for he viewed the victory with mixed feelings himself. He was much concerned that Albany was receiving the French Ambassador more and more frequently at the Scottish Court while Border raids by strong forces of Scots did not improve the tenuous relationship between his own and Henry's kingdom.

Since Windsor his conception of Henry had altered completely. He no longer saw him as an oppressive jailer bent on keeping him a helpless captive but rather as a young man with high ideals who intended to make his country great at the same time restoring James to his rightful throne from where he could govern a friendly Scotland. In Henry he saw, with his natural logical brain sharpened by the legal training he was receiving, his main hope of returning to his inheritance. If Albany persisted in establishing his ties with France it might be Henry would further James' cause.

Despite this in the following May Murdoch was released from the Tower under escort to begin his journey northwards. He was to await at Warkworth the news of Henry Percy's arrival at Berwick where the exchange was to take place.

James stood with the Constable of the Tower as his cousin was handed over to two esquires and bade him Godspeed with as much grace as he was able. He comforted himself with the knowledge that Murdoch had had four more weary years in captivity than he had and that when he did arrive in Scotland the Regent would not be able to make use of his son whose physical and mental state had so sadly degenerated during his long imprisonment.

News soon came to James that Murdoch was not to have an easy journey home. Crossing the Yorkshire moors he was captured by a band of Lollards who overpowered an armed troop supplied by the mayor of Newcastle. James and William found it difficult to suppress their mirth at the thought of the flabby Murdoch intimidated by his tough and fanatical captors.

The Lollards success was short lived for Murdoch was quickly released by a company of soldiers under Ralph Pudsey and taken to the Castle of the Earl of Westmorland at Raby.

Here he stayed for over six months until the arrival of Henry Percy at Berwick in the following February. It was generally believed that if the Neville family did not enjoy having the Regent's son imposed upon their hospitality he would gladly have stayed there longer for the Earl had several daughters all having reputations for great beauty.

At Berwick the ill gotten ransom monies were handed over and Murdoch proceeded to Scotland.

In London King Henry impatiently awaited the arrival of Henry Percy to pay him homage. He waited for some weeks, for Percy, arriving at the Westmorland home fell in love with Eleanor, a widowed daughter of the Earl and married her. After much feasting and rejoicing they travelled south together to pay their respects to Henry obtaining at the same time his pardon and the return of the Northumberland inheritance.

Henry, after recovering from his annoyance at Percy's tardy appearance could only be pleased with this turn of events for the bride was a niece of the Beauforts and thus forged a strong link between the throne and the newly returned Earl.

James had spent some time in Pevensey Castle while King Henry had been fighting in France but he returned to the Tower in 1416.

He found on his arrival here a fellow prisoner with whom he was quickly on good terms. Charles, Duke of Orleans, had been the most illustrious captive after the Battle of Agincourt. Many of his fellow noblemen had been killed or seriously wounded in the engagement while the less important ones had been ransomed for high prices.

Charles was about three years older than James but in experience was certainly many times his superior. He had married his cousin, Isabella widow of Richard II of England, when he was only fifteen and had been devastated when she had died a short time afterwards. After the Dukes of Burgundy and Brittany he was the most important noble in France for the King was a nonentity, suffering as he did from recurrent fits of madness. Although he was espoused to the daughter of the count of Armagnac who was the true leader of the Orleanist faction, he was not really politically minded and it was most unfortunate for him to be captured after a battle in which he had had no particular desire to fight.

He and James soon discovered they shared the common interest of writing poetry and James learnt much from the older man in the matter of style. Charles was not prepared to languish in captivity and was horrified to hear of the years of privation his fellow prisoner had suffered.

'I do not care,' he said waving his expressive hands, 'if it adds huge sums to my ransom but I do not intend to sit back and wait for my countrymen to release me. I have already asked King Henry for the best horses and hawks he can procure and I shall use them as often as possible. These chambers you are using are disgraceful! My servants are at this moment in the city purchasing damasks and silks to make new hangings. How you have endured I shall never know.'

Looking at it from this nobleman's sophisticated angle James began to wonder indeed. But for all his high flown plans, which certainly matured as time went by, Charles was never happier than when he and James had quill and ink before them and sonnets and ballads flowed from them.

Amid this new found interest John Lyon and another retainer of James called John of Alway were given safe conducts to go to Scotland while at the same time permits were issued for the Earl of Douglas and his supporters to come to England to treat with Henry on James' behalf.

As these journeys and the ensuing discussions were taking place Henry was entertaining Sigismund, King of the Romans, at the English Court. Although Henry lavished hospitality upon him he would not agree to Sigismund's plea for a total cessation of war between the warring Christian kingdoms. He did however promise to observe a truce from October until the following Candlemas. As Scotland was included in the general peace a faint glimmer of hope, once more, appeared to James.

This was strengthened when Henry sent for him early in December. He went with pleasure and greeted the young king with unfeigned courtesy. Henry was leaner and browned from his campaigning but he was in good spirits and clasped hands with James in friendly fashion.

'My Lord,' Henry began. 'We are happy to tell you that negotiations for your release have reached the stage when I think it would be beneficial to your cause for you to go North. Archbishop Beaufort and I have therefore arranged for you to be escorted to Pontefract to await there the eleven Scottish nobles who this day have been given safe conducts to come to your presence.'

'Your Grace!' James stammered, unable to believe what he heard. 'I can never thank you enough!'

'Not too fast, my Lord. This is only a preliminary — perhaps a temporary liberation to see to your affairs from your own country. Rest assured that we have made all arrangements for hostages should you not return by any date which may be specified. But go in peace and may God prosper you.'

James knelt swiftly and pressed Henry's hand to his forehead then rushed from the audience chamber. His one thought was to find William and Charles and tell them the unbelievable good news.

To be allowed home! The thought was breathtaking. Once in his own country he would be able to put his case to those nobles loyal to himself and force Albany to raise his ransom through the Burghs. As he was taken back to the Tower he was certain in his own mind that he only had to make personal contact with his people to ensure he was never sent back to England. In his absence it was only too likely that waverers to his cause should incline to the Regent but given a few weeks in which to show his strength he would stiffen their support.

On 12th December, in excellent spirits, he left London. Although the weather was cold and forbidding he hardly noticed it in his delight to be going North.

After they had spent Christmas en route James sent John Lyon and Alway ahead of him to Scotland to speak with the eleven delegates who were to meet him in the Border country. With them he sent several of his thoughtful and well penned letters putting with great tact his thoughts and wishes.

William saw the two leave with his blessing and bade them keep him well informed of the true feeling of the Scottish nobility for his hopes were not as sanguine as James' and he feared there would be no speedy solution to his King's misfortunes.

It was two months before James was in sight of Pontefract Castle and the further North he came the more the burden of his long imprisonment slipped from him.

The gentle hills and sweeping dales reminded him nostalgically of his childhood and he pushed onwards as eagerly as was possible in trying and difficult conditions. His party was met in a downpour of needlelike rain by heralds of the referees who were awaiting them at Pontefract.

When James heard that the Bishop of Durham and the Earl of Westmorland had Northumberland as the third member of the English representatives who were to negotiate with the Scottish ambassadors he turned joyfully to William.

'We are indeed fortunate! This must be a happy omen for our cause. How long is it since he and I parted at St. Andrews?'

'Far longer than I care to remember,' William answered drily. 'All of eleven years it must be.'

'He will be much altered, as I am,' James said. 'Do you think he will have his bride with him as his father-in-law is here also?'

But Eleanor was not with Henry Percy as he came swiftly to greet James when he dismounted at the Castle door.

Neither of the young men spoke for a moment; each taking quick stock of the other and noticing in a glance the changes and the familiar. Then they clasped hands and slapped shoulders shouting with pleasure.

Percy called loudly for wine and led James into the Hall which seemed full of people. Pushing their way through the throng to the hearth they found Westmorland and made the formal presentations. This over James noticed the easy fellowship which existed between Percy and his father-in-law. This was hardly surprising as they were both northcountry-men and steeped in the traditions of their vast tracts of land.

James was pleased to discover Henry was hardly taller than he and his build was almost as burly. His hair was tawny and his eyes the same colour, the skin around them crinkled with humour. He promised James a quiet pot of ale when the formalities of the evening were done. They had so much to talk over and remember since that long ago day when James had set out for France.

'Where are the delegation from Scotland?' James asked. A quick look around the hall had told him no Scots were present and although he feared this meant they had not yet arrived there was the chance they were keeping to their chambers.

'They are not here but they'll come within a day or two,' Henry said cheerfully.

'They have had plenty of time,' James protested.

'Oh, the roads are practically impassable with the thaw setting in. Don't you fret; we'll have them among us soon enough.'

But a week went by and there was no sign or word from the delegation. Unable to admit they were probably not coming at all James prevailed upon Henry and Westmorland to send word to King Henry that he wished most strongly to go further North to be closer at hand. Now somewhat concerned at the unexplained delay the Earls consulted with the Bishop of Durham and agreed to take James to Raby while a messenger was sent to London.

Henry was secretly pleased at this move for he had left his wife with her mother, Lady Joan, at the Westmorland stronghold and he was missing her sadly. He was also glad to have something definite for James to do for the young King was showing every appearance of disillusionment with the whole project.

James at any other time would have enjoyed the ride through the grandeur of the Yorkshire dales but he was impatient to reach Raby. Arrived at the mellowed grey stone castle he was cheered considerably by the Neville family for he liked Eleanor on sight and the other young daughters made it their business to pamper him. He relaxed in the family atmosphere which had become so strangely foreign to him and for a brief hour forgot the reason for his coming. Although there were other girls in the household spending several months as guests while pursuing their studies with the Nevilles James saw them all as from a distance. Not one of them roused him as even the cleaning girl had done.

Word eventually came from King Henry that he might stay a week or until Easter if James did not consider the seven days long enough. If the Scottish delegates had not arrived by the feast he was to return.

Henry Percy grieved over this news but he was well aware the King of England was making all preparations to war against the French once more and it would not do for him to have James out of his surveillance at this time.

James felt a frustration which threatened to rob him of his reason. He grew angrier with Albany as the time limit ran out and a quiet, steel hard resolve formed in his mind that when, if ever, he went back to Scotland he would make the Regent and his family suffer for keeping him shut out of his native land and from his rightful throne.

A subdued company celebrated Easter with James trying to push his thoughts of vengeance away from him. When it was over Henry Percy, not daring to disobey his King's command, formed up his troop to escort James on the first part of his journey back to London.

Burning with indignation James took his leave of the Nevilles most reluctantly, thanking them sincerely for their kindness.

'I shall never forget,' he told Lady Joan who was sister of Archbishop Beaufort. 'What it has been to be among a family again. One tends to forget the gentleness of women shut away as I am.'

'Do you not mix with the court in London at all?'

'Rarely. Perhaps at Christmas time. Once I went to Windsor and the King took me hunting but I have my books and there are friends in the Tower,' he added hastily not wishing Lady Westmorland to think him full of self pity.

'I must send word to my sister-in-law, now Duchess of Clarence, for she has a young family and perhaps could persuade the King to grant permission for you to visit them.'

'That would be most kind,' James said gratefully.

On his return to London Henry was, however, too pre-occupied with affairs in France to worry over much about the social side of his illustrious prisoner's life. He continued to pay through his Exchequer the 13s. 4d. which was James' daily allowance, kept him out of the Lollards way as much as was possible and was as kind as he was able. He had indeed, been genuinely sorry for the young King when he had been forced to come South without having had any contact with his Scottish Ambassadors.

His sorrow turned to fury when Albany sent several raiding parties deep into England and at one stage he was obliged to send ships to support Percy who was hard pressed rousing the support of the loyal men in the North. Of all times, at the moment when he was prepared to land in France, he could not afford to have trouble on his Border.

The situation did not improve when the Scots increased their pillaging and burning and Henry received information that the French were sending a fleet to transport a large force of Scots to assist them in France.

Almost at the same time Henry learnt Albany had offered 30,000 livres to the French. This when he had been unable to raise the ransom for the return of his rightful King. Henry left for France with the Scottish monarch very much on his mind.

His last act before departing to attempt the conquest of Normandy was to send James to Kenilworth where he hoped the young man might be reasonably happy and well occupied.

9

While the war in France took its entangled course James made the most of the more pleasant imprisonment at Kenilworth. The castle had been renovated and enlarged and it was generally believed that when Henry eventually resolved the French situation he would live more often in this quiet retreat.

Since the fiasco at Raby James had no further doubts concerning the enmity of Albany and although he sent John Lyon again and again to Scotland during the next two years he regarded his missions as hopeless.

His monetary affairs were at this time at their lowest ebb and had he received any summons to visit the Somerset family he would not have had the temerity to go for his wardrobe was threadbare and hopelessly outmoded. He had even swallowed his pride sufficiently to ask Douglas to intercede with the Estates to grant him an allowance, however small, to implement the meagre amount granted him by Henry.

No such help was forthcoming but Douglas sent a crumb of comfort in the news of Murdoch's inept effort to assist his father in the rule of Scotland. Albany was in despair at his son's inefficiency.

In France Burgundy defected from his English ally and made war on the Orleanists alone. The fight now became three cornered.

Henry, in possession of most of western Normandy, was worried by Burgundy's hold on the garrisons of Rouen, Varon and Mantes. The situation looked serious indeed when John the Fearless led his Burgundian troops into Paris. Henry now saw even greater danger in an alliance between the two French factions. His army was fighting separated from its main base and would be completely outnumbered. As he feared the Orleanists and Burgundy lost no time in calling a truce and joined forces along the Seine.

Henry did not hesitate. He took the Pont de l'Arche and succeeded in crossing the river, making Rouen his objective.

The unfortunate townsfolk held out here against the English Army entrenched outside from 30th July 1418 to 19th January 1419. The people were near starvation by October and were reduced to eating cats, horses, dogs, rats and mice in an effort to stave off their pitiless hunger. With the lack of food came disease and the strong were forced to watch the elderly, the sick and small children die of hunger.

In December, when malnutrition made it difficult to move, the Captain of the defenders issued an order to put the oldest and weakest outside the wall. In helpless sorrow the relatives saw their loved ones depart.

Outside Henry of England looked on with mounting anger. He ordered his troops to push the outcasts back into the town but as quickly as they were returned the defenders ejected them. Henry refused to allow them through his lines but he was unable to see them starve and the besieger's rations were stretched to feed them.

The garrison finally surrendered with hardly an able bodied man in the place. The bedraggled party who came seeking peace held up the white flags with emaciated hands purpled with cold.

When the English soldiers entered the town Henry gave strict orders for no plundering and allowed food to be given to the inhabitants but despite his help they died in large numbers for days after the capitulation.

While Henry was looking to the refurbishing of his army and his own defences, itinerant troubadours, who were a useful source of information to both sides, reported large movements of Scottish troops coming to the aid of his enemies. Throughout the summer men were being shipped into France and at the beginning of June Scots were attacking forts of Lower Normandy with the Orleanists. Their success encouraged the French who retook several towns.

The capacity of the French for double dealing was never stronger than during this time when, somewhat to Henry's amusement, both Orleanists and Burgundians were sending secret envoys to him in an effort to halt his campaign.

Eventually after much torturous negotiation a meeting place on the Seine was arranged for all the leaders to review the situation while a truce was proclaimed.

In complete contrast to the ugly devastation of war the gathering was a scene of great splendour. Pavilions and tents in gaily coloured canvas and silk were erected and brave banners fluttered in the wind. The King and his brothers, with Archbishop Beaufort to support them, brought out their finery which had been stowed away since the beginning of the campaign.

Henry was always grateful afterwards that he had taken some trouble with his appearance and had bathed in the river before putting on his gold stitched doublet, for on the third day of the parleying the King of France presented his daughter, Catherine, to him.

Henry, looking at her after many months of privation and hard soldiering, found his heart touched by her ethereal beauty and charming manner. He had no difficulty in agreeing to consider the terms of the King's party which included the hand of the Princess among them.

Unfortunately however, although the French were ready to cede Henry's claim for sovereignty in Normandy they demanded he should give up any other claims in Anjou, Maine, Brittany and Touraine. These terms were not acceptable to Henry despite the pull of Catherine's attraction and the meeting was disbanded. Not, nevertheless, without a secret treaty being signed between the Orleanists and John of Burgundy behind Henry's back.

This uneasy alliance lasted for two months until the Dauphin lured Duke John to Montereau where he had him treacherously murdered.

Henry took quick advantage of the chaotic situation that developed and while vengeance was being demanded from all sides issued his terms for a treaty to weld together the French King's party and the new young Duke of Burgundy.

Only too happy to have a strong arm on which to lean, his proposals were hastily agreed upon and so it was Henry gained the hand of Catherine and the promise that their children should be heirs of the kingdom of France for ever.

Henry saw in this the realisation of his dream of a united England and France which had now become an overriding passion with him.

The Dauphinist faction soon let it be known they had no intention of allowing this to happen and they consolidated their forces and doubled the garrisons at Meaux and Melun. Masons and stoneworkers worked night and day to strengthen the fortifications of the towns. Once again Henry's attention was drawn to the large number of Scots who were taking part in these exercises.

Infuriated by Albany's insolent help for his enemies Henry was at a loss to know how to deal with the situation, when quite suddenly he was struck with the idea of sending for James and using the young King to appeal to the Scottish troops to return home.

A messenger was despatched at once for England.

At Kenilworth James looked up in amazement from the letter breaking this news to him. During the two years he had lived among the fields and woods of Warwickshire he had drifted in a state of half contentment, half furious occupation and this despatch caught him unprepared.

'It appears,' he said to William Giffard. 'I am commanded to go to Henry in France. Not, as this letter states, as a prisoner any longer, but as an ally of the King. Henry is perturbed by the large number of our countrymen who are fighting for the Dauphin and he thinks I should be able to use my influence to order them to cease fighting. All things considered I suppose I should feel flattered that anyone thinks I have any influence. How does it strike you?'

'As a very difficult task if the reports of the behaviour of the Scots in France are true. It is said that they are highly unpopular with the peasants who rush to lock up their wine and their women when they know the Dauphin has the Highlanders with him!' Giffard laughed but went on more seriously. 'But you can certainly try.'

'Listen to this,' James said reading from the parchment which was covered in Henry's own vigorous writing.

'There is a purse for me with this letter containing twenty marks and I am to be fitted out with horses, armour, tents and banners as well as new clothes. William, I confess I am a little bewildered, what shall I do?'

'Go, of course,' William said drily. 'There is nothing else you can do and while you are gone I shall beg your permission to go to Scotland to see at first hand who is for you and who against.'

'No one cares other than for his own wellbeing,' James answered, turning to look out on the trees rustling in the gentle breeze.

'That is not the case, my Lord and the day must come when your supporters are able to oust Albany and acclaim you their King.'

'You are a comfort William, as you have been all these long, weary years and it will be strange without you but it certainly would be good to have accurate information from you.'

'Thank you, my Lord. Now, what is to do about your journey?'

'The letter states I am to set out at once for Southampton in the company of one John Waters who brought the message here. It should not take over long to pack up either your or my possessions for they have grown pitifully scanty during the last years.'

He set out from Kenilworth, guarded but no longer treated as a prisoner, and arrived in the Hampshire port in the early part of May 1420. James had then been in the keeping of the English for fourteen years.

Within the walled town he spent more

money in three crowded days than in the rest of his life. Armourers came to take measurements and worked all night to fit him a currass and helm and tailors found him doublets in unaccustomed rich fabrics. James could hardly believe his ears when he learned the price of the garments and thought somewhat guiltily of the added amount to his ransom.

After choosing a tent for his personal use he was taken to select a destrier from the castle stables. He had no difficulty in picking out a dappled grey, sturdy and broad of shoulder who trustingly nuzzled James' hand as he stroked him.

He had been permitted to bring several attendants from the household which had been gathering round him during his stay at Kenilworth and although he missed William's care and companionship the young John Alway, supported by Alexander Ogilvy and Walter Forstare, filled the gap most adequately.

As he boarded the ship which was to take them to France he could not help thinking of the odd quirk of fate that made his present destination the same as the only other voyage he had ever made.

Unlike the previous journey the crossing was calm and uneventful and they reached harbour under tranquil skies. Stepping on to French soil James realised a sensation of freedom coupled with the pleasure of partaking in the world's daily life. He had for so long been a helpless onlooker. The garrison captain of Harfleur informed them Henry awaited the King of the Scots at Troyes.

James' party arrived there to find the town in a flurry of preparation for the marriage of Henry with Catherine. He admitted to himself he was interested to see the bride who had captured the heart of the warrior King and he was not disappointed when he saw her at the Nuptial Mass celebrated by Henri de Savors, Archbishop of Sens.

Viewed from his place in the Cathedral she appeared a delicate being in a magnificent dress of silver brocade, her shining hair crowned with a diadem.

The ceremony was conducted with great pomp and although the precincts of the Cathedral were strongly guarded no shadow of the Dauphin's enmity was allowed to fall on the Mass or the feast that followed.

Much to his surprise James was given a place of honour close to the bridal pair. Henry was obviously proud of his new Queen and presented her to James saying that later he would have time to outline his plans for his help in the war.

At first he felt strangely ill at ease in feminine company after so long a confinement in Kenilworth but Catherine made shy conversation with him, speaking slowly so he could understand her.

'Do you know,' she told him. 'Henry does not speak French very well and I have so little English. You find that amusing I see!'

'Only because his father spoke French so perfectly that he once thought it unnecessary for me to come to France to learn the language when he could be my tutor. Do you think you will like living in England?' he asked hastily to change the subject.

'Yes,' she said, hesitating for a moment. 'That is if Henry is with me and the weather is not as damp and depressing as we hear. I must confess also that the reputation the English have for hauteur and coldness equals that of their weather and this dismays me a little for I am affectionate by nature and like to have my affections returned,' she blushed and looked away from James as she spoke and he made some smiling, non-committal reply. There was time enough for her to discover once she was surrounded with Henry's love, the prosaic English.

He had cause to think of her many times in the days that followed for although Henry gave every appearance of doting upon her, he did not give up his relentless perusal of the Dauphin's forces and only two days after the marriage took his bride with her mother and James and all their vast entourage to besiege first Montereau and then Melun.

Henry had found time to call James to him and explain his reasons for bringing him to France. The Scots support of the Dauphin under the leadership of the Earl of Buchan, another of Albany's sons, constituted a real threat to England's success. Henry was confident that the northerners, confronted with their true sovereign would listen to his orders for them to return to Scotland. James wished he held the same belief.

Montereau fallen Henry pushed on to his next objective of Melun, leaving Catherine and her mother, the Queen of France, with their ladies in waiting at Corbeil.

James watched their leave taking and against his will saw the look in Catherine's eyes as Henry embraced her and leapt to his horse. He prayed silently that when he met the woman he would make his wife he would never surprise a similar expression of frustrated bewilderment on her face. But she waved gaily to James as if nothing had occurred and he kissed her hand wishing her well. On the road to Melun he examined recovered to take some supper. Although most of the faces in the dimly lit hold were still pale, the strain was eased and an air of gaiety was apparent. The younger men talked of the fabled beauty of the women at the French court and told James that they envied him the prospect of a prolonged stay with them; more than one of them regretted that they would have to return to Scotland once they had safely delivered the young prince to Paris. James, whose limited experience of women confined him to memories of his mother, nurse and sisters, felt slightly uncomfortable when the discussion became freer as the wine went to the men's already unsteady heads. He smiled when they asked him if he did not consider himself most fortunate and thought privately that he would rather return to St. Andrews to Henry's companionship than go to France whatever the extent of French hospitality. It was in this mood of relaxed relief that the party settled down for the night.

They were awakened, in the grey light of morning, by a jolting crash that jarred the Maryenknyght from stem to stern. This was followed by the rattle of chains and loud thuds on the deck above them accompanied by cries of anger and shrieks of pain. James' escort, rubbing at their eyes stumbled to their

Henry's marriage with an analytical eye and
was forced to the conclusion Henry was glad
to be free of ...ving encumberance of a
wife and ... on an adventure much
mor... ...mes allowed himself
...He had come in the
...rospective delving
...om moment to
...to himself that
...wife and had
...not yet seen
...ld care to
...This, he
...rmission
...rance
...ty of
...oth
...n,

and he was thrown into the preparations for its capture.

The city, standing on the upper Seine, commanded the access to Paris and was strongly fortified by the Dauphinists under the leadership of the Sire of Barbazon.

James watched with admiration as Henry set about the siege in his usual businesslike manner and posted his forces under the commands of his own brothers, the Duke of Bedford and Clarence and Catherine's brother the Duke of Bavaria.

On the vital North East side Henry positioned the young Duke of Burgundy, somewhat mollified since the fall of Montereau and the punishment Henry had meted out to anyone who had partaken in the murder of John the Fearless. To support him Henry sent the Earls of Huntingdon, Warwick and Somerset.

Of all the Englishmen he had met, John Beaufort Earl of Somerset, nephew of Archbishop Beaufort and the Countess of Westmorland, attracted James the most. He was a tall, handsome young man with the ruddy gold colouring of a Plantagenet stock from which he sprung. Despite his youth he was a capable soldier and Henry instructed him to take James with him and explain the mechanics of the siege. James listened attentively as Somerset pointed out the cannons being rolled into position and the mining operations already under way.

'The long slope of ground up to the battlements that you see over there is called a glacis and has been thrown up there by the defenders so that when we attack we are constantly under fire from the ramparts. The Dauphinists have worked hard here and they say the Sire of Barbazon is a tough fighter who will not give in easily, but King Henry will not allow that to disturb him; he is used to long sieges and he believes starvation is the best weapon in his armoury.'

Sympathising with the inhabitants of the town James asked Somerset how many Scots were supporting the garrison but the young man did not know.

'It must be sufficient to warrant you being here,' he said smiling.

'I hope they will listen to me and I can help Henry to hasten the taking of the place and curtail the suffering, but you see, my people do not know me and I am afraid I shall have no influence.'

James could not keep the bitterness from his voice and John looked at him quickly.

'You were with my aunt at Raby,' he said, 'and she sent word to my mother to make an effort to — ' he broke off awkwardly, unwilling to appear patronising to an older man who was, at least in name, a king.

He relaxed as James smiled.

'Your aunt was most kind and perhaps one day I shall be able to visit you and your family.'

With the capture of Melun as their present objective this seemed a far off time indeed but at least he now had suitable clothes in which to present himself.

Acting on the English King's orders James issued a proclamation telling all the Scots bearing arms in the Dauphin's army to return home.

Buchan, in charge of the soldiers refused to obey the order, claiming it had been issued under compulsion. This was exactly what James had feared would happen that when Henry sent for him he expected to be told of his speedy return to England and captivity.

When he had paid his respects to Henry, who looked, James thought, far from well, the King made no mention of this and bade him be seated.

'Bring in Sir John of Lethe,' he called to a page who hovered at the tent's mouth.

James knew Sir John as an esquire who often carried messages for Albany and he greeted him with controlled curiosity.

'Sir John has business with you, my Lord,'

Henry said. 'Tell your King what you have just told me.'

The squire made James a slight bow.

'I regret to inform you, my Lord James, of the death of your illustrious uncle, Duke of Albany.'

Involuntarily James gasped. He received the news without a vestige of sadness for the passing of his late father's brother and was gratified at the prospect of the way being cleared for him to return home.

But later when Sir John had departed and he and Henry were alone it was soon made obvious that the English King, despite the failure of James' proclamation, was not going to allow him to depart from France.

'When the war is over,' Henry said quietly but firmly, 'We shall begin negotiations for your immediate release and reinstatement. From what I hear Murdoch will be no success as Regent in his father's place and the Estates will be only too happy to raise the money for your ransom.'

10

The capture of Melun proved a longer affair than had been anticipated and it was hunger once more which caused its eventual fall.

When the surrender terms were given by Henry, mercy was extended to all, except those who were implicated in the murder of John the Fearless and the Scots mercenaries who had not obeyed their King's command to cease fighting.

James was forced to watch as gallows were erected and twenty of his countrymen hanged. He felt sick with disgust, not only for the waste of life, but for the discovery in himself of a sense of power that exulted in punishment being meted out to the men who had defied him.

When he realised the full enormity of his sin he went in haste to the nearest chapel and stayed on his knees in prayer until his limbs were heavy with cold. He suffered an agony of repentance and when he was calmer could understand more plainly why it was that self understanding was the most tempering of all knowledge.

Once Melun was restored to some kind of

order Henry set out for Paris.

He entered the walled city with the King of France and the young Duke of Burgundy. Their triumphal procession was greeted everywhere with joy by the populace who doubled their enthusiasm when Catherine and her entourage joined them. James did not accompany them but was sent on to Rouen to await their coming, for once the visit to Paris was over Henry intended to return to England for the Coronation of his Queen.

He enjoyed the respite in the ancient capital of Normandy, now restored to the rhythm of everyday life. He wandered through the narrow streets and stopped often to lean against a wall and watch the people going about their daily business. He watched fascinated as women brought live hens, squawking disapproval, in baskets to the market while hawkers shouted their wares. Peering in cavernous doorways he could make out in the gloomy interiors huge barrels of wine and bushels of wheat which the prudent townsfolk were storing against any further threat to their peace. He stood for a long time close to the Porte de la Grosse Horloge and saw the minutes go by on the two dials of the clock which topped the arcade spanning the street.

In the Cathedral, where pale sunlight

filtered through the rose and blue of the great windows and the ring of the mason's hammers echoed to the roof of the nave, he found the Lady Chapel behind the altar a peaceful haven. He knelt again to beg forgiveness for his lapse from grace at Melun and in the unhurried tranquillity recalled his complete indifference to the news of his uncle's death and his subsequent pleasure at the prospect it opened for him. He wondered uneasily if his long imprisonment had deprived him of the gift of charity.

When Henry and Catherine came he journeyed with them to Calais where they crossed the Channel to Dover.

Here the people's adulation was such that Henry and his Queen were not permitted to walk ashore but were carried shoulder high.

Henry was anxious to make certain all preparations for the coronation were in hand and he went on alone to Westminster leaving Catherine with James at Eltham, a pleasant palace in gentle countryside where James had spent a long ago Christmas.

Before he left Henry gave orders to the Master of the Wardrobe to send for tailors to make several fine doublets and a fur cape against the cold for James.

During the journey through France and England James had plenty of time to study the new Queen of England. She became his first woman friend and he watched her relationship with Henry with the anxious eye of a loving brother. It was not difficult for him to come to the conclusion that his earlier fears on her behalf were well founded. She gave every appearance of being only too willing to give her heart to Henry completely but held back as she realised he did not really need it.

It was not that Henry lost his attentiveness towards her or ever treated her with discourtesy and it was probable that anyone less sensitive than James would not have noticed anything amiss. No word was spoken between them of her lack but Catherine knew James understood. When she was especially quiet and he saw the slight droop of her lip he would pick up his lute and sing the lighthearted airs he composed especially for her. She would relax under the spell of his music making and reward him with her radiance restored.

Never at any moment was he in love with her. She was altogether too ethereal and melancholic for his sturdy frame and own introspection but she touched him neverthe-less with her defencelessness.

For her part she worried for him that he had no amoureuse of his own. As they set out for Westminster she laughed up at him and wished him success with the fair sex at the banquet after the crowning. He answered her gaily, confident and dashing in his new apparel and promised he would do his best.

Alighting in front of the Abbey Church of St. Peter Catherine walked the short distance to the West Door under a canopy of rich velvet. Here she was met by two Bishops and entered the Abbey to a Te Deum sung by the monks and choristers of the school of Westminster. The vast congregation standing elbow to elbow caused her to hesitate a moment but, smiling resolutely, she began the long walk to where the Archbishop of Canterbury waited to place the consort's crown upon her head.

Henry watched her gravely as she knelt before the Archbishop and joined her as they went to receive communion together.

At the great feast in Westminster Hall which followed the ceremony James sat on her left hand while on the right she had the Archbishop of Canterbury and the Bishop of Winchester.

Every effort had been made to honour the occasion and the Duchess of York, the Countess of Huntingdon and the Countess of March attended her while the Earl of March and the Earl Marshall knelt before her with a sceptre. The King's brother, Duke of Gloucester, stood behind her chair and pages hovered near to gratify her every whim at the marble table. Catherine looked more vital than James had ever seen her before. She talked with animation to those around her and watched with wide eyes as the Earl of Worcester rode about the great hall keeping order among the hundreds of guests with the help of men armed with tipped staves. She showed great interest in the Mayor and Aldermen of the City of London who occupied seats of honour near the royal dais in the company of the Barons of the Cinque Ports.

To James as well as Catherine it was a first experience of a grand English banquet and he enjoyed the almost military precision with which course after course followed one another into the Hall.

It was Lent and all the fare was of fish but such care of preparation had been bestowed on each huge trencher that there was no sense of fasting. Catherine wheels were much in evidence as garnish and an image of St. Catherine in sugar and almond paste brought the long meal to an end.

While he sat at the royal table James had realised he was the subject of much interest. More than once he saw girls in rich dresses of silks and velvet glance his way and whisper behind soft hands. Their laughter sent the gauzes on their head-dresses shimmering in the dimly lit hall.

When at last the lavish feast was finished and the older folk settled back to gossip or doze in a haze of completion the younger ones moved around greeting friends. James found himself the centre of a group of girls and was amused and secretly flattered by the artifices they used to catch his attention.

One girl, with the high plucked brow of extreme fashion, complained of a speck in her eye and proffered her kerchief for James to remove it for her. Laughingly he entered into the spirit of the charade and having dealt with the non-existent particle willingly accepted the kiss she gave in gratitude.

In no time he was engulfed with fluttering squares of lawn while eyes of all colours developed urgent need of attention. The situation looked highly complicated for James until a disconsolate male on the outside of the circle snatched one of the kerchiefs and called loudly for forfeits. At once the young woman who had lost her kerchief was clamouring for its return and a rapid exchange of possessions with suitable payments followed. James took his fair share of both.

John Beaufort told him later that he was a source of much interest to the ladies of the court who sympathised with him in his plight and admired him for his poetic skill.

'Judging by my lack of success in returning to my kingdom or finding the woman of my heart 'twere better they had heard of my love of jurisprudence!' James laughed.

'That has not escaped them or your prowess as an athlete. It would seem you have all the attributes for success with the ladies.'

James blushed.

With the coronation celebrations completed Henry set out on a tour of the country. He wanted to show off his bride and at the same time assess the state of the domains. He went into Wales, to revisit his birthplace, pointing out with nostalgia the countryside around Monmouth where he had spent much of his childhood and early manhood.

With James accompanying them the Court spent Easter at Leicester. Here Henry washed the feet of some of his aged subjects on Maundy Thursday and when he and Catherine dispensed the bounty afterwards James was able to give fifty shillings and one penny out of his own funds. He enjoyed the unusual pleasure of generosity for although he was by no means wealthy Henry now saw to it that he received a regular allowance.

While they had been making their progress Henry sent an envoy to Scotland with the French ambassadors and John Lyon to express his displeasure at the help being sent to the Dauphin's party. The need was as pressing as ever because the Earl of Buchan had recently been in Scotland and returned to France with huge reinforcements of troops. Before the embassy was able to accomplish anything tragic evidence of the bearing the Scottish mercenaries had on the war in France was brought home to Henry with force when he heard of the disastrous defeat of the English Army at Bauge.

He and his Queen with James were on their way to Windsor for James to receive his knighthood when the news of this major catastrophe was brought to him. Saying nothing Henry left the company quickly and shut himself away in his room, unable to pass on the contents of the message which at one and the same time brought him a blow to his dreams born at Agincourt and the ill tidings of the death in the battle of his brother Clarence.

When he was sufficiently in command of himself on the following day he hurried to Windsor, his face set and haggard with lack of sleep.

However, he did not forget in his grief that

he had promised to bestow knighthood upon James and conducted the ceremony despite the intensified preparations he was making to return to France.

Catherine gave James a jewelled belt to mark the occasion.

'I shall not be coming with you to France,' she told him when he went to thank her for the gift. 'I am enceinte and Henry does not think it would be wise for me to travel at the moment.'

'This is wonderful news!' James exclaimed. 'Will you be able to join us after the child is born?'

'I hope so,' Catherine said.

Amid all his other making ready Henry found time to send a detachment to the support of the Earl of Douglas who was now in open conflict with Murdoch. Henry gained the valuable promise from Douglas of assistance to him for the rest of his life.

Although he was very quiet and withdrawn during their journey to Southampton for embarkation Henry sought James out and gave his word that on their return from this campaign he would do all in his power to restore James to his throne.

James, with a following of loyal Scots who had been drifting to him during the past months, therefore set out in good heart and gave Henry all the assistance he was able as they fought a difficult passage to the gates of Meaux.

Here Henry drew up his army and stationed the troops for the reduction of the town.

It was here, quickly stifled by their superior officers, that murmurs were heard among Henry's men of the King losing the great spirit which at Agincourt had carried them to such a tremendous victory. James, looking at Henry's lined face and missing his ready smile hoped this was not the case and was heartened when he realised that such was the King's magnetism that the soldiery did not falter in their loyalty towards him.

This was fortunate indeed when illness began to attack the waiting army. Many of the men succumbed to dysentery and some died while others with recurrent flux had to be sent home to England.

Morale began to slip a little, then, in early December, word was brought from Windsor of the safe delivery of a son to the Queen. This heartened the English considerably and Henry was loudly cheered when he doubled the issue of beer.

James went to congratulate Henry in his tent and found Bedford and Gloucester with him. A restrained silence fell as he came in.

'My Lord, may I offer you and the Lady Catherine my heartfelt congratulations on the birth of an heir,' James said as he knelt to the King.

'Thank you,' Henry answered. 'It is an occasion for great joy to know the succession in France and England is assured. If only I could rid myself of an unwelcome premonition which refuses to leave me.'

'God's oath, Henry,' Bedford interrupted passing his brother a goblet of wine. 'Drink this and several more like and forget about your womanish nightmares. They were probably caused by the foul diet we are forced to eat here.'

Henry took the cup and held it from him looking into the red depths of the wine. After a moment he shook his head and shrugged his shoulders as if to shake off a clinging memory.

'If only the child had been born in any other place but Windsor,' he said so low the others only just caught the words.

'Windsor!' James echoed. 'But I have always found Windsor the happiest of your castles.'

'So had I until I had this unfortunate dream of disaster for any heir of England born within its walls. I cannot understand Catherine not fulfilling my wishes. She knew full well I asked her to go elsewhere before the time of her delivery.'

'Perhaps her pains were on her before her time,' James comforted him, unable to imagine Catherine flaunting her husband's commands.

'Possibly, possibly,' Henry said in a colourless voice. 'But I wish it were otherwise.'

Gloucester went out and returned with a musician and James and his brothers remained with Henry until he seemed in a more cheerful frame of mind.

James thought later he had never seen the King so low and dispirited and reluctantly came to the conclusion that the rumour circulating among the troops of Henry suffering with the flux as well as they must be true. What else could account for his melancholy when he should have been jubilant at the birth of a son? James felt his pride on such an occasion would have known no bounds wherever a child was born.

By February the cold and sickness had reduced the besiegers to an almost inadequate force but they were able, nevertheless, to withstand an attempt made by the beleaguered garrison to escape. In the fighting which took place the defenders were pushed out of the outlying parts of the town into the market where they held out for a further two months under unbelievable conditions.

When they finally gave in Henry offered them fair terms of surrender and only executed five men. James, who had dreaded being forced to watch more of the Scottish mercenaries hung before his eyes, was spared this ordeal as Henry ordered them to be kept as prisoners at his will.

Leaving troops in occupation Henry departed for Vincennes where Catherine awaited him with his brother John, Duke of Bedford, who had gone to England to bring her to France.

Together with King Charles the two courts went to Paris and stayed until the heat of an early summer sent them to rest at Senlis. The streets of the capital had been airless and evil smelling and had brought a sense of apathy to the company. Rejoicing at the capture of Meaux had been brief and a mere shadow of the exultation expressed after the fall of Melun.

At Senlis, which lay in a valley bordered by three vast forests, Henry and his Queen took up residence in the castle. Within the strong walls of the city they tried to forget for a time the stresses of the present situation. Together they explored the remains of the once Roman settlement and Catherine would sit by his side in the gardens of the castle as Henry dealt with the day's business. They were both very quiet.

Catherine confided to James her delight at the birth of her baby son and how she had longed to come to Henry and share her joy.

'But he is not well,' she said pitifully. 'And it takes all his strength to attend to these never ending papers and documents. He is proud of our child, of course, but he does not seem to listen when I tell him of how he grows and tries to smile at me.'

'He will be interested when you are able to return to England and show him his son,' James told her. 'Few of us can resist a baby when we see them.'

'Pray that may be soon James, for Henry is sick and the physicians and surgeons do not seem able to help him.'

Their rest at Senlis was interrupted by a plea for help from the young Duke of Burgundy who was being harried by the Dauphin's army close to Lyons. He sent word to say he was at present besieged in Cosne.

Henry took immediate action. Stirring himself with difficulty he rode out to succour the Burgundians but after a day in the saddle he felt too ill to continue and cursing himself bitterly for showing weakness before his troops had a litter brought up and climbed wearily into it.

At Corbeil he admitted to feeling too weak to continue and ordered John of Bedford to take over his command. Bedford went with great reluctance for his brother looked desperately ill but Henry insisted and rather than risk angering him and worsening his condition he departed.

Henry fought against his malady and growing weakness for several days and then asked to be taken back to his Queen at Senlis. His retinue, with mounting anxiety, decided to take him by water and found a suitable boat. Although they chose this method to save him suffering even the gentle movement was too much for his aching, sore body and he was hardly conscious when he was carried ashore at the Castle Chareton.

Urgent summons were sent to John of Bedford and he left the siege of Cosne to come to Henry.

He fell on his knees beside the still form in the darkened room unable to see for the tears which blinded him. He was horrified at the change which had come over Henry in the short days since he had left him.

Gathering his failing strength Henry gave his instructions for the carrying out of his will and his wishes for the Regency during the infancy of his baby son. Bedford, unable to grasp the significance of what he heard, was made Governor of France while Gloucester was to be Deputy Regent of England while Bedford was overseas. The care of his son Henry gave to Thomas Beaufort, Duke of Exeter.

Exhausted by the effort of making plain these tremendously important plans for the future Henry fell back into the pillows and Bedford motioned to a priest who hovered near to come closer. The man began to intone quietly from the psalms.

In the stillness of the night the proud victor of Agincourt died in his thirty-fifth year. Although his brother was with him at the last his Queen came too late to see him alive.

11

James never forgot the extraordinary sense of loss he experienced when he heard the news of Henry's death. It was as if some link with his past was severed for ever.

This affection he had discovered for Henry deepened during the campaigns in France and James now regarded the dead King as a perfect example of a leader of his people. Henry had been thorough in everything he did and was scrupulously fair. His self discipline had been a shining example to the men under his command.

It was only in his dream of French domination and a coupling of the crowns of the two realms James thought he had been unwise and he feared for the future without Henry's strong hand to guide his brothers and the nobility of England.

Bedford was a brave man in the field but lacked the vision of his kingly brother while Gloucester was volatile and inclined towards the sophisticated pleasures of music and acting. It was common gossip that he possessed a reputation of arrogance and self advancement and his recent liason with the

169

estranged wife of the Count of Brabant was an international scandal. He had never been popular with the English people as Bedford or the dead Clarence.

Perhaps his most serious deficit was the lack of sympathy between himself and the Beauforts. His half uncles had never regarded him with favour and now much would depend on the harmonious working together of these extremely influential men and the Regents of France and England. James could only hope Henry's brilliant leadership was not to be wasted and that the new Governors would honour the dead King's promise to return him to Scotland.

James was appointed one of the chief mourners with Bedford, Burgundy and Exeter and before the leaden coffin was finally sealed he went to pay his last respects to Henry.

In the gloomy chamber so markedly different from the warm, scented summer outside he knelt beside the catafalque and looked down on the emaciated features of the man he had first seen on that long ago day in Nottingham. He had seemed so young and so vigorous then and it was impossible to imagine the closed eyes twinkling with laughter as he told James of the difficulties the French peasants had with the Scots troops when they were on the march.

'No wife is safe,' he had said, 'when the red giants from the north have drunk deeply of the goodman's wine. I am not the only one who will be glad to see the Scots go back to their homes! You are not like them, James, which is just as well!'

Now, rising from his knees, James shook his head in disbelief. What would life be like without the man who had caught up England in his hand and showed them their true destinies? What would his own future be now that the elder brother figure of Henry was gone? What of Catherine and the babe?

As swiftly as she came to mind he remembered she would be arriving before nightfall and he knew she would look to him for comfort and support.

When she arrived quiet and very pale James helped her from her litter and went with her into the small private solar of the castle. She seemed bewildered and lost and did not ask to visit the coffin. It was obvious she had been weeping but James felt it was in hopeless sadness for the ending of Henry's life rather than from the suffering of a personal tragedy. She and Henry had had so little time to grow close and in the last days at Senlis she had tended him with the devoted care of a nurse rather than as a wife. It could be her grief was more for her son and the uncertainty which lay ahead for them both. This was confirmed to James later when they sat together on the battlements in the fading light, looking out over the forest of trees which stretched as far as the eye could see.

'I know too much,' she said, 'of the governing of a country where the sovereign is young or weak. My father of whom my mother sends to tell me, is ailing once more and he has periods when he is incapable of ruling. It is always during those times that trouble is fomented.'

James murmured his sympathy recalling only too easily his own fate for the very reason she was giving. He said nothing not wishing to interrupt her as she talked to ease her anxiety.

'I know little of my lords Exeter, Gloucester and Bedford and yet they are to have so much influence on my son. How will they treat my baby and me?'

'They will surely bring him up to be worthy of his father.' James glanced quickly at Catherine as he spoke but her expression did not alter. 'And the English treat their women-folk honourably — if a little stiffly,' he added drily.

'Oh, well,' Catherine sighed. 'I'll meet what comes and I have at least my baby to love. We must go to our rest, James, for the journey ahead of us to London will be long and demanding I fear.'

James thought of what she had said many times during the two months it took to escort the funeral chariot back to Westminster Abbey. He was glad that Catherine's party followed at a distance behind for he found the continual sight of the effigy of Henry on top of the catafalque distressing enough and feared she would have been overcome by it.

Two hundred mourners escorted the procession and at night torches were lit which lent an eerie dimension with wreaths of smoke snaking in and around the shuffling people and the high chariot.

The progress was agonisingly slow and Catherine grew impatient as endless masses were said at every stopping place.

At St. Denis a High Mass was celebrated and she took leave of her family who had come to take part in it. Her mother, Isabella, was distraught for she saw in the death of her son-in-law the removal of the chief support to her failing consort Charles, King of France.

Bedford parted with them at Rouen for he had to remain in France to take up his duties as Regent. He knelt to Catherine, kissing her hand and avowing his loyalty to her son and herself. He expressed the wish he could accompany her to London and turning to James he entrusted her welfare to him.

Once in England the funeral services continued with no sign of abating. Huge congregations were present at Masses held in Dover, Canterbury, Rochester, Dartford and St. Pauls. The sad procession passed through mile after mile of sorrowing silent people. Many wept as they saw the young queen wrapped in mourning white. It seemed only yesterday she and the victor of Agincourt were taking the road for London amid the rejoicing of their people and now she was no longer wife of a King but the mother of a young and helpless monarch at the mercy of fate.

At last the final Mass had been said in the Abbey Church of St. Peter and Henry laid to rest beside the Confessor.

Almost at once Catherine left for Windsor with her baby, whom she could hardly recognise, and Thomas, Duke of Exeter. James took his leave of her, glad that she would now be able to rest in some kind of privacy.

'Come to see me, James, as soon as you are able. I shall feel so strange and alone at Windsor.'

Looking down at her in the heavily curtained litter he promised to present himself at her court as soon as he had ascertained his own position and had been granted permission to come.

She smiled her gratitude and lay back among the cushions, exhausted with the ordeal of the past months.

'It will seem a long time until you come, James. You have been a great comfort to me and helped me through these unhappy days. I shall always be grateful and remember your kindness in the uncertain future. Le Bon Dieu tu remerceria.'

Rather to his surprise he had found when he arrived in England that Gloucester and the Bishop of Winchester were ready to consider the plans Henry had mooted for him and James saw this as the moment to press forward his demands for repatriation. Letters from John Lyon confirmed Murdoch's inadequacy to rule Scotland and stated Douglas was pleading James' cause and meeting with considerable support for the exiled monarch.

'Although I must confess,' he wrote in his clerkish hand, 'affairs here are this way and that. Albany was an ineffectual ruler but commanded a certain following and the nobility are so intermarried to make it difficult to decide where loyalty lies. Your homecoming cannot be a day too early and to that end Alexander Seton and Water Ogilvy are eager to come south to treat with the English Council on your behalf.'

James, staying in the home of Sir Water Merying, spent every waking hour writing letters to the Estates, his uncle Earl of Douglas and to the growing number of Scottish supporters of whom John Lyon and William Giffard sent word.

By the time Christmas, kept very quietly, was over and the New Year well advanced he began to hope for the first time since his ill fated journey north over seven years before of seeing Scotland within a reasonable time.

His hopes were reinforced by Bedford's urgent requests to the Council to do all in their power to stop the flow of Scottish troops who were still crossing the Channel to aid the Dauphin. If James were permitted to return home conditions of his homecoming would include a truce between Scotland and England and a promise to withdraw at once all the Scots mercenaries.

It was springtime before James begged permission to go to Windsor. He felt now that everything had been set in motion for his release. A considerable number of his countrymen were coming to Westminster later in the year to escort him north to meet other delegates at York to discuss terms for his repatriation and the ransom required by the Regent and his advisors.

With the lift in his heart that the prospect of a visit to Windsor always gave him he rode out of London through the hamlet of Chelsea in warm sunshine. Since he had journeyed from France with the sombre burden of Henry's cortege the earth had reawakened and banks and hedgerows were bright with tender flowers.

The harrassing months of correspondence and negotiation he had just spent dropped from him like a mantle and he found himself wondering why he had bothered to put so much effort into obtaining his repatriation when just to be alive was enough.

The entourage who accompanied him were in a gay mood and they laughed and sang their way to the castle, clattering over the drawbridge and bringing servants hurrying from all directions to help them alight and unpack their baggage.

The green lawns of the bailey were filled with throngs of brightly dressed people, gossiping and strolling in the evening air. Several of them came up to the newcomers. One especially pushed his way to James' side.

'Well met, old friend!'

'Orleans! By all that's wonderful!' James

clasped his hand. 'This is good news indeed. I did not look to see you here.'

'I do not spend so much of my time in the Tower of late,' Orleans told him. 'Perhaps the little Catherine has had something to do with that.'

'How is she?' James asked quickly.

'She is recovered from the shock of Henry's death,' Orleans replied. 'But she is very melancholic — '

'Not like the late king, her father?' James interrupted.

'Oh no, not at all,' Orleans hastened to reassure him. 'This is a sadness of the heart. She broods about the future when she fears her baby son will be taken away from her to be brought up according to Henry's will. Also she is very young to be a widow, James — and to remain so!'

'Remain so?' James echoed.

'Yes, the English forbid their Queens to marry again.'

'A heartless custom,' James said frowning. 'But I suppose a logical one when one considers the ramifications of the claims of any other family.'

'Come,' said Orleans. 'Let us make haste to ensure that you and I share a room or are at least near at hand.'

They went up to the turret where Orleans

had a chamber and John Alway quickly staked a claim for James.

As it was late food was sent up to them and they talked deep into the night. Orleans was thirsty for news of France which James could give him from first hand experience while James was anxious to have Orleans' view on the affairs at court.

He knew that Gloucester had secretly married Jacqueline of Brabant in March but Orleans was able to fill in much of the background of the infatuation which had led up to the annulment that had shaken Europe.

The rift, which had always been apparent between Henry Beaufort, Bishop of Winchester and his nephew, widened considerably and Gloucester became so unpopular that there were rumours for the recall of Bedford.

Bedford was already embarrassed enough by his brother's behaviour because the Lady Jacqueline was a first cousin of the Duke of Burgundy and it was feared the marriage would shake the Duke's alliance with England.

'Not that that worries me unduly,' Orleans said with a smile. 'Especially since Catherine's child was acclaimed King of France as well as England when her father died. For me — a life of peace to hunt and write. As long as one lives — that is all, I find.'

However, although he professed not to care what became of his inheritance, his provinces were administered during his absence by the Dauphin's officials and he was anxious to have James' opinion about the outcome of this long and weary war. Skirmishes and raiding were still common and there seemed no end in sight although it was common knowledge that the Dauphin was no adversary for Bedford. The young prince was reputed weak and vascillating.

'The French have no real leader,' Charles said.

'The English have Bedford,' James added slowly. 'But he is not of the same mettle as Henry.'

He went on to tell Orleans of the rigours of the campaign in France and the events which culminated in the death of Henry. Charles listened in silence, occasionally turning his head with a direct and sometimes quizzical expression.

'It would seem, friend James,' he said at last in his lazy drawl. 'As if your opinion of our late illustrious captor changed over the years. If I remember you were not always so full of admiration for Henry.'

'You are quite right,' James agreed. 'But it must be admitted Henry had a certain quality which singled him out from ordinary men.

Towards the end of his life he treated me very well.'

'He had every reason so to do,' Orleans said drily, but seeing the expression on James' face he added hastily, 'but do not misunderstand me, I, too, admired Henry and am sorry for his death, if only for the sake of the little Catherine.' Changing the subject he asked James what he thought of his chances of returning to Scotland.

'From what I hear,' he said, 'they must be improved. The continuing use of Scots soldiers against the English has at least brought it home to the Council that they must encourage the true King of Scotland to return and oust the odious Murdoch. Ugh, how I detested the shambling young man when we were in the Tower. Not a cultured thought in his head.'

James laughed, although somewhat sleepily. The oil in the little pottery lamp was almost spent and the light was growing feeble and wavering.

'For the first time in years I dare to hope I may be in Scotland soon. It seems a strange irony that the man who least wishes me there should be instrumental in bringing it about.'

'You will be wanting a queen to share your throne,' Charles said on a yawn. 'It worries our little Catherine that you have no lady love.'

'She always worried for me about my lack of lovers,' James said. 'Married as she was to Henry she does not understand I am searching for an ideal.'

'Then your heart is still free to bestow?'

'Yes,' said James softly. 'My heart is still free to give.'

The wick burnt out and the soft summer darkness wrapped the chamber in quiet. James slept.

12

He awoke to sunlight streaming through the casement and lay for a long time revelling in the tranquillity. Distant sounds underlined the peace rather than disturbed it and he dozed again before stretching lazily and rising slowly from his bed.

Still wrapped in the half-awareness of waking he went to the casement, now without its winter shutters, and leaned out, resting his arms on the ledge.

Below him was a walled and secret garden, closed in with flowering trees, sweet scented in the morning air. He let his eye linger on the blossoms, hearing a cuckoo calling across the woodland. A thrush fluttered into a bough with a flurry of wings and a small movement close under the window attracted his attention.

He caught his breath in the surprise of the moment for seated with carefree abandon on a garden seat was a girl who glowed golden in the sun, the little hat she wore on her abundant hair shining as its beads caught the light. Bright dyed feathers curled downwards over her cheek and shadowed the half closed eyes but James saw the outline of the cheek and the rounded chin.

In the certainty of her privacy she had unlaced her bodice and exposed her bosom to the sun's warmth. James watched its rise and fall as she breathed evenly with now and then a deep ecstatic sigh of contentment.

How long he watched her he could not afterwards tell, but he feasted his eyes on her beauty, lost in the delight of her being. Her dress of shimmering gauze fell softly to reveal her limbs stretched with ankles crossed. There seemed about her an aura of wellbeing and wholesome loveliness.

James smiled, unwilling to move, and heard voices calling from afar. She heard them also and unhurriedly laced her dress and stood up, raising her arms above her head.

'I am here,' she called and moved gracefully to a door set in the wall.

James longed to beg her to stay but she was gone while he searched for a name to arrest her.

He turned away, trembling, and sat down on his ruffled bed. Here was his golden girl; here was the woman he had searched for down the years. The woman! Near panic seized him as he realised she was no child and might well be claimed already.

Amazed at the way his thoughts were

outstripping his reason he sprang to the door and went to call Orleans, but with his mouth open, he stopped. It was better not to know yet whatever the experienced Frenchman could tell him of his love. Better to dream before the heart's shattering.

He returned slowly to his own room and found quill and parchment which the thoughtful Alway had set out for him.

In the first wild burst of love for his unknown the pen raced in his hands. The stanzas taking their own form.

'And therewith cast I down mine eye
  again
Where she had come walking under the
  tower
Full secretly, now coming here to play.
The freshest, the fairest young flower
That ever I saw, methought, before that
  hour.
For which sudden shock, anon it sent
The blood of all my body to my heart.
And though I stood amazed a moment
No wonder was: for why? Why, wittis all
Were so o'ercome with pleasure and
  delight
Only through letting my eye behold her
That suddenly my heart became her
  thrall'

He sat with the pen poised and looked up startled as Alexander Ogilvy brought in some ale and bread to break his fast.

'Working early, my Lord,' he said somewhat surprised for he had thought James had come to Windsor to rest.

'Not work,' James cried exultantly, 'but poetry, Alexander.'

'Indeed, my Lord,' said Ogilvy politely. 'It is most certainly a beautiful morning and the Master of the Horse bids me tell you a horse has been put at your disposal by Queen Catherine so that you may fully enjoy both the weather and the countryside.'

James patted him indulgently on the shoulder and agreed that a ride through Windsor Forest in the sharp new green of late Spring was a most happy choice for this moment.

A small party of men and women awaited him and he joined them in the best of spirits, looking around unashamedly to see if his golden girl were among their company. But she was not and he comforted himself that she was certainly of the household and that they must meet at some time.

He could not bring himself to question any of the company he knew, not wishing to hear her name from any lips but her own.

He rode with fearless pleasure exulting in

the sight and fresh purity of the sweeping paths through the woods. They came upon glades where the white windflower trembled in the wake of the horses and they saw, under the new leaved trees, the bell-like bluebell dappled in sunshine. Startled deer faded into the boles of the forest and birds swooped low across their path. It was a day of beauty, made for living and the new sensation of happiness that had so recently come to James washed through him.

He was still glowing when later he went to pay his respects to Catherine and escort her to the midday feast. He was pleased to see her manner was less tense and her face regaining its comeliness.

She greeted him with real happiness, kissing him on both cheeks and then leading him to admire her baby son.

'How is it with you?' she asked, talking quickly and not keeping still for a moment. 'You look better than I have ever seen you. Is it good news you have from Scotland and the Council?'

'I hope so,' James replied. 'Safe conducts were issued just before I left Westminster for an embassy to come to Pontefract for discussion on a treaty of liberation and this time it looks as if agreement may be reached.'

'That is good,' Catherine said. 'It bears out

the news Bishop Beaufort has given me from time to time when he has seen you in London. He hinted your future was looking less bleak than hitherto. Oh, James, will it not be wonderful if you are soon able to go home!'

'Yes,' he agreed lightly for he saw a shade of dark cross her eyes momentarily. 'Tell me what you do all day.'

'I have my babe,' she answered. 'And that takes up all my time. Come. Let us go to our dinner.'

She took his hand and he noted the resolute set of her chin. He could not break the spell of this magical day by enquiring deeper into her feelings. Time enough for understanding when she asked for it.

James was given the place of honour next to the Queen Dowager and was greeted by Henry Beaufort, Bishop of Winchester and the Earl of Westmorland who hurried forward to meet him.

'There is a chance Northumberland and I shall be your hosts again in the Autumn,' he said. 'Let us trust this meeting will be more fruitful than your last journey north.'

'I pray it will be,' James said earnestly. Thomas, Duke of Exeter was also present but James realised that Humphrey of Gloucester and Jacqueline would not choose to be of the same company as the Beauforts and were therefore absent.

As he took his place Alway brought him a silver bowl in which to wash his hands and Alexander gave him a linen towel. This finished he looked quickly down the high table and saw with quickening pulse that seated at the further end was his girl of the morning talking with a handsome, splendidly attired middle aged woman. As he watched, John Beaufort Earl of Somerset, came into the hall and throwing a leg over the form dropped lightly on the other side of this lady who smiled at him affectionately.

Catherine spoke to James at this moment and it was a long time before he could look in the girl's direction again and when he did so it was to find her looking straight at him. His heart raced and he smiled. Quick as the bat's dart in the summer evening she smiled back.

'James,' Catherine said gently, 'my Lord Bishop desires to know if you have news of Bishop Wardlaw.'

'Yes.' James replied bringing himself to pay attention with considerable difficulty. 'He and I send messages as oft as safe conducts are granted.'

'Touché! my Lord,' Henry laughed. 'You must beg an interview of him from me when you are returned home. He and I have much in common with our university life.'

That is about as far as it goes James was able to think in the delightful confusion of the moment and although he talked dutifully with the Bishop and with Catherine he was longing to steal another look to the end of the table. When at last he was able to the girl was conversing with her other neighbour and was turned away from him but he enjoyed the curve of her neck and the shining gold of her hair caught softly into a fillet.

She could not be married he told himself, exultantly, for her hair was unbound and the smile she had given him was not sullied with guile. He almost brought himself to cut across the polite conversation drifting around him and ask Catherine to tell him her name but he hesitated like a youth tongue-tied in calf love.

'Will you come to my solar this evening, James? Several of my household will be there and perhaps you would sing for us.'

'Of course,' he replied and knew that his lovely girl would be of the number.

He dressed with such meticulous care, splashing about in the garde robe and discarding shirt after shirt until he chose one of finest lawn that John Alway and Alexander regarded him with astonishment. He had never been a vain man, even since his fortunes had improved, and they had to admit that when he troubled he was a handsome one.

'Not over tall of course,' Ogilvy hastened to say when James had departed, in case the other Scot thought him fawning. 'But of good figure and when one comes to think on it he has had precious little call to dress himself up.'

'Perhaps it's a woman!' Ogilvy said, wondering.

'Perhaps,' Alway agreed. 'It's about time.'

When James climbed the stone stairs to Catherine's private room which looked westward towards the river's source it was bathed in the dying light of the day. Rosy and warm, there was a stillness in the air, almost of expectation.

He bowed over the Dowager's hand and she motioned him to find a place in the solar and he sat at her feet.

When the company was assembled Catherine raised her slender white hand and called for quiet. As the chattering hushed she passed him a lute. He began to sing, without restraint, one of the haunting melodies he had learnt in his far off boyhood. The plaintive air went softly round the room and all listened. James could smell the burning peat in the great hearth at Linlithgow and see his mother's eyes, tranquil for once, as she had crooned the same melody for him. He was almost unaware the song was finished, so lost he was in the happiness of yesterday and today blended together.

'Again!' they cried but rousing himself he laughingly protested it was enough and gave the lute to Catherine to hand on. As a young woman put the silken cord round her neck and picked out a chord he turned to find his girl of the morning beside him. He could swear she had not been there before and guessed she had moved towards him when he was occupied in passing the lute.

'My Lord,' she said softly and inclined her head slightly. James bowed to her and the new song lilted about them. Both listened and applauded when it was finished; before there was time to speak together someone had struck up a roundel and as they came to the chorus James picked up his companion's hand and waved it in time to the music. He smiled down at her afraid she might take it away but she made no protest and indeed did not withdraw her hand when the singing was done and the men and women drifted into small groups.

James helped her to her feet and found an embrasure cut deep into the wall where a little of the day's light still cast a glow on the stonework. She was as lovely as he had first thought and on closer inspection her skin was smooth and bloomed with health. Her eyes were bright and her mouth upcurved and full, her body supple and strong. She watched him as he looked at her, unashamed of the scrutiny.

'Do I please?' she asked gently, amused.

'Please forgive me,' James stammered.

'There is no need, my Lord. I watched you at the dinner this day, quite unheeded. You have known the Lady Catherine for a long time haven't you?' she asked wistfully, her head on one side.

'Since her wedding day,' James agreed. 'But I have never been — ' He faltered.

'You do not need to go on,' she broke in. Then added. 'They tell me you have hopes of returning to your kingdom at last. May I wish you well?'

'Thank you,' James said quietly. 'Now, may I ask you a question?'

'Certainly,' she said, sitting up a little straighter and looking at him intently.

'What is your name?' he asked.

She relaxed and laughed softly.

'Jane,' she said. 'Jane Beaufort.'

'Then you are Somerset's sister,' James said wonderingly. 'And had I been able to visit you when Lady Westmorland commended me to your mother, all this time would not have been wasted!'

Jane took his hand and cradled it against her cheek.

'I promise you,' she said so softly he could hardly catch the words, 'to make up for any time lost.'

Around them the company were making their adieus and they joined in with the others thanking Catherine for her hospitality.

Orleans was at the Queen Dowager's side and she looked happy and pleased with the success of her evening.

Outside the night was warm and sweets-cented.

'May I walk with you to your chamber?' James asked.

'With pleasure, my Lord,' Jane replied. 'It is not too far distant if we take the left hand path.'

'Then let us take the right hand,' James said.

Jane laughed and when he took her hand moved nearer to him.

James found himself unable to talk. Although there was so much to say to this girl whom he had known for a few short hours only, words seemed superfluous. It was almost as if she had been waiting for him as he had for her. She had accepted the relationship as if it had been predestined. There was between them a bond of what Catherine would have called 'sympathie' and it obviated the necessity for the usual preliminary skirmishes which marked the beginning of any man and woman association.

They walked very slowly, the starlight lighting the gaps in the pleached garden. Once he raised her hand to his mouth and kissed the back of it. She turned it over and held the palm under his chin, cradling his face against its warmth. James closed his eyes, experiencing happiness he had not known existed. To his dismay he found tears pricking his lids and chided himself for growing soft in his imprisonment.

Despite their unhurried pace they arrived at her room with what, afterwards, seemed extraordinary haste and she stood in the light of the cresset beside the door to bid him goodnight. James regarded her, still without speaking then stooped and kissed her swiftly on the brow.

Lying sleepless in his chamber he went over again and again the sequence of their meeting, delighting in the intimacy which already existed between them. As the dawn broke in the East he went to the casement and looked down on the little private garden. Remembering her as she had sat earlier that day he cursed himself for not taking her in his arms as he had bade her sleep well. He knew she would have responded with joy to his caresses but later, when he fell exhausted on to his bed, he realised he was glad something had restrained him. There was always tomorrow and a lifetime of days to be spent together. Comforted with this knowledge he slept.

Awakening he found Alway moving quietly about the chamber putting out fresh linen and carrying towels to the garderobe.

James, checking a desire to rush to the casement, asked instead what hour it was.

'It is late, my Lord, but it seemed a pity to wake you when you were sleeping so soundly.'

'Thank you, John.'

There was a knock on the door and Orleans came in.

'Come on, sluggard! You are wasting this beautiful day. Catherine sends word she is having a feast spread out for us *en plein d'air* deep in the forest of Windsor and you lie here wallowing in sleep. Time enough for that when this benighted island is covered in its winter mists and soaking rains.'

James sat up and stretched luxuriously.

'Who goes with us?' he asked nonchalantly, pulling on a lawn shirt handed to him by Alway.

'You do not deceive me, James Stewart,

with your air of disinterest! But have no fear, if the little Jane is not already of our number, I'll make it my personal concern to see she goes with us.'

Humming the chorus of a popular lover's ballad of the moment he went out with a flourishing bow.

In the bailey horses awaited them and the men of the party were gathering, some with their falconers. John Beaufort came up to greet James, his left arm covered with a strong leather glove. Behind him stood one of his men, similarly gloved and bearing on his extended forearm a hooded goshawk.

'No hunting for you, James?' Beaufort asked.

'I have no hawks,' James answered. 'And I prefer to ride free this day.'

Orleans joined them and they stood discussing the bird merits as their owners brought them to the group. James was only half conscious of the earnest conversation for he was watching for the arrival of the women.

They came in an assortment of brilliant dresses, rivalling the birds' plumage, chattering and laughing together. Catherine greeted the men who awaited them and her Master of Horse assisted her to the huge, ornately worked saddle of her mare.

James picked out Jane from the lively

flurry of women and when he saw her groom help her mount, he sprang lightly to his horse and went to her side. She bade him welcome with pleasure, looking into his eyes with candour and pressing his hand as he took it to kiss.

He stayed by her side as they moved off and rode with her at the gentle pace set by Catherine. It was admirably suited to the day for the sun was warm and shone in a cloudless sky.

Jane was dressed in a gown of amber, girdled with a belt finely wrought in gold studded with seed pearls. A cap of gold mesh also set with pearls held her hair. James noted she rode well, her back straight and her hands light on the reins.

Unlike the previous evening James talked to her without restraint and she listened intently, commenting when necessary. Gradually it became as if the others were of a different party and James and Jane fell behind until, at last, coming to a small clearing James put his hand on the bridle of her horse and brought it to a halt.

Suddenly quiet he slid off his mount's back and put up his arms to help Jane down. As she slid to the ground he held her against him, still saying nothing but savouring the delight of her nearness. She did not move but stood in tranquil acquiescence as his arms tightened round her. Then as his mouth sought her she put her hands to the back of his head and kissed him tenderly.

Far off the crackling of twigs and muffled bursts of laughter told of the rest of the party but James and his love did not heed them. The world had shrunk suddenly to the small confines of the forest clearing and the trees, pressed close together, were as secret as a turret room.

'I do not have to tell you what is in my heart,' James said softly. 'For you have known since the moment our eyes met at the table yesterday, but I have loved you since I first saw you sitting in the little garden beneath my window.'

'You saw me — yesterday?' she asked somewhat breathlessly, colouring slightly.

'Yes,' James agreed. 'And a prettier sight I had never seen before. I hope you will always make it your custom to sun yourself in the garden beneath my chamber.'

'Oh, James,' she whispered, hiding her face against his shoulder. 'You must think me wanton!'

'That I do not,' James assured her emphatically, adding hastily, 'but of course, I should not like to see you so attired before others. I think when we are married I shall have to have a secret garden especially made for your sun-worshipping; although,' he said, suddenly gloomy, 'from what I remember of it, Scotland is not all that suitable for sunning oneself.'

For the first time his return home seemed to have disadvantages but he was not able to dwell on the subject for Jane had heard the word of marriage so casually dropped.

'Married. When shall we be married?' she asked quietly.

'As soon as I am freed,' James said. 'Now I have more reason than ever to press my claims for repatriation. You will share my throne with me Jane, won't you?'

Struck with the precipitous nature of the wooing which had brought them within a day to be speaking of their marriage he held her at arms length, regarding her quizzically, afraid to mar the perfection of their understanding by haste.

'I do not rush you, sweeting?' he asked.

'No,' she answered smiling. 'Your thoughts and mine run together. My only concern is that marriage may not be an advantage to you in your homecoming.'

'On the contrary,' James said as a fresh aspect of the situation came to him. 'It might suit the King's advisers to have the Scottish throne wedded to a Beaufort.'

Holding her close again he kissed her on the brow.

'I do not think, sweetheart, we shall meet much opposition to our plans here. As far as Scotland is concerned my position can only be strengthened by bringing a consort home with me. It will do away with any jealousy that could be caused by the King marrying into one or other of the families who are continually at one another's throats and the more I think of it from England's point of view the more advantageous it appears. It is likely Gloucester may have doubts but he is taken up with the trouble his marriage has caused and the possibility of having an English queen of Scotland will be so acceptable to the Council that, with your uncle leading them, they will not favour Gloucester's opinions.'

Later as they rode homewards towards the castle he said,

'Undoubtedly, my love, you have altered the contrary fates that govern my life for you have bestowed upon me the double blessing of being the most adorable woman in England and being the most suitable bride I could have chosen.'

And so it seemed during the rest of the magical month James spent at Windsor. The long, sunlit days were filled with joy and the court smiled benignly on the Lady Jane and the transported James. It was the happiest period of his life, during which he shed the remnants of the tense strivings which had beset him through so much of the latter years of his captivity. He discovered depths of feelings for Jane which he would have thought impossible a few weeks before. He lived for her, seeing the world through her eyes, accepting almost as inevitable the favourable progress which was reported to him of the negotiations for his release. All must go well with them now!

No official word was spoken of his desire to marry Jane but it was obvious that Winchester and Westmorland, with Exeter and Somerset regarded his suit with favour. When word came from Westminster summoning him to return to put in motion the final arrangements for the meeting of the English and Scottish envoys he was torn between leaving Jane and working for what would be their future together.

Jane, perhaps even more glowing than when he had first seen her, did not weep as they parted but she was unusually quiet as she stood at his horse's side, one hand on the stirrup.

'Do not be absent too long,' she said. 'For my heart lives only in thee.'

James found himself unable to answer her and unsmiling bent down and kissed her before the assembled company then spurring the horse turned abruptly and rode off.

13

He missed her with a physical and spiritual sense of loss, cursing the slow machinery of government as it drafted the proposals for the meeting of the representatives which was to take place as soon as could be arranged in Yorkshire.

The days, still wrapped in Summer's blood-quickening beauty, were only made tolerable by the knowledge that a climax in his affairs was approaching and the awareness of the mutual love flowing between himself and Jane. In the short nights he slept easily, his mind more at peace than it had ever been before; plans for their future in the unknown Scotland lulling him in hopeful dreams.

His life at Sir William Meryng's underwent a subtle change for he was cosseted as never before. When the evenings became cool fires of well dried wood were lit and his diet was more varied than at any time since his imprisonment. Exotic delicacies which he found hard to name, such as heron, porpreys, merlings and conger eels loaded his table. He could only assume that this fare, which he knew perfectly well was being meticulously charged against his ransom, was being supplied, literally, to leave him with a good taste of English hospitality.

Needless to say, Ogilvy and Alway did not enquire too deeply into their change of fortune and ate with relish any succulent dish set before them.

The news from Scotland, reported by John Lyon and William Giffard, was of growing dissatisfaction with Murdoch, now Duke of Albany. It appeared all feuds had been forgotten, however temporarily, in the desire to oust the Regent and crown the rightful king. Of Murdoch himself James' correspondents reported he was too apathetic to realise what was afoot.

At the beginning of August James left London for Pontefract accompanied by Philip Morgan Bishop of Worcester. He was joined in the imposing castle crowning the steep hill by Henry Percy who brought with him further representatives of the English Commission in the Bishop of Durham and John Wodeham.

The two friends met with real pleasure but were unable to find time for private matters as the Scottish ambassadors arrived almost at once. These were also headed by a Bishop Lauder who was supported by several abbots and knights and Murdoch's own secretary,

Patrick Houston. This was bewildering if encouraging.

Any doubts James experienced when he saw March was not with them were dispelled when the Scottish Commissioners greeted him with unfeigned pleasure. His spirits soared and as the meeting progressed he knew, almost by intuition, that whatever terms were dictated to them they would accept as a means of recovering their rightful King. It was at one and the same time a flattering and humbling prospect and showed only too plainly the unsettled state of Scotland.

When the first long, engrossing day was finished James and Henry sat comfortably relaxed on either side of a glowing fire. Alway had brought them wine and James had sent him to bed.

'Well James, at last! What do you think of your chances now?'

'Very good,' James replied. 'The terms, I believe are stiff and the ransom exorbitant but — '

'What do you call exorbitant?' Henry broke in.

'The Bishop of Worcester mentioned £40,000!'

'Great heavens!' Percy said on a long whistle. 'Where will they raise that?'

'That is certainly the most difficult question,' James agreed. 'And it is not made any easier in that it has to be repaid within six years.'

'An uphill task indeed,' Henry said. 'But the Scots — your people,' he added hastily, 'can scratch in their herring barrels and woolfells and find every last penny of it for the tardy way they have left you to rot in England. Not that you look very wasted! In fact I have never seen you better.'

'Well,' James said slowly, 'I have found a girl who will be my wife.'

'By Our Lady and you keep this from me until now! James, by all that's wonderful — and is she as you expected? Who is she? Is she suitable?'

James laughed as Henry sat forward eagerly firing questions.

'Yes, most suitable for she is the sister of John Beaufort.'

'A Beaufort! By all that's Holy, James, you're a canny quiet one. Or,' he broke off, 'did the mighty Bishop of Winchester engineer the whole affair?'

'Indeed he did not,' James said indignantly. Then sat back as he thought of Jane being pressed into her uncle's service to entrap him and how well she could have carried out his plans.

'No,' he said smiling and shaking his head. 'You need have no fears on that score, Henry. My future wife has a mind of her own, like most of the Beauforts and our happiness seemed almost — ' he hesitated, 'preordained. Oh, Henry,' he continued quickly, 'perhaps only you know how I have longed all my life to have someone of my own who cared for me.'

'Yes, I think I do,' Henry said quietly, seeing in the dark recesses behind the leaping flames the young James as he had been in their last days together at St. Andrews.

'She is everything and more than I have dreamed and since we have met it seems as if the tide of fortune is flooding in my direction. But you must have met at Court!'

'Perhaps, perhaps,' Henry said. 'But you know how it is when one is married. Wives, even the best of them, don't take too kindly to a wandering eye. Be warned, my boy, be warned!'

Henry leant back against the cushions of his chair and drank deeply of his wine, and on a more serious note went on to ask James about the official views of his marriage.

'There is a very guarded clause about an English lady of rank being most suitable for my consort. This goes on to say that I must make the choice as English grande dames are not in the habit of offering themselves in marriage.'

Henry shook his head in disbelief.

'What lawyer's brain thought that out, I wonder?' he said. 'Is there mention of hostages and a truce?'

'Both,' James answered. 'The English marriage is to encourage peace and the hostage to ensure it.'

The short night was almost ended as they bade one another good night and sought their allotted chambers.

As James had expected it became obvious during the next few days that the Scottish Commissioners were eager to come to agreement. They accepted the terms put before them and made no effort to cut the ransom. When they were questioned about the method of raising the money they expressed no doubt of its promp payment. James when he heard this could only marvel at their naivete but excused them on the grounds of little or no experience of extorting money from the common folk. His tuition at the English Court told him that this was going to be one of the most difficult and urgent problems he would have to face when, eventually, he came to govern.

The Commissioners were equally con-vinced they would have no trouble in finding the required number of hostages and they eagerly agreed to send ambassadors to make the final arrangements for James' marriage.

James parted from them on the best of terms and it was settled they should all meet again in the following March when the hostages would be exchanged for James at Brancepeth.

He set out for Windsor taking with him several more Scots who had expressed their loyalty towards him during the past days. He enjoyed their company, questioning them closely about their country's affairs and so engrossed was he in the subject they arrived in Berkshire almost as swiftly as he wished.

There was no need to send word of their coming for watchmen on the high round tower had seen their train with its bright new banners from afar and a large company awaited them on the winding hill.

One sweeping look found Jane in the centre of a small group where she waited until he came up to her. Only he knew the control she exercised for he longed to take her into his arms and the quick little breath she drew as he knelt to kiss her hand told him her thoughts.

It was not until the September dusk was falling and wisps of white mist crept up from the river that they were alone. Without speaking they walked to the secret garden beneath the tower of James' room.

Here she sat on the bench and looked up into his face.

'Are we really together,' he said wonderingly. 'It seems an age since I have held you in my arms. I have missed you so much, but God willing we shall not be parted for long now.'

'Was the marriage definitely arranged?' she asked when, a little breathless, she drew away from him.

'It was all most diplomatically broached and discussed and Scottish ambassadors come to London next month to settle the matter. Do you think Queen Catherine could spare you to accompany me when I go to Westminster to meet them?'

'The Queen Mother with all the court is going to Hertford for Christmas and it is usual procedure for us to spend a few weeks in London before we go to the chosen palace so there will be no difficulty. Oh, James I must be wanton for life is not the same when we are apart!'

They spent as much time as possible in each other's company during the next month and when James left to be in Westminster to greet the envoys they were not separated for long as the court followed almost at once.

Great cordiality marked the discussions, both the English and Scottish ambassadors showing unfeigned pleasure in the choice of the Lady Jane as the future bride of the King of Scotland.

James thought she had never looked lovelier than on the raw November morning when he presented her to them. She glowed with an abundance of health and happiness, her radiance filling the room. She wore a golden velvet surcote trimmed with white fur enhancing the warmth of her skin and had bound her hair in a fillet of gold. Her open smile quickly melted the taciturn Scots and she was at ease with them immediately. James watched her with admiration as she moved among them deferring to their superiority but preserving at the same time a youthful dignity. Several times she found him looking at her and her smile deepened.

The ambassadors set out on their tedious journey to the North well pleased with their future Queen and the generous remittance of ten thousand pounds of the ransom made by Bishop Beaufort as a dowry for his niece. As many of them as possible agreed to return to London for the marriage which was to take place in the following February.

The court returned from Hertford, where it had spent a quiet Christmas, glad to have the excitement of a royal wedding to occupy the dark days after Twelfth Night. Quite suddenly James and Jane seemed unable to find time for more than snatched moments of each other's company.

She was in constant demand to make decisions about chattels and furniture to be taken with them on their journey to Scotland and her mother the Duchess of Clarence insisted upon providing her with an ample trousseau.

The English Council had also shown its genuine approval of the coming marriage by giving James sufficient money with which to buy suitable garments. Amused at his own vanity he chose a length of cloth of gold for the doublet, his years of deprivation convincing him this was a wise choice as he would be able to wear the same clothes for his Coronation later in the year.

His time was also much occupied with the question of finding suitable hostages. These were slow in forthcoming and James could understand only too easily the reluctance of heads of families to part with their heirs. Not only did it mean weakening the strength of the family but it entailed the payment of quite large sums of the ransom. Patriotism, surprisingly enough, won the day all the same and the Bishop of Glasgow reported the list almost completed as the marriage day came.

Close covered barges hung in velvet waited at the steps of the Palace of Westminster to carry the bridegroom's party to St. Mary of Overbury at Southwark where the Bishop of Winchester waited to marry his niece to the King of Scotland.

Before taking the cloak Ogilvy had ready for him James thanked his squires for their devotion to him in the difficult and trying days of his bachelorhood, and looked forward to their continuing service in the unknown days ahead.

As he went down the stairs to the waiting barge Ogilvy turned to Alway.

'Let us pray the days before us are not as difficult as those we have come through. At least we can thank the Almighty he has chosen to marry a real woman and his fancy did not light on any of the other bedizened females who throng this court. They sicken me with their ridiculous headdresses and plucked foreheads.'

'They all look to me as if they live in a state of perpetual fright,' Alway said.

'Perhaps they do,' Ogilvy chuckled. 'We men are not always the parfait knights their childhood dreams led them to expect.'

Unconscious of their ribaldry James threw himself on to the cushioned thwart unable to think of anything except that in less than an hour he would belong to someone for the first time in eighteen years. The loneliness he had experienced was something which he could now put behind him for ever.

Despite the cold a large crowd had gathered, curious to see Beaufort's niece married to the King who had been England's prisoner for so long.

James ran up the stairs of the landing stage and was met with goodnatured whistles and subdued cheers. He was vaguely conscious of empurpled faces beneath hoods of coarse wool and was grateful for the press of bodies which protected him from the icy wind. The Bishop's chaplain led him to the large porch of the church and he did not have long to wait for his bride as he heard the crowd's roar and saw them fall back as the bridesmen made up a path for her.

James took her hand and held it tightly as Bishop Beaufort began the time honoured words. For James they held special significance and he responded in his turn with joy. He partook of the Eucharist which followed with true thanksgiving and promised to bestow his constant care on the woman who knelt beside him in solemn devotion.

In the barge he kissed her swiftly as they were joined by Ogilvy and some of her

215

women. They did not talk but kept their hands closely linked oblivious to the others' chatter.

Beaufort had prepared a magnificent feast for his niece in his Palace at Lambeth and had dug deeply into the coffers of his own estates and that of the See of Winchester to provide her with a banquet befitting her new rank as Queen of Scotland.

Not since Catherine's coronation had James seen such sumptuous dishes and intricate arrangements of marchpane and sugar. A seemingly endless stream of servants bore aloft dishes of succulent roast beef, mutton and piglet while down the long boards went a succession of silver platters piled high with eels, larks tongues, lampreys, boiled oysters and breasts of ducks. These were followed with pies and fruit both fresh and candied. Ewers of wine were passed from hand to hand while jugglers, tumblers and lutists ran, leapt and sang wherever space was available.

Jane sat on a raised dais beside James, radiant with happiness in her bridal gown of brocade overlaid with silver and gold gauze. On her head she wore a diadem of pearls and topaz which was a gift from her uncle.

James was still quiet, eating very little but drinking deep of the wine. Once he passed the cup to her and she drank, looking steadily into his eyes as she did so.

When at last the women came to take her to the chamber already prepared with great care for their bedding he had a swift glimpse of those same eyes now wide and limpid. His heart lurched in his breast and he became completely abstracted from his surroundings. When the gentlemen of his bedchamber came to escort him away he almost forgot to pay his respects to Beaufort and thank him for the magnificence of his hospitality.

Beaufort accepted his gratitude with the benevolence he had displayed throughout the proceedings. It had been a day very much after his Plantagenet heart where splendour had been mixed with political gain.

James kept his patience as well as he was able as his squires helped him with his disrobing, laughing at their well meant advice and pointed humour. After what seemed a most unnecessarily protracted time they assisted him into the new chamber robe he had had made and he allowed them to carry him to the door of the bride's room. Here he gently, but very firmly, dismissed them and watched them as they stumbled away from him laughing and gay. When he could no longer hear them he opened the door with some hesitation.

He dreaded finding waiting women still in the chamber but a quick glance told him none were present. Soft light from a well tended fire and several tapers played on the luxurious appointments of the room. Damask covered the walls and was caught in a ring in the ceiling to fall round the bed in folds of gold and amber.

He did not speak but dropping the robe beside the fire opened the curtains and climbed upon the bed.

'James.'

He caught the soft whisper as her hand found his and drew him beneath the silken sheets and soft covering. He came close to her, the warmth of her naked body enfolding him, welcoming him. Her arms came round his neck, pulling him to her and he buried his face in the abundance of her sweet-smelling hair, murmuring her name.

As her arms tightened round him and he turned her face to meet mouth with mouth he knew this was where his life began. All the agonising, frustrating years of his imprisonment had been worth waiting for the experience of sharing his future with the woman who lay beside him ready and willing to transport him. His hands caressed her, then caught her to him bind her to him until they were really of one flesh.

Afterwards he clung to her as if his life depended on her nearness and she lay quiet and acquiescent until she felt him relax. When she was certain he slept she pulled the covers over his shoulders and nestled against him her hair entwined about him. In complete happiness she closed her eyes and slept also.

14

The marriage took place on Sunday the thirteenth of February and the next day James was back in the company of his ambassadors drafting final instructions for the Durham exchange of hostages.

His years of discipline now stood him in good stead for he was able to concentrate on the serious business being transacted while he longed with all his being to be with Jane.

He had woken in the grey light of the morning and had found her sleeping curled beside him, the smile of contentment still on her lips. He had not disturbed her but lay watching her in the dim, close bed living again the happiness she had given him. He found it impossible to express the peace she had brought him and his poet's command of words deserted him. He only knew since the first moment when she had smiled at him at Windsor until now she had eased the burden of his existence and finally removed it. In its place she had given him courage and strength to return to Scotland and face whatever lay before them.

Although he had given passing thought to

the new life ahead of his bride he had pushed away from him any fears of what the future might hold for her but now, seeing her lying so trustingly beside him he was smitten with the selfishness of his own actions. Full of remorse he saw how truly great her sacrifice was, for she was leaving the pampered security of the English court for the uncertain Queenship of Scotland. He was ashamed that in the overwhelming happiness he was experiencing he had overlooked how much she was sacrificing on his behalf. Tenderly he put his arm about her and kissed her on her forehead. She roused momentarily, long enough to return the pressure of his embrace and slept again.

Returning from the warm delights of his very new marriage he heard Gloucester granting him permission to go to the Tower and secure the temporary release of two of the sons of the Earl of March, David and Nicholas Dunbar.

The meeting dragged on for what seemed interminable hours but eventually the Council expressed its satisfaction with the arrangements being made for the settling of the hostages in various castles throughout the Midlands. James was called upon to witness his intention of carrying out his side of the bargain and this done the Assembly gave their

221

final blessing and wished him Godspeed.

James hurried to the Tower to release the two Dunbars. He had met them briefly during their mutual confinements and he could well understand their joy at being released. Before embarking in the waiting barges they fell on their knees and expressed their unfaltering loyalty to their sovereign.

Catherine sent for them on the following morning as they were about to set out on their long journey. Kissing Jane she wished them well in their new life together. She took a brooch handsomely wrought in gold and set with pearls from a box on a nearby table, and pinned it to the bodice of Jane's gown.

Thanking her Jane saw tears, hastily blinked away, in Catherine's eyes. The dowager Queen turned quickly to James and he raised her hand to his lips.

'Thank you, James, for your support to me in those dark and difficult days. You will always have my gratitude as from one stranger to another.' She hesitated, 'Go with God and may Our Lady protect you and your wife in your new life and may the happiness you now enjoy stay with you always. Au revoir, mon ami!'

Helplessly James made his farewells, unable to wish Catherine anything but a peaceful and contented life with her baby son, the King.

'Poor Catherine,' Jane said as they rejoined the party awaiting them. 'She is so very young to be set aside in widowhood and in a foreign court where loyalties may shift from day to day.'

'There is always Orleans,' James said somewhat lamely.

'But he is not for her!' Jane cried. 'He is a bon viveur, a man incapable of real emotion, living only for the moment. The Queen needs the comfort of a man — '

'Let us hope she will never find him,' James interrupted her quickly. 'For it will be the worse for her — and for him, if the Council should hear of it. They cannot afford to have the power of the Regency undermined by the King's mother gathering support.'

He helped her to her horse for she had said she would rather ride than be jolted in a litter on the ice bound roads.

At first they rode silently still troubled by the unhappiness of the dowager Queen but the crisp air and the pleasure of each other's company soon revived their spirits.

Leaving the village of Westminster the countryside was beautiful with the stillness of winter. Frost sparkled from the grasses and a pale sunlight bloomed the frozen puddles.

Blackbirds lumbered from the hedgerows and pairs of partridges circled in the fields. Only a tiny sparrow broke the silence, undaunted by the cold.

They spent the night at Hatfield, coming on the nestling palace of the Bishop of Ely in the quick falling evening.

'James!' Jane said to him, turning eagerly in the saddle. 'Do you realise you are on your way home!'

'Yes,' he answered. 'And after all these years I would gladly elect to remain in England if it meant choosing between you and Scotland.'

'Oh, James,' she said softly. 'Thank God you have not to make the choice.'

'Thank God, indeed,' he replied. 'For by His Grace you are beside me now!'

The journey to Durham took them two weeks, hampered as they were with laden mules carrying silverware, cloth, linens and provisions. They trundled through the towns of the Great North road passing Huntingdon and Stamford and throughout the tedious travelling seemed to be surrounded with fellow companions. Even at night they found it was necessary to separate and share sleeping quarters with squires or ladies in waiting.

Marjorie Norton, who had been nurse to

Jane since she was born, clucked her disapproval and tried to find private chambers for her mistress but it seemed it was forgotten that the marriage of the King was but a week old in the business of getting from one resting place to another. Keeping out the cold and finding sufficient food were of prime importance to the other members of the company.

Brancepeth was a haven which could not be reached quickly enough for James and Jane.

The crossing of the Trent near Lincoln threatened to delay them even further for the bargemen demanded an exorbitant sum for handling the mountains of baggage. John Everton, in charge of the expedition, refused to be browbeaten and eventually succeeded in persuading the men to accept five shillings. Although this was considerably less than their original demand it was still a great deal of money. The head bargeman seemed in no way satisfied, however, and grumbling and muttering to himself superintended the stowing of the heavy chests at a maddeningly slow rate. He made no haste to return for the men and women of the party and by the time they were ferried to the northern bank it was night. It was not surprising that it was the first day of March before they came upon

Brancepeth Castle. Breasting the last hill and looking down over the rolling moorlands to where the castle lay enfolded and solitary James reined in his horse and put out his hand to detain Jane's mare. As the others rode on past them he stared down the valley to their destination and then drew close to Jane and cupping his hand round her chin bent swiftly and kissed her hard on the mouth.

'Now,' he said vehemently. 'They may protract their negotiations as long as they care while my wife and I have a chance to be alone.'

When they came up with the rest of the party and entered the yard of the castle their hearts sank as they saw the occupants drawn up to greet them. In a quick estimation James reckoned there were upwards of a hundred and fifty knights and men at arms. Before he was able to comment to Jane he saw Ralph Neville detach himself from the ranks to come forward to welcome them.

'My Lord,' he said with real pleasure. 'At last we see the dawn of your return to Scotland and you bring Jane with you to be your wife and Queen. Welcome, my lady!'

He bowed over her hand and turned with twinkling eyes to James.

'I know what you are thinking James, but

fear not, you will not be worried with the courtesies while you are here. My wife is at Raby. She protested it was early in the year for travelling and remembering you were but newly married thought you might care to be on your own for a while. She sent her felicitations and hopes to meet you both another time.'

James thanked him, laughing, and they dismounted and entered the castle.

While Ogilvy accompanied them to the sparsely furnished but comfortable and warm rooms put at their disposal Alway set himself to find out the situation regarding the arrival of the hostages at the Castle.

He carried the somewhat gloomy news of the presence of Patrick Lyon, heir of Glamis and Alexander, Earl of Crawford. This was the sum total of the Scottish hostages to date. Two out of an expected twenty-seven was discouraging to say the least but to his surprise James did not appear to be as concerned as he had expected.

'He's a queer one,' he said later to Ogilvy. 'I'd die of frustration if I'd been nearly eighteen years a captive to arrive here and find but two of the hostages had appeared.'

'Well,' said Ogilvy slowly. 'Thinking it over, perhaps if you had a new wife and had not had more than two or three uninterrupted nights with her since you were wed you'd not be over bothered with another small wait.'

'But it may not be a short time; it could go on for months!'

'Fash not and leave him be. Time alone will tell,' Ogilvy said and was proved at least partly right when later James requested supper to be served to them in their private solar.

'And you need not stay to wait on us either,' he told the two squires and the pages. 'We'll manage for ourselves.'

With rather a smug expression Ogilvy gratefully closed the door behind him, he had been proved right and the night was young enough to seek the pleasure of the company of some of the ladies in waiting.

Ralph Neville had had his seneschall send up a well cooked duck and a flask of claret warmed and fragrant. James and Jane ate and drank with pleasure. When they were finished she pushed the table away and stood up and stretched luxuriantly, her eyes heavy with sleep.

'Unlace my dress,' she said turning her back on James and trembling slightly he found the strings and the heavy dress fell to the floor. Jane stood in her shift, young, appealing and infinitely desirable. With one swift movement she drew off the linen shift and ran towards the bed.

'Oh James,' she called. 'They have even been thoughtful enough to warm it for us with stones wrapped in wool. Come and take them!'

He carried them to the hearth and returned to her where she sat enthroned in the curtained bed. For a moment he could not move, entranced with the sight of her demurely holding the covers to her chin, while her eyes no longer sleepy, sparkled up at him. Slowly he came in beside her and with a moan of delight gathered her to him.

This was to be the pattern of their life during the month that followed and their love deepened with their mutual knowledge. The long wasted years were forgotten in the newly awakened world Jane discovered for him. His roused passion, dormant during his young manhood, was perfectly attuned to her abundant and generous vitality. She gave unstintingly of her love, melting away the loneliness he had walked in.

The hostages found him understanding and sympathetic and he pledged his word to have them replaced as quickly as was practical. To Jane he confided that he thought several of them looked far from strong and would find the confining restrictions a tax on their strength.

He questioned them all closely about the situation in Scotland and they confirmed the despatches John Lyon sent him. They were unanimous in their opinion of Murdoch, now Duke of Albany and Regent, stating they did not think him vicious as perhaps his father had been but completely incompetent to hold high office. It was generally believed the coffers of the country were empty and lawlessness abounded. Many of the young people could speak of parents or friends who had suffered some wrong at another's hand and had been unable to find redress in a court of law or by applying to the Regent. Coupled with his inefficiency Murdoch had not altered his personal habits and his life was notoriously profligate.

James was gratified to discover among the hostages some who had attended the university at St. Andrews. They told him it was flourishing and attracting men from as far afield as Paris and even Rome. Bishop Wardlaw was respected and admired. In the second week of their stay at Brancepeth James received a letter from his old tutor welcoming him home and stating his wish to perform the coronation ceremony if James so desired.

'I have not thought much of the coronation,' James said to Jane.

'It will be an opportunity to wear our wedding finery again,' Jane said. 'It always seems such a waste to put it on only once.'

They were standing at the window of their room watching snow fall on the moors. The huge flakes drifted down obscuring the light, covering the heather and stunted trees.

'We are imprisoned here,' James said softly. 'In an Ice King's palace while the key has been spirited away by one of the hobgoblins who live on the moors. Let us hope whatever good fairy is sent to find it they do not accomplish the task too easily!'

He looked down into her upturned face.

'I do not have to ask thee if thou art happy,' he said. 'For your eyes tell me enough. But are you sure you have no regrets about leaving the luxury and safety of the English court in company with a King who does not know his kingdom and will undoubtedly have a difficult and perhaps even dangerous time ahead?'

'No regrets. No regrets at all,' she answered quietly putting her arms round his neck and pulling herself close to him. 'In the month since our marriage your love has given me more happiness than I knew existed in the world. Our life is complete in itself and the strength that love gives us will help us to face whatever the future may hold.'

'Dearest love,' he whispered and found himself unable to continue for the tightening of his throat.

'See James, it is dark enough for night.'

He stooped and lifted her to the bed.

At the end of March the required complement of hostages had arrived at Brancepeth and James was summonsed by the English Commissioners to present himself at Durham for the final signing of his release. As he left the castle with Westmorland the Earl told him there had been moments when the London delegates had been minded to return to Westminster cancelling the proceedings altogether.

It was not so much the slow arrival of the hostages which had upset them but the news they had received of a large force of Scots under Murdoch's son Sir Walter Stewart and the Earl of Douglas arriving in France.

James could well understand their fury at Douglas' treachery but he read into their decision to carry through his release a favourable omen for his own future for it meant the English were so anxious to have peace on their Northern border they were prepared to overlook this flagrant breach of the as yet unsigned treaty.

He went to Durham and received permission to proceed to Melrose Abbey where he was to put his name to the ratification. He was well content with the meeting and came back to Jane in Brancepeth in high hopes.

'There, my love,' he said. 'Now we are completely free to return to Scotland. The snow has melted and nothing stands in our way. I must admit that now my homecoming is so close the prospect invites and appals me at the same time. I can only hope God grants me the health and wisdom to give my country the guidance she needs. Stay close beside me won't you?'

15

While he had been at Durham Henry Percy had arrived to accompany him to the border as part of the English escort.

'Marriage suits you, James,' he cried. 'As I knew it would! What news have you from Scotland?'

James told him what he had learned from the hostages and that Bishop Wardlaw was coming to Scone to perform the crowning.

'Is there a chance of you being there, Henry?'

'With a truce for seven years anything is possible,' Henry replied. 'Have you much baggage to take with you to Scotland?'

'Not as much as we transported here,' James laughed. 'All the silverware and linen lent to us for the journey has been returned. John Everton has not been idle while we have been here, however, and has brought large quantities of coal and fish as well as other provisions.'

'I suggest you send them on to Edinburgh by sea,' Henry said. 'Otherwise our progress will be painfully slow.'

With his journey through England fresh in

his memory James agreed with him and was thankful for the advice when they came to the undulating country of the desolate Northumbrian uplands.

After the gentle dales with their thickly wooded valleys through which the company rode on the first days of leaving Brancepeth the empty vastness of the moors towards Otterburn was startling. They crossed mile upon mile of hills, barren and wrapped in mist. Here and there a lonely crow flapped in the biting wind and when they came on a small homestead it was so hidden in the folds of the earth to resemble from the distance the stone outcrops surrounding it. When the inhabitants were visible they showed a wary interest in the travellers, biding within the shadow of their dwelling and keeping their offspring hidden. They had been subjected to too many raids from both north and south to trust any strangers and the Scottish King's banner meant little or nothing to them.

Jane was full of pity for the people clothed in coarse cloth and pieces of fur and was conscious of the richness of her velvet surcote and the sable lining of her mantle. The meanness of the hovels and the poverty of the dwellers reminded her of the wretched years James had passed in penury.

Redesdale Forest was hardly more comforting with its dark trees giving perfect cover for an ambush but they traversed it in safety and Henry told James the higher hills visible in front of them marked the border and Carter Bar where he would be leaving them.

Gaining the moors again they climbed until they seemed to have gained the highest point of the world where they could look down in one sweeping arc to both England and Scotland.

Scotland! James caught his breath and let his eye travel to the furthermost horizon. He was home.

Henry took his leave of them reluctantly for he would have liked to continue with them to Melrose but his instructions had been to accompany them to the border and this he had done.

He rode off with his troop of some sixty men and James gave the signal to begin the descent into Jedburgh. Here he was greeted by a small number of townsfolk who stared in disbelief at the banner proclaiming the return from exile of their rightful King. James returned their salutations, holding Jane's hand and showing her to the people. By the time they were moving off a crowd began to gather and faint cheers followed them down the road to Melrose.

James had time during the ride through the place to note the disrepair of the castle. Here was proof of Murdoch's incompetence in not strengthening this vulnerable fortress. He must make its reparation one of his first duties.

They came to the beautiful Cistercian abbey as the sharp Spring twilight threw the buildings into relief against the paling sky. It was possible to pick out the graceful church and the ruins of chapels destroyed in earlier days.

The monks had prepared a simple but sincere welcome for them and the food they provided was ample and well cooked. James and Jane were given an austere chamber with a small unyielding bed. They were so tired they sank gratefully into it and with arms about each other fell almost at once to sleep.

'We're home,' she murmured against his cheek.

He tightened his hold of her.

'Yes,' he said sleepily. 'Now we shall not have long to wait to find out what Scotland has in store for us.'

The next morning he signed the confirmation of the treaty and left at once for Edinburgh. On the outskirts of the city they were met by John Lyon and representatives of the Scottish Council who led them to Holyrood.

James was overjoyed to have Lyon with him again and they talked without ceasing until they clattered over the cobbles of the narrow streets and came to the Palace.

Apartments had been prepared for them and although James had been expecting less elegantly furnished and appointed rooms than those of Windsor or Westminster he was dismayed at the cheerless and comfortless chambers. He had not looked to find brocades and silken hangings but he was shocked at the dingy curtains and threadbare covers on the beds and settles.

As if sensing his disappointment Jane threw wide her arms and surveyed the room.

'What a beautifully shaped room!' she cried. 'Marjorie Norton and the other ladies and I shall have plenty to occupy our time while you are busy. How fortunate John Everton was thoughtful enough to send so much linen for we shall be able to make new hangings.'

'When Everton returns to London he can order brocades and silk,' James said hotly.

'What will he use for money?' Jane asked quietly.

'When I call my first Council I'll make it of prime importance to look into the coffers and see how cousin Murdoch has provided for the country and for the Royal Household,' James promised grimly.

His first meeting in the sombre council chambers of the Castle was well attended, most Earls present in the country coming to pay their respects. Among them were his uncle, the old Earl of Atholl and Murdoch.

They greeted him affably enough and Murdoch seemed to bear no resentment for being relieved of his Regency. The most notable absentee was Walter Stewart, heir of Murdoch. Later, when James questioned Lyon about his whereabouts, he learned he had gone to Falkland since announcing his intention of joining Douglas in the sending of troops to France.

James made no comment either on his non appearance or his breach of the recently signed treaty but determined to act immediately after the business of the meeting was concluded. He had attended sufficient of Henry V's Councils to know how he wished to conduct his own and started as he meant to continue by showing his authority.

He named the day on which he wished his first Parliament to meet and then called for the Rolls of the Exchequer. Murdoch refused to meet his eye as the heavy parchments were brought in and handed to him by his new

Chancellor Bishop Lauder. Forgetful of the eagerly watching faces he concentrated on the documents and was quickly left in no doubt of his cousin's incompetency as he realised the extremely low state of the country's funds. Jane had been only too right when she had asked how he intended to finance the restoration of their living quarters.

When at last the Council adjourned all present realised a new force had come to govern Scotland. The lax, easy going days of the Regency were at an end. This was welcomed by the progressive, younger Earls but some murmuring about new brushes could be heard from the cronies of Murdoch. James ignored the comments, announcing the twenty-sixth of May as the meeting of the first Parliament following on the Coronation which was to take place five days before.

Comment about the efficacy of new brushes was swiftly silenced when James sent to Falkland and arrested Walter Stewart and sentenced him to confinement on the Bass Rock.

'I must show them who is master,' he told Jane when she protested at his action.

'But he is your cousin,' she said.

'Family relationship did not stop my uncle Albany from causing the death of my brother or from keeping me a prisoner in the English court for eighteen years. I must make an example of Walter. It remains to be seen now if Murdoch will knuckle under or prove troublesome as a result. It sometimes follows that when weak people are roused they become vicious.'

'Let us hope that is not to be,' Jane said.

The following two months of her marriage were totally different from the idyllic happiness of the time spent at Brancepeth. James worked at fever pitch to produce the Statutes he intended presenting to Parliament when it met at Perth. During the day he ate snatched meals taken in to him at his desk.

Jane had expected this preoccupation would interfere with their private happiness but she was proved wrong. She lay awake for him the first time he had stayed closeted with Lyon until well after midnight and had anticipated he would fall into bed, weary with his law-making and the harrassing task of raising the money for the ransom. To her surprise, finding her not asleep, he had drawn her to him, wordless, and made love to her with a passion in no way lessened by his application to his work. Later he talked quietly of the day's problems seeking her advice and opinion. She came to understand then that their life was something apart from the happenings outside the walls of their apartments and that nothing could detract from their mutual joy in each other. She realised also that James' strength, physical and mental, was enhanced by her love.

During this time great preparations were being made for the crowning and summonses were sent throughout the kingdom.

When the day dawned at Scone, cool and bright, hundreds of people were already threading their way through the forest to the Abbey. Those privileged to take part went into the chapel and the others gathered in their multitudes on the mound which sloped down to the river.

Bishop Wardlaw had arrived on the previous evening and had greeted his former pupil with restrained affection. He had gone to considerable pains to find out the correct ceremonies to be observed and subjected James and Jane to a thorough rehearsal of the traditional rites to be performed on the following day.

He carried through the coronation with great dignity and the waiting crowd of nobles and commonfolk saw James and Jane receive their crowns in a well ordered ceremony.

Murdoch, perhaps mollified when James had knighted his younger son, Alexander, along with twenty-six other young men, had claimed his ancient right of placing the newly crowned king on his throne. It appeared as if differences were set aside for the day and Atholl beamed on all present as if the proceedings had been largely his own idea.

Oxen were roasted whole in the meadow and beer was freely poured for all comers. In the Abbey a lavish feast was held for the nobility. Only James and Jane knew the extent of the credit they had had to beg to provide the hospitality but the goodwill it engendered seemed worth the pawning of her jewels and some inherited family plate.

Later that night, when at last their guests had gone home or to bed, she told him she was expecting a child and that it should be born at Christmas time.

To his surprise James found his eyes full of tears.

'This is wonderful!' he cried. 'But you must take great care of yourself. If I had known this before you undertook all the excitement of this day I should have been crazed with anxiety for you.'

'And that is just why I did not tell you until now,' Jane said laughing. 'I am very well, as you see, and you did not notice anything amiss, did you?'

'I have been so selfishly taken up with my law-making and arrangements for the corona-tion I have had no time to think, except how bonny you are! But I'll make up for my lack now.'

'There is no need,' Jane told him softly. 'You go about the business of your kingdom and with God's help I'll produce a son or daughter in due time.'

'Have you told the physician or the midwife yet?'

'Not yet, but my women know and now that I have told you we'll tell the midwife.'

James held her at arm's length looking down at her, searching for a difference.

'Take that worried look off your face, my love, and come to bed. Today was your coronation and you are also going to be a father. This is a day of days, let us not spoil it in needless anxiety. I shall not shatter like crystal, James.'

But it was some time before he could rid himself of the anxiety he felt for her. His need of Jane was so great that the thought of life without her filled him with real terror.

Before Parliament met he made a swift journey to Dundee where he had inaugural meetings in connection with the burgh's contribution towards his ransom. He came away pleased with the result of his mission but rode with all speed to Scone to see how his wife fared in his absence. To his relief he found her very well and to his inward mortification more able to comfort than to require solace from him.

Buoyed with this encouraging knowledge he opened his first Parliament.

He began in the established manner by upholding the power of the Holy Church throughout the land and went on to make no secret of the fact that the husbanding of his country's resources and the raising of the ransom was his chief concern. He announced levying of taxes on land, wheat, rye and other grains. He appointed assessors and valuers to determine the amounts to be paid and laid down the penalties which failure to settle would bring on the defaulters. Some of the money, he told the Three Estates, would go towards improving the status of the crown, but the majority would be used for the benefit of the country and the paying of the ransom.

When his audience had listened, half incredulous to his proposals, he outlined some of the measures he intended instituting to strengthen the well-being of the realm. It was now forbidden to trap salmon with nets or to burn heather or let rooks build in trees where they might prey on crops.

In order to keep as much wealth in the country as was possible James forbade the export of gold and silver and outlined punishments for those who sought favour from the Papal Court by sending there large sums with which to purchase dispensations and favours. This measure caused many lifted eyebrows but weighted in James' favour when it was realised he must be fairly sure of his own strength to risk the displeasure of the Roman See.

At the same time he proclaimed a new coinage was to be minted and all mines were to become the property of the King. He further stated that severe penalties would be incurred for the theft of Church land and announced the forfeiture of estates of any who rebelled against the Crown or fought personal battles between themselves.

With the military example of Henry V very much in his mind he forbade the playing of football and golf and ordered the setting up of butts on village greens for the practice of archery by every able bodied man.

He spoke throughout with no heat but with the manner of one who knew his cause was just and destined to succeed. His listeners heard him in silence, warming to him as he roused their latent patriotism until at the end of the session they went home well pleased with the Sessions business. Most of them had suffered from the weakness of Murdoch's rule and welcomed the evidence of a strong hand.

James accepted their protestations of support knowing full well that dissension was reduced to a minimum by the absence of many of the nobles in France and as hostages in England. He listened with wry amusement to Lyon when he told him of the cynics who had admired his policy but doubted his ability to enforce his new regulations. This he realised was the most difficult part of his task.

It was not long before the assessing of lands brought to light several vast tracts which had previously belonged to the Crown and were now claimed by other owners.

The Earl of Lennox, father-in-law of Murdoch, and Sir Robert Graham were two of those who, when questioned about their possession of some such lands, refused to answer any enquiries. James, acting as he had promised in his Parliament, lost no time in arresting them both.

Rather pleased with his showing of strength he was nettled when a few days later Lyon reported to him that a messenger had arrived from Stirling bearing the news that Sir Robert Graham had affected an escape and was highly incensed at James' action.

'We'll not worry about him,' James said. 'It is more than he dare to return to his own castle and he is unlikely to rouse up much feeling against me. All the same it would be as well to find out his whereabouts and keep an eye on him.'

Later in the year James was saddened to hear of the death of Douglas who was killed in France with his son and son-in-law. While harbouring no illusions about the Earl's inconstancy he had been a brother of his mother's and one of the few who had worked in however a small way to aid his repatriation. The Douglasses had died in a great French defeat which had practically annihilated the Scottish force who had left only in the previous December to support them.

He spent the remaining time before Christmas when his child was to be born, travelling up and down the southern part of his kingdom. He met and spoke with as many of his people as was practical, listening to their grievances and capturing their imagination and loyalties with short, carefully worded speeches. He left behind him a sense of goodwill and a new born pride in their country. The commonfolk liked him for he did not hide from them the poverty he had suffered in his youth and they realised he understood their difficulties.

Among his new measures he had ordered the building of alehouses for every village and town. This he had devised as a method of keeping travellers from seeking shelter from nobles in their fortresses where they might be pressed into taking service in a private army. He visited several sites where building had commenced and brought ale to cheer the workmen.

He visited all of the Border strongholds, ordering the repair of broken down walls and the forming of glacis and the deepening and widening of moats. He rode back to Edinburgh satisfied with the first stages of his plans for Scotland.

He found Jane full of energy and ready to listen to all he had seen and accomplished. He talked earnestly while she lay propped beside him in the great bed they shared. He had enquired minutely into the state of her health but she laughed off his anxiety with gentle assurance of her well being and he had to admit she did not appear to suffer unduly. Her only complaint was the difficulty she had in bending down to retrieve dropped objects.

He had been home with her for several days when she woke him to say her pains were beginning. He leapt from the bed calling loudly for her women who dismissed him to the anteroom.

The wind howled outside and the fire had died down so that the bitter cold penetrated the room. James summoned his page and spent the time until the logs crackled again pacing up and down. Rubbing sleep from their eyes Alway and Ogilvy came to keep him company bringing with them mulled wine and bread to toast at the fire. They told him Sir John Forrester the Chamberlain, had aroused the household who were waiting below for news of the birth of an heir or heiress.

They had not long to keep vigil for Jane, with a minimum of fuss, gave birth to a daughter. The Chamberlain went to the Palace gate to order the guard to pass on to the Watch, who huddled from the searching cold in the corners of the wynds, the good news.

James, now in a turmoil of excitement and gratitude, hurried into the bedchamber as soon as he was bidden and went quickly to the bed. Jane smiled up at him as he bent over her.

'A daughter, James. I am sorry it was not a son, but we'll hope for that next time.'

'I am as delighted with a daughter as I should be with a son. All that concerns me is that you are well.'

'I am certainly that, a little tired perhaps but that will pass. Do you not want to see our daughter?'

'Yes,' James said without taking his eyes from her face.

'Well, kiss me then,' Jane said sleepily. 'And go over to the fire.'

Reluctantly James stooped and kissed his wife and crossed to the fireplace where several of Jane's women were clustered. Marjorie Norton was swaddling the babe as it lay on her ample lap.

Shyly James looked down on the tiny, red faced creature and was conscious of the women regarding him.

'Isn't she lovely?' one of them asked.

'Yes,' James replied, somewhat to his own surprise.

'What will you call her, my lord?'

'Margaret,' James said, for this was the name he and Jane considered the most suitable for a Scottish princess.

With a backward look at the now sleeping Jane he went out of the bedchamber and had a bed brought into the ante-chamber where he spent the remaining hours of the night.

It was not long before Jane was up and about again, her vitality restored and her beauty softened. To James she was more heartrendingly dear than before. Motherhood suited her and she glowed with the fulfilment of her natural function. She scorned a wet nurse for the infant and delighted in suckling her, telling James this was her duty while he was preoccupied with the matters of the realm.

Preoccupied he most certainly was for he had soon discovered the cynics had known their subject when they prophesied the difficulty he would have in enforcing his laws. He spent hours closeted with his Chancellor, John Lyon and the secretaries who grew in number by the day. The most troublesome question to be faced was the gathering of the ransom; while money for it had been coming in fairly satisfactorily it was generally considered that the second levy would be most unpopular. Weary hour after weary hour was spent in devising means of finding the money without undue hardship to the people. In his heart James could understand only too well the reluctance to part with their hard gotten earnings to foot the English Bill.

With this in mind James called his second Parliament and restated his previous statutes bringing in stronger measures to improve further the productivity of the land. Each owner of land was required to dig or plough a certain amount each day, leaving no part uncultivated.

He spoke of his concern at the quarrelling which still seemed to be prevalent between his nobles whom, he contended should be better employed looking to the husbandry of their estates. His representatives from Inverness, given leave to speak, then spoke of much unrest in the Highlands.

Dismayed, James was about to announce a visit to the North of his kingdom when shouting at the door of the Council Hall interrupted the proceedings. John Lyon hurried to ascertain the cause of the noise while James called for order. John Lyon returned to the dais to report that word had come from Falkland of a rebellion instigated against him by Murdoch and his youngest son, together with two other Lowland knights.

Hot anger surged through James as he listened silently to what Lyon was telling him, but his mind remained clear. Every lesson he had learnt at the English court told him he would have no peace to govern while Murdoch existed as a figurehead for trouble-makers to set up against him. Any idealistic plans for a peaceful Utopia in Scotland were impossible with such opposition. He gave orders for troops to be sent at once to Falkland to take into custody Murdoch, his sons and those implicated in the plot.

He had Murdoch and the others taken to St. Andrews in safe keeping, while he dismissed Parliament and closely investigated the truth of what he had been told. It would be most unwise for him to take further disciplinary action before finding out the true facts of the case. He was always glad afterwards that he had had the foresight to do this for it transpired the Lowland knights were guiltless and that Murdoch and his son were the only instigators. The knights were released at once but Bishop Wardlaw was instructed to tell the others that they must set about preparing their defence for their trial which was to be held in Stirling in the following May.

Before this date Murdoch's only remaining son still with his liberty raised a rebellion and marched against Dumbarton hoping to stir up the entire Lowlands against James. James did not hesitate for here was proof of what his reason told him and he acted swiftly sending his best troops to quell the disturbance. Most of the offenders were caught at Inchmurrin but Murdoch's son escaped to Ireland.

'There is no help for it,' James said to John Lyon and his confessor. 'I shall have no peace until the Stewarts are dead.'

'Do nothing hasty, my son,' his confessor replied. 'God says that he who lives by the sword shall surely die by it!'

16

James kept this act of gross treachery from Jane for as long as he was able. She was happy and contented with her baby daughter and he hated to disturb her with the problem which refused to leave him night and day. He knew she would help him, giving him the comfort of her strong mind and body, but he knew also her prime concern was for the peace of his realm and woman-like she abhorred bloodshed and would never be persuaded to see the necessity for its occasional use.

He called Parliament for the first of May, in Stirling, and made it known the chief business was to be the trial of the Albany family. Twenty one nobles were summonsed to the Court at which James would sit as the head. In doing this he was only too aware he was providing a cover for himself if the accused were found guilty and a sentence of death was passed. The knowledge of his weakness did not improve his troubled state and as the time approached he grew very quiet.

Jane was not deceived for it had been

impossible to keep from her the reason for the trial and she understood the agonies of mind her husband was suffering. She suffered with him, recalling only too vividly his confession of the feeling of power he had experienced at Meaux at the sight of his fellow countrymen hanged for disobedience.

Now she attempted to divert him with her own interests and begged him to come and visit their daughter at least once a day but this was a new James, almost beyond her reach, struggling with a demon over which he had no control. With the other disclosures he had made to her he had told her of the melancholia which gripped him during periods of despondency in his youth. She saw how it could still affect him.

She wisely did not ask to accompany him to Stirling but she kissed him with great tenderness when he came to bid her farewell and was shocked at the pallor of his face and the unnatural brightness of his eyes.

'God bless you,' she said. 'Whatever happens will be best for Scotland and that is what concerns you most. I shall pray for you, my love.'

Her words stayed with him as he rode to Stirling, oblivious of the countryside waking into life and the clear blue sky above him.

Parliament was duly convened and Murdoch and his sons and their grandfather, Lennox, were brought before the nobles and charged with treason.

It soon became obvious that no one present had any idea of acquittal for the accused. The actions of the family since James had taken up the ruling of his kingdom had been constantly against him and their peers thought they were better removed.

The Albanys showed no sign of repentance and would make no protestation of loyalty when pressed to do so and James was asked to bring in a verdict of guilty with a sentence of death. All he had dreaded had come to pass and he felt numb with shock as he spoke the words condemning his cousin and his family.

The Court had sat for little less than a week and as soon as sentence was given the four accused were beheaded. James was forced to watch from the walls as a great throng gathered to behold the executions. He felt no upsurge of power as he had had at Meaux but as he looked at the men, strangely dignified in death's shadow, kneel to the block only a tremendous sorrow at the need to take life to ensure the safe-keeping of his kingdom.

Jane did not have to ask how the verdict

had gone when he returned to her. She prepared a sleeping potion and mixed it with wine. He drank it, wordlessly, and stumbled into bed where he slept for the best part of two days.

Jane sought out John Lyon and begged him to have ready a full day's work for James when he awoke. Lyon assured her this would be easy enough for Lancaster King at Arms who had been their guest during James' absence had come to discuss the tardy payment of the ransom and the pressing necessity for an exchange of hostages.

James came out of his deep sleep to find her sitting beside him. His head felt heavy and his eyes burnt in their sockets. As he stirred she bent over and cradled him against her bosom.

'It was terrible,' he said thickly. 'I hope I may never be called upon again to pass sentence of death.'

'Don't fret, James, it is all over and behind you now and you have at least more freedom to govern as you think best. They were, after all, nought but common traitors to the kingdom you love so well. None of them had anything in their hearts but self advancement and the common weal was of no meaning to them.'

James muttered some incomprehensible

words and she continued with difficulty.

'Lancaster Herald has come in your absence and doubtless there is much for your attention, but what do you say, when it is completed, to taking me to Linlithgow? I have heard much of your favourite residence but we have not yet been there together.'

'Yes,' James said as he roused himself and stretched his arms above his head. 'It would be a good idea. Heaven knows we need to have a little time together.'

Lancaster Herald soon made it plain when James granted him an audience that the English Council were far from satisfied with the payment of the ransom money and the slow rate of the exchange of hostages. James hastened to reassure him by telling of the large amounts of marks coming to the English exchequer through the Flemish merchants acting for the Scots in the matter. He said also that all the hostages at present in the south were due for repatriation except the Master of Atholl who was behind with his quota.

James experienced a momentary uneasiness as he passed on this information for he had sensed of late a subtle change in the manner of his uncle Earl of Atholl. James was not certain if this were due to the trial and subsequent beheading of Murdoch and his family or to James' determined effort to restore crown lands to himself. He dismissed his fears as being consistent with the low state in which he felt at the time and gave his attention once more to Lancaster Herald.

In hours of talk and discussion James noted for future reference the number of times the growing feud between Gloucester and Beaufort was mentioned; this he imagined could be used at some juncture for Scotland's benefit.

When at length Lancaster Herald was convinced of the assurances he received about payment of James' dues he left on the first stage of his journey back to Westminster and James went gratefully up to Jane's parlour.

He found her sitting on the floor at an open casement with a rug spread beside her. On this their daughter kicked in carefree abandon, gurgling and cooing to her mother. The domestic scene was so peaceful after the ordeals to which he had been subjected at Stirling and with the English emissary that it caught at James' heart and he dropped down beside them in an uprush of emotion. He put out a tentative finger to the baby and she clutched at it focusing her round blue eyes on him. As a small smile curved the corners of her mouth he gathered her up and held her close to his face, where, crowing happily she clutched at his hair.

Jane watched, leaning back against the wall, as her husband and daughter played together for the first time. Here, restored to her, was the true James. James the gentle husband, the passionate lover and sharer of her dreams; gone for the moment was the lawmaker and stern disciplinarian.

'When do we go to Linlithgow?' he asked.

'Whenever you are ready,' Jane replied.

'Let us make it the beginning of next week and take Margaret with us.'

On the journey to the castle Jane experienced the regard the common folk were discovering for their king. James had instituted in his last parliament measures providing a lawyer to assist the poor when they had reason to come to court. This had been the only time a monarch had considered his meaner subjects worthy of being given a hearing and his stock had risen sharply.

All along the way small groups of town or village folk came out to greet them, pulling branches from the trees to festoon the roads. Now and again James would call a halt while he talked with the people and showed them their queen.

Jane heard James promise to look into several cases and she knew he meant what he said and would deal with the matter promptly on his return to Edinburgh. He had experienced too many disappointments in his own life to risk causing hurt to others.

Jane wondered, as they came through the narrow street of the village of Linlithgow, if she could care for the castle about which James had told her so often. She knew it had been his mother's favourite and for that reason she was interested to know what had appealed to Queen Annabella. There had been a serious fire in part of the palace during the Christmas of the previous year but it had not touched the rooms they intended to use now.

She was not to be disappointed for when the cavalcade took the right hand road leading up the hill on which the fortress stood she gasped with pleasure as the wide loch came into view. She turned impulsively to James.

'It is lovely!' she cried. 'Almost as if it were a fairy castle.'

James had taken much trouble to ensure her comfort and the chambers prepared for them were luxurious compared with Holyrood. Brocade hangings covered the walls and the windows and Jane discovered when they went early to bed that even her feather filled mattress had been brought with them.

The few days they spent beside the loch were warm and sunny and they rode and walked together. James practised at the butts and tried to teach her to throw stones into the loch.

'Women can't throw,' he said laughingly as they stood on the beach while little waves broke at their feet.

'Watch!' he cried and picking up a pebble threw it far out into the sunlit water.

Obediently she watched and chose another smooth stone and gravely imitating his stance put her entire weight into projecting it. To her chagrin a melancholy little plop about twenty feet from where they stood told her she was not a very apt pupil.

'Oh, well,' she sighed. 'It all goes to prove you are the superior sex, I suppose.'

Arms round each other they made their way back to the Palace and joined Marjorie Norton who was sitting under a gnarled tree with the infant princess beside her. They stayed here, quietly absorbing the peace of their surroundings, until the nurse said she must take her charge into bed before the damp of the evening.

Later as they listened to a small group of musicians Jane asked if she might stay more often at Linlithgow.

'Gladly,' James replied. 'We'll leave the

furnishings we brought with us and I'll have some of the bales sent by Everton brought on to you here. I ordered some silks for you too, so that you may make a new gown for Christmas. I have thought perhaps we might celebrate the festival at St. Andrews this year. It will be a compliment to Bishop Wardlaw and we will hold our first Court at the same time. I'll do my best to show my nobles we are not far behind the English when it comes to doing things with style.'

'It sounds wonderful, James, but can we really afford to spend lavishly yet awhile?'

'Yes, yes, of course,' James said somewhat tetchily. 'If the English have to wait for their money it will not hurt them, they only want it to continue their never ending war in France. After all they kept me eighteen years. A little of their own treatment will not go amiss.'

Jane changed the subject by referring to the silks he had ordered and asking for his opinion on a style for a gown. He had a surprisingly good eye for what became her and this was the first new dress she had had since her marriage. He was easily diverted.

Before he left Edinburgh he had arranged a meeting at Berwick to discuss with Lancaster King of Arms the two border towns of Roxburgh and Berwick. These towns were a thorn in the flesh of each country for the

Scots had always enjoyed free access to pasture around them but marauders from both sides continually broke the truce-making terms of the Durham Treaty.

He left Jane at Linlithgow for she said she would prefer to remain in her new found home while he was absent and he was glad when the discussions became protracted and wearisome that she was happily settled there.

Throughout the Autumn which was marked by unseasonable thunder and rainstorms James was heavily occupied with affairs of state. His household, constituting the chief officers of the government, worked with enthusiasm. John Lyon remained as his personal adviser but much of his daily work had been taken over by a bevy of clerks who were directly responsible to him. It was a compliment to James' acquired skill that executive affairs ran smoothly. This was a comfort at least, for all else seemed fraught with difficulties.

He was glad when Christmastide came and Jane arrived in Edinburgh to travel with him to Perth. He had visited her in Linlithgow as much as possible but he grudged every hour when they were separated, more so when she had discovered she was pregnant again and not as well as she had been before.

However, he was relieved to find her

radiant and looking forward to the holding of their first Court.

Awaiting them at St. Andrews were the new Earl of Douglas with the Earls of Mar, Angus and Moray. Most of the other nobles resident in Scotland had also accepted the King's invitation and they mingled with merchants from Flanders and scholars of the University.

The twelve days of Christmas were celebrated as James had promised with overflowing hospitality and good cheer. All present joined in the merrymaking and the festivities were gay and friendly. The scholars gave added pleasure to James for he sat talking with them long into the night, his enquiring mind stimulated with their controversies and logic.

Jane wore her new gown and accepted the compliments she received, wisely saying nothing to James about the cost of the festivities for he was so obviously enjoying himself. He sang when it became his turn to do so and delighted his listeners with the melodious quality of his voice. Jane heard him laugh more often than since the early days of their first meeting. She prayed fervently for his wellbeing and did not grudge him one moment of his pleasure. She had seen too much of his hard work on Scotland's behalf and the depth of his despair when his conscience went against his judgement to spoil his fun with doubts about the paying of the accounts.

He returned to Edinburgh with renewed vitality and plunged headlong into the preparations for the next meeting of Parliament. He had received during the last months evidence of church lands being surreptitiously stolen by greedy nobles and a certain amount of money being filtered to the Papal Court. He drew up further strong measures to protect Holy Kirk at the same time keeping the power of the Church as much Scottish as he was able. He realised only too readily that any recognising of Papal authority weakened his own.

When, before Parliament met, a second daughter was born to them he told Jane he was delighted as if it had been a son, called her Isabella and sent word to the Kirk that from now on he would like a special prayer said for the Royal Family such as was customary in the English churches.

'It won't hurt them to remember their benefactors,' he told Jane.

Later in the year, when time permitted him a little respite from the everpresent and growing problem of the raising of the ransom, he was able to turn his attention to the Highlands where lawlessness abounded and homesteads fell into ruin. He travelled as far north as Aberdeen, seeing for himself the state of this wild part of his domain. To set a good example he ordered the rebuilding and setting in order of his stronghold at Inverness.

The ransom became an increasing burden and throughout the year Lancaster King at Arms and James' own clerk Thomas Roulle were back and forth between London and Edinburgh. The money was increasingly difficult to gather and James was forced to throw his net wide in an effort to bring in more trade from such countries as Scandinavia and the Lowlands.

These measures met with some success but he would still be unable to complete payment as he should do by the end of 1429.

In the February of 1427 he heard with concern that the English were strengthening their garrisons at the controversial Berwick and Roxburgh. James redoubled his efforts to find hostages with sufficient wealth to replace those now long overdue to return to Scotland.

In the Spring Garter King of Arms came north to express in no uncertain terms his Council's deep displeasure at the tardy payments and James' inability to keep his side of the treaty. He was particularly displeased with the very slow replacements of those unfortunate hostages who had died of the plague when it had swept through London during the past winter.

For the first time James lost his temper and retorted that if the young men had been removed to the country they would not have succumbed to the loathsome illness which carried them off. Garter King at Arms, lost for an answer for a brief moment, recovered his wits sufficiently to protest neither Bedford or Gloucester, or any of the rest of the Council for that matter, had seen fit to go out of London and that the hostages had not been subjected to close imprisonment and had been free to move about and look to their own health.

James did not pursue the argument and promised to try and find substitutes of sufficient rank and wealth. This was now practically impossible and he was reduced to seconding two young men in the place of one. He knew this would be unpopular and he was not slow to realise he was being regarded by the families of the chosen youths with increasing resentment. Hostility was not open but fathers avoided his eyes and mothers came less and less to court. His sympathy was with them but he had pledged his word to find the ransom and he had to raise it somehow.

He had gathered most of the next instalment together when he received word of a massing of Highland barons, including the young Lord of the Isles and his mother, the Countess of Ross. He was forced to spend the hard gotten money in raising an army with which he hurried north to confront the ringleaders and their followers.

His journey to Inverness was plagued with the realisation he would be facing, in the near future, a further test of his ability to govern with a strict hand.

He summonsed the culprits into the newly roofed hall of the castle and sat regarding them for a long minute. Most of the Highland nobles were of large stature, clad in a strange assortment of clothing. They gave him back stare for stare undaunted by his kingship.

The Lord of the Isles, son of the man whose emissary had visited James so long ago in Nottingham Castle to protest his loyalty, was not cast of the same metal as his father. He was a weak, headstrong young man possessing a doting mother who with pride and ambition, turned a blind eye to her son's loose morals and shortcomings. When he had been visited by Huntly and other barons who proposed to overthrow James he had listened eagerly to their plans without realising the full implication of what he undertook.

As he stood with the others James, who had husbanded his anger until it was in full spate, felt a stirring of pity for the handsome young renegade. He had already made up his mind to put to death the three ringleaders and he now told them his intentions in a voice hard and unwavering. Softening a little he told the Lord of the Isles he was bound over in good behaviour as long as he returned to his lands, then abruptly turned on his heel and left the assembly.

While the sentences were carried out he shut himself in a small chamber on the opposite side of the castle and had the accounts of the ransom brought to him. He searched through them with all the concentration he was able to summon hoping to find any sums overlooked before. He was disappointed.

Leaving strict instructions on the fortifying of Inverness he returned to Edinburgh.

Jane was in residence with their daughters Margaret and Isabella and the two other girl babies born to them in the past two years. He fell into her arms more despondent than at any time since he regained his freedom.

'I am beginning to think it is hopeless,' he told her. 'The nobility may enjoy my hospitality but they resent me and my new fangled policies.'

'They will come to appreciate your work when they see how Scotland benefits,' Jane comforted him.

'No,' James said sadly. 'They have been allowed to do as they pleased for so long they find it impossible to discipline themselves, let alone their followers. As I see it the only salvation for the country is to institute a parliament on lines akin to the English where the people are represented and can hear for themselves what I purpose.'

'That would be difficult to bring about James,' Jane said slowly as she weighed up the possibility. 'But surely you are not without loyal supporters? The household are behind you and the new knights you created at the Coronation are for ever expressing their devotion.'

'You are forgetting Alexander Stewart,' James said bitterly. 'Although apart from that faithless creature, these are the only loyal men I have, I think. This insurrection in the north is only typical of what I fear is common throughout the country. I regret I find it increasingly difficult to trust anybody. God alone knows who is plotting my downfall at this very moment; it is my intention to put a Statute through the next parliament giving you the full powers of Regency should I be deposed.'

'Do not speak like that!' she cried in sudden anguish, amazed by his thoughts. 'You have no personal enemies. Those who are against you would be against any man who set up a strong authority.'

'I would not be too sure,' James said grimly. 'Stewart's still alive, here or in Ireland and the relatives of those I have just beheaded in Inverness have no love for me while Sir Robert Graham and my uncle Atholl with his son still languishing in the Tower would be happy to see me gone.'

Jane did not reply but led him to the nursery where she hoped the sight of his daughters, growing into sturdy children, would heal his hurt.

Nothing, however, seemed to relieve his despair and she was consumed with anxiety for him when help came from a most unexpected quarter.

Ambassadors arrived from France and begged James to give them an audience. He granted it out of sheer curiosity but had uneasy moments when he recalled Garter King of Arms might appear at any time to renew the omnipresent discussions of the ransom and hostages.

Three Frenchmen, Regnault de Chartres,

Conte d'Evreux and Alain Chartier elegantly clad but wrapped well against the notorious Scottish mists presented themselves and bowed low over his hand.

James offered them wine and almond sweetmeats, hastily ordered from the kitchens. He wondered for some time the purpose of their visit as they spoke of general matters and complimented him on the tasteful decoration of his apartments. At length Regnault leant forward and spoke earnestly to James.

'Our master has sent us here to enquire if you would be willing to agree to a marriage between your elder daughter and the Dauphin, Louis.'

James sat back and regarded him quietly. The proposal was completely unexpected and took him for a moment off his guard. He had rehearsed careful speeches about recognising the pulling power of the Auld Alliance while gently rebuffing the requests he had expected for troops to fight in France. This he had not anticipated.

'This would need careful thought, monseigneur,' he said at last. His heart raced at the prospect of severing his pact with England and renewing the forbidden alliance with France. Let England sing for the rest of the ransom! It was a most tempting and alluring thought.

'What terms would you suggest?' he asked cautiously.

'The king of France would settle a handsome sum in the event of the consummation of the marriage whether or not your daughter ever became Queen.'

Without showing any emotion James said. 'How much?'

'Sixty thousand pounds,' the ambassador replied. With difficulty James restrained himself from shouting aloud although this enormous sum could only mean the French King was in extreme difficulties and required of James something he might not be prepared to encompass.

'What would be my side of the bargain?' he asked, wincing at his callous dismissal of his daughter's future as a matter of barter.

'The French King would not expect a great settlement but would be happy to have your moral support and a small force, of say, six thousand men,' Regnault said sauvely.

'I see,' James answered. His supposition was correct and the French, suffering heavy defeats, were casting about to find help from any quarter. The Auld Alliance seemed to offer more solid reason for support than any other.

'Perhaps we may discuss this further when

I have had time to consult my advisers,' James told the three men. 'Please remain here as my guests while I call a meeting of my Parliament.'

The Scottish Council did not take very long to make up their minds. Their mutual inclination towards France was ready to welcome overtures of a friendly nature. They chose to ignore any implications of what English reaction would be to this further breach of the Treaty of Durham. James told himself that he had only signed a truce for seven years and this would surely be up by the time his daughter would have to leave for France.

He reported his country's acceptance of the offer of the French marriage and signed a formal document marking the betrothal of the two infants. He closed his mind to the time, far distant he prayed, when he would be called upon to furnish the necessary troops.

'I wonder how the English Council will receive this piece of news when it is reported to them by their spies,' he asked Jane with a rueful smile. 'It should take their minds off the failure of my goverment to send the instalments of my wretched ransom. That's worth a great deal, at least.'

'I do hope you are doing the right thing for Margaret,' Jane said, her English blood rising at the worsening of relations between their two countries. 'France is in an unhappy state and she is such a baby to leave us yet. When did you say you had agreed to let her go?'

'Not yet,' said James a little hastily. 'Next year was mentioned, but don't start grieving yourself for it is a long time until then and many things might happen.'

Events proved him right. Beaufort announced he was coming north to enquire personally into the controversies which seemed to be splitting the two nations and France found a new saviour in a peasant girl who heard voices leading her to guide the French nation to restore sovereignty over its own soil.

The marriage of the Scottish heiress to the French heir suddenly became less urgent.

17

James went to meet the great English statesman at Coldingham. When the talks had first been mooted it had been suggested that Durham should be the place of rendezvous but James was wary of setting foot again in England and had insisted upon his own country.

Beaufort arrived with great pomp, accompanied by a huge escort. James was pleased to see the banner of Northumberland among those fluttering in the sharp breeze. Here at least was a man whose continuing friendship was a source of satisfaction. James only hoped the harrassed English Council did not regard Henry with suspicion for this reason. Henry's own devotion to the Crown was beyond doubt but his family's record was sufficient to keep his life long fellowship with James under the surveillance of the Council.

There seemed no sign of this when, the preliminary formalities completed, James and Henry sat together and talked until the early hours of the morning. Henry's only complaint was with Beaufort who had kept him waiting at Berwick for sixteen days.

'I had a hundred horses to stable and as many men kicking their heels and getting up to all the mischief in Christendom. I'll wager there isn't a virgin left in the town. The old man has this crazed idea of going to Bohemia to put down the Hussites for the Pope and nothing else matters. Ever since he received his Cardinal's hat he has been obsessed with the Crusade of the Roman Church.'

'I would not regard that with much favour here!' James said. 'What do Bedford and Gloucester think of him drawing off troops to fight a senseless war when they are so hard pressed in France?'

'Not much, as you can well imagine,' Henry said. 'The feeling between Beaufort and Gloucester has not improved. They like each other even less than before. All the same I still don't believe Beaufort will ever take his troops to Bohemia; it is all a wild dream to satisfy his vows to the Pope. Anyway, let us not talk of the wearying subject, let us talk about ourselves! Tell me about yourself. We hear so many stories. Are you still happy now you have been home so long?'

'If you mean personal happiness,' James answered slowly, 'there is no question.'

He spoke with constraint for he had never before discussed his marital state.

'Jane is a perfect wife; loving, kind, forgiving — '

'Forgiving?' Henry said with a quick upward glance.

'Not in the way you mean,'James said hastily. 'It is my temper. It gets worse as I get older.'

'And fatter!' Henry laughed. 'You certainly don't look starved, James.'

'No,' James agreed ruefully. 'It's all this sitting at conferences and councils. There isn't sufficient time for sports and riding even if I felt free to indulge in them.'

'Free?' Henry echoed.

'Well,' James said, 'since I forbade my subjects to play football and instituted a weekly visit to the butts it doesn't seem fair for their sovereign lord to waste his time. Thank Heavens you only inherited an earldom, Henry, the way I am plagued sometimes anybody would be welcome to take over the government of Scotland.'

Henry laughed again and sat back regarding James. After a few moments companionable silence he leant forward and threw a log on to the fire.

'You've certainly put the tinder to the kindling with your daughter's betrothal. You would have been quite flattered with the stir it caused when the news filtered through.

Beaufort could not rest until he had confronted you with it. I am not sure if it is England's cause he is concerned with or if he has his eye on your six thousand troops. No wonder they have no time for football if you can amass an army as large as that to send to France.'

'I did not know anyone had heard of that,' James said somewhat shamefaced.

'No one talks of anything else. Unless — ' he stopped.

'Unless what?' James prompted him.

'Unless it is about the Queen.'

'What's that?' James asked quickly.

He had hardly thought of Catherine in the hustle of the years since he and Jane had taken their leave of her but Henry's words recalled her poignant face and the unhappiness she strove so hard to disguise.

Henry glanced over his shoulder into the dim corners of the chambers.

'Well,' he said slowly. 'It appears Catherine has taken a lover.'

'Hardly surprising,' James said. 'Who is the man?'

'Owen Tudor,' Henry replied.

'That is an odd name! Tudor,' James said.

'Yes, he is a Welshman; claims descent from Pendragon. He came to Court in Henry V's time as a squire and lately was made Master of the Queen's Wardrobe. He seems to have succeeded in the task pretty well.'

'Poor Catherine,' James said quietly. He recalled the time in Windsor when Orleans had told him of the law which forbade dowager Queens of England to remarry.

'It is poor Catherine,' Henry agreed. 'She was kept so much in the background and was even more lonely when Gloucester took her son away from her.'

'That was inhuman,' James cried.

'The Council thought it was time he was given the touch of a man's authority. They were afraid he would become too soft if he remained with Catherine and her women.'

'What is the child like?' James asked.

'I have only seen him once or twice and at his Coronation, which incidentally, was performed by Beaufort,' Henry said. 'He seems a quiet child. Doesn't take after his father.'

'A pity,' James said.

'Tell me about your family, James,' Henry said in an effort to dispell the misery which seemed to have crept into the room.

'Four daughters,' James said smiling. 'No sons yet but Jane is expecting another child in the Autumn and we are hoping that perhaps this will be the time. She is not with me because we thought it unwise for her to travel. Also it might be better for her not to hear too much of what transpires between her uncle and me!'

There was plenty of talk in the ensuing days. Every aspect of the Treaty of Durham was brought up and discussed at length.

Beaufort put very strongly the English resentment at James' failure to fulfil his obligations. James was left in no doubt about his shortcomings.

Summoning all his powers he put his case as well as he was able, expressing his regrets and explaining his difficulties. Rather to his surprise Beaufort listened with sympathy.

James began to realise what made the old man the great statesman he was. Not only was he possessed of considerable talents of organisation and patriotism but he had deep human kindness. James did not underestimate the iron will and the ruthlessness which could be called upon at any given moment but he was genuinely amazed at the scholarly slant he brought to bear on the problems discussed. It was obvious his interest and teaching in Oxford had been genuine enough.

This became more apparent when Wardlaw arrived from St. Andrews and the two clerics spent hours cloistered together talking about the multi-faceted subject of the Church. James was not present on these occasions but he gathered from Lyon that the two strong willed old men were not always agreed upon what influence Rome should have upon their respective Churches but that they enjoyed to the full the power of each other's thoughts.

These interesting hours did not detract from the real business in hand and when Beaufort returned to England he had wrung from James his assurance of keeping the peace at Berwick and Roxburgh and his promise to replace with speed the hostages still in London.

James went home and let the French negotiations slide for the moment. He would not have admitted to anybody that the Cardinal had intimidated him but he knew Beaufort had revived in him, however temporarily, the old affection he had always felt, despite himself, for England. If he had been called upon to analyse his true feelings he would have admitted, however grudgingly, he was against falling out completely with his wife's kinsman and the country he represented.

He returned to Jane and the next month travelled with her to the castle of Michael Ramsay who had lately been appointed guardian of his daughters and who had the care of them when their parents made their progresses through the countryside. They were happy to be a family again and James saw how Jane had lost her anxiety for Margaret now the threat of her leaving them for France had been removed for the immediate present. He did not hesitate when she begged of him to allow Ramsay to accompany them to Linlithgow with the children for the summer months and they set off in high spirits.

Settled in her favourite palace Jane spent as much time as she was able with the little girls and on the first Sunday gave an especially large donation to the church of twenty shillings as a token of her earnest prayer for the child she was carrying to be a son. It had not worried her unduly when the first two had been daughters but she had been a little disappointed when the third, who had been named Eleanor, was not an heir and had experienced real dismay when the fourth had been a girl also. It was not that James reproved her in any way but she felt she failed him by not fulfilling this vital need.

She hated also to add in any way to the burden he bore and sometimes felt sapped of strength as she tried to bolster him against the disillusionment that daily crept into his public life.

She knew he was losing hope of ever

providing Scotland with the stable government and economy he had envisaged for her. He had come to regard his people as children to whom he had given every care and attention but who resented his authority and took every opportunity to flout him and squabble among themselves.

To counteract this frustration Jane knew his private life was one of complete happiness. Instead of his affection for Jane waning as his absorption in his country's affairs became deeper it deepened also, compassing every facet of a man and woman's love; passion, understanding, companionship and common interest.

Her strong personality gloried in his ability and ideals while her tender heart grieved for his high hopes when she saw them wilt for lack of support. She coped with his bouts of temper with a calm which surprised herself. She, had, once or twice, shouted back at him like a fishwife, but soon realised this did them both harm. His wrath was an outlet and it was better to allow him free vent to it.

One of the tasks she had undertaken for James was guardianship of the young Lord of the Isles who had come to court after serving a short period of his banishment. James hoped his youthful exuberance would be tempered by a stay with more sophisticated people and Jane would influence him for the good. This had undoubtedly been the case but despite the royal support the courtiers made him a butt of their wit and never lost an opportunity of referring to his attire and country habits.

Jane found this cruel and exasperating, knowing as she did how new found was the polish of most of those who made up James' court. In an endeavour to offset his unhappiness she taught him to play the lute and when he sought her parlour, as he did more and more frequently, she was gentle and kind and encouraged him to talk to her and amuse the little girls when they were present.

'He is only a child himself,' Jane told James.

'That's what I believe and it probably explains why he cannot apply himself to anything for any period of time. Even the smallest task seems beyond his powers.'

'He is very unhappy,' Jane said.

'Unhappy!' James exploded. 'I was very unhappy for the best part of my youth and young manhood but I did not allow that to interfere with my studies. I forced myself to see imprisonment as a means to an end.'

Jane told him quietly the Lord of the Isles was not comparable with him in any way and James was restored to good humour.

She was not surprised however when the young man was reported missing from the palace and she could well understand when, later in the year, James flew into a veritable tempest of fury at the news of the burning of Inverness under a force headed by the Lord of the Isles.

James lost no time in amassing a force and hastening north, where, after a pitched battle he succeeded in once more capturing the wayward young Lord. He brought him back to Holyrood and threw him into a dungeon. Neither James or Jane mentioned the subject but one of her pages brought word to her that the Lord of the Isles begged her to come to him. She took herself down to the damp, sour smelling prison and had the guard admit her to the cell. The young man, pale and thin, threw himself at her feet and poured out a flood of self incrimination laced with promises of future good behaviour. With a twinge of disloyalty to James she felt drawn to forgive the foolish boy and longing as she did to give life to a manchild felt a superstitious horror of depriving anyone of that precious gift at this moment.

Without promising him anything she told him to spend his time in prayer and meditation and to go to his trial when summoned in a spirit of true humility.

For days she could not rid herself of the sight of his anguished face and spent much of her time on her knees asking for guidance.

On a still, peaceful summer morning James called the court into the chapel at Holyrood and sent Walter Ogilvy, who had lately been made Controller of the Household, to order the guard to bring up their prisoner.

The Lord of the Isles presented a pathetic enough picture when he appeared clad only in his undergarments, carrying a sword with the handle extended towards James. This he obviously intended his sovereign to understand as his acceptance of punishment worthy of his crime.

James, who had been steeling himself to pass sentence of immediate beheadal, felt his determination falter. He looked down at the kneeling youth who had now pointed the sword to his heart and made a half-hearted attempt to grasp the hilt.

As he did he was conscious of a movement at his elbow and saw out of the corner of his eye his wife lifting a hand to her throat.

'My Lord!' she cried softly.

The air in the chapel matched the quiet of the day outside as all present waited for James to act.

In a flash of insight he saw the repercussions if he ordered the execution to proceed.

Yet another list of names would be added to the growing number of his enemies. Looking at Jane, almost in desperation, he saw her imperceptibly shake her head.

He grasped the sword and handed it to Alway.

'We shall spare your life yet again, my Lord,' he said coldly to the youth. 'But if I have the slightest cause in the future to doubt your loyalty you will be beheaded without trial. Go to your Isles and learn to govern them in peace.'

The young man rose from his knees, stammering his thanks and stumbled from the chapel.

James made irritable signs to his confessor to begin the Mass.

As they knelt to pray Jane took his hand and pressed it for a moment.

The well known phrases droned over their heads as James cursed himself for a sentimental fool but he recognised only too well he had few enough friends to risk making any more enemies. The consequences of Beaufort's visit were being felt now with the removal to the Tower of the Master of Atholl and three other important prisoners. This meant their lives were literally in his hands for if he committed any indiscretion of which the English did not approve they would not hesitate to behead their prisoners. James knew himself caught in a maze having no exits. His uncle Atholl was increasingly absent from the Council with his excuses becoming weaker with each occasion.

Word had also been brought to James of support being sent to Ireland for Albany's surviving son. This not only from the English but also from some disloyal Scots.

The English Navy out in strength in the English Channel to intercept any attempt to take the Princess Margaret to her marriage with the Dauphin added to the cares of a harrassing summer.

James admitting himself checked, however temporarily, wrote with secret relish to the French King, Charles, informing him of his decision to keep his daughter for a time at his side until he and her mother were assured she had reached sufficient maturity to fulfil obligations.

He was relieved he had resolved this before Beaufort was persuaded, as he waited at Rochester to embark for Bohemia, to take his enormous army to the relief of Bedford who was reeling under the new found strength of the French Army. Henry Percy's prophesy had come true.

'The English have enough on their hands and the French also to keep them from being too interested in our affairs at the moment. Let us hope it may continue thus for a very long time,' James told Jane.

However, negotiations on both hostages and the vexatious question of the border towns went on throughout the summer and the English were not too encumbered to have forgotten that most of the huge debt of James' ransom was still unpaid and their representatives pressed for payment while James pleaded again and again for grace. He despaired in long sleepless hours of the night of ever finding the sum he still owed.

He was reprieved from complete dejection when the English Council surprisingly suggested the truce should be extended for a further ten years and invited James to consider the marriage of one of his daughters to the boy King, who was taken to France for his crowning in accordance with the treaty signed between his father and grandfather. James realised this was an attempt by English to show their authority when it obviously being undermined by the success the French who were going from strength to strength beneath the banner of the Orleans who led them forward in the direction of her heavenly voices.

With this knowledge came the understanding of why the English had chosen to press for a truce and marriage into the Scottish house. Trouble on their northern boundaries would be very unwelcome. James sent his Herald with haste to the Council with instructions to settle a limited truce and give his assurance of considering the subject of marriage.

This slightly improved situation was in being when Jane woke him in the night of October 15th to say her pains were starting.

He sprang from the bed, hastily dragging on a robe and shouting for her women sleeping in the next room.

'The midwife,' he called. 'Someone find the midwife.'

He came back to the bed and took Jane's hand; it was hot and limp. He bent over her and kissed her forehead.

'Don't go too far away,' she pleaded as her women came in.

'No, I will not,' he promised. 'I'll have my papers brought up to the anteroom.'

Alway appeared at the door.

'Send a page to build up the fires and have someone prepare us some mulled ale.'

He went into the anteroom and two pages came in rubbing their eyes. The laces of their doublets and shoes were untied and their hair tousled.

'More light please and one of you wait on

the women to see they have all they want.'

Alway brought his rolls and he pulled up a stool to the table and spread them around him. The first one he undid concerned the revenue of the Royal Mint, usually an engrossing subject but now he found the figures swimming before his eyes in the flickering light of the tapers. After a few minutes he pushed the scrolls away and walked to the fire where he kicked the logs into a blaze.

When the beer arrived he asked Ogilvy and Alway to sit with him. They sat talking quietly until the dawn broke, sending a cold, cheerless light into the room.

James rose abruptly and went into his wife's room.

Jane lay on the great bed, pale and waxen. She gave him a shadow of a smile and suddenly James was afraid as he had never been before in his life. He felt almost unable to breathe. Suppose Jane died! He went cold with fear, and turning hastily to the midwife he beckoned her from the throng of women around the bed.

'Why is the labour so prolonged?' he asked.

'Och, your Grace, it's not that long. Just because the Queen has always produced her babies with such ease before does not mean it will always be like that. There may be — '

'May be what?' James said controlling himself.

'Nothing, my lord, perhaps something had made her tired and she is not able to put all her usual strength into helping herself. Don't fash yourself, your Grace, we can manage, whatever it is.'

She glanced towards the bed as Jane cried out and groped for the hand of one of her women.

'Is the physician here?' James asked.

'Yes, he is preparing a physic for my lady. Ye go back to your papers and don't fret. We are used to childbirth and ye are not.'

James went, reluctantly, back to the anteroom but made no attempt to work. He took up instead a manuscript of some of his poems, untouched for years.

'Are you god Cupid's own princess?
Come to loose me out of band,
Or are you Nature's own goddess,
That has furnished with your hand
The beauty of this garden fair?
What shall I think? What reverence
Shall I minister to your excellence?'

He dropped the paper unable to read more for the tears in his eyes. He could remember as if it were yesterday the small, secret garden and the first sight he had ever had of Jane as she had sat, so trusting and innocent, enjoying the warmth of the sun. Don't let her die, he prayed. I don't deserve her, but spare her to me.

Food was brought to him but he sent it away untouched. He completed the business of the day as Lyon brought in urgent matters for his attention and went for a brief spell to the chapel. He hurried back to the anteroom hoping the child had been born in his absence but Alway shook his head when he asked for news.

It was not until dusk was falling one of Jane's ladies came to summon him to the bedchamber. He felt, for the first time in his life, old and drained of energy.

He saw nothing as he came into the room but Jane sitting propped against pillows, pale but awake. He stumbled towards her and oblivious of the watching women gathered her in his arms. She felt his hot tears on her shoulder but said nothing, weakly caressing his arm.

At last he looked up into her face.

'Do you not want to see your sons?' she asked.

For a moment he did not understand, then slowly released his hold and sat back on his heels.

'Sons?' he echoed.

'Yes,' she said, her voice a whisper. 'No one knew it was to be twins and that is why I suffered a little extra; but it is over now and, think of it James, we have two sons!'

'My love!' he said.

Marjorie Norton came over to them with the newly washed infants wrapped in fleecy shawls. They were very small with wrinkled red faces and masses of dark hair.

'They are not like you, or the others,' James said lamely.

'But they will be just like you,' Jane said and lay back on the pillows.

James was instantly on his feet.

'I have tired you,' he said. 'Rest now and we'll talk tomorrow. Good night, Jane.'

He looked back from the doorway and saw she was already half asleep.

He called for his confessor and went back to the chapel where he gave sincere thanks for his wife's deliverance and for the birth of not one but two sons.

Jane's condition improved rapidly within the next few days and she was strong enough to attend the infants' christening, a most lavish and hospitable occasion. The importance of the birth of an heir was marked by the effort the court made to appear in their finery and to forget, for the moment at least, their quarrels and grievances.

The royal daughters were delighted with their new brothers and spent much time hanging over their cradles with hands firmly clasped behind their backs as they had been taught by Marjorie Norton. They had some difficulty pronouncing the name Alexander which James had chosen for the elder twin but found the more homely James quite simple. It was easy to distinguish between the babies as James was larger than his brother and had a small birthmark on his cheek.

James thrived at his mother's breast but it soon became obvious all was not well with the little Alexander. He could not digest properly the smallest quantity of milk and did not cry with the same lusty abandon as his brother. Jane could not disguise her anxiety and did not need the physician to tell her the baby would not survive. She had been very subdued since the birth of her sons and now sat by their cradles for most of the day keeping that of Alexander by her through the night. James protested to Marjorie Norton that she was taxing her strength but the old nurse told him to bear with her for she did not think it possible the baby could live.

She was unhappily proved right in the third week when Alexander died. James, watching over his wife thought she lost for the first time since their marriage a little of the golden patina which had always clung to her. It was as if she realised death was something even the most disciplined self control could not overcome.

When the baby James gave every appearance of continuing to make progress his father told Jane, as gently as he was able, he thought it time for him to go with his sisters to Doune Castle into the care of Michael Ramsay.

She did not query his wisdom in coming to this difficult decision but agreed to start looking immediately for a wet nurse.

It did not take long for a suitable woman to be found and brought for Jane to interview. Janet de Liddale was a burgher's wife from the Wynds who had lost her own child on the previous day. Jane liked her open countenance and obvious competence and while she was modest and respectful she was not cringing. Jane sent for her son and when she saw the look on the woman's face as she cradled him in her arms Jane knew she could care for him as her own.

Within a few days the children and their nurses left for Doune with a household of servants and governesses under the care of Michael Ramsay. Provisions and linen had been sent ahead of them and the tenor of their life would be much as it was whether she was with them or not but Jane saw them go with a heavy heart although she knew beyond question they were safer at Doune.

When they had gone she redoubled her efforts to help James in his duties of government. She went with him whenever he asked to Perth or St. Andrews and Inverness when once more rebellion was threatened there.

A peace with England was signed finally in 1431 and James scratched in his coffers to send a part of the still unpaid ransom. He had done his best to keep the terms of the truce and the English had succeeded in their efforts to subdue the border towns.

Despite their mutual endeavours however, raiding did take place into the Scottish lowlands and Scottish ships were attacked by pirates. James did not hesitate to send protest to London; it was so rarely he was given the opportunity.

Having placated the rebels in Inverness other small rebellions broke out from time to time throughout Scotland. The grievances were mostly on trumped up issues and James, in desperation, put into motion his threat of seizing the lands of the culprits.

'We shall see if this will teach them who is master,' he told Jane.

'They may call you master but they will not love you for it,' she said.

'I have long since given up expecting love or gratitude,' James answered. 'My popularity with my barons has never been lower. Like a strict tutor they resent me. The only people who think well of me are those whose plight I have, perhaps, improved a little. The nobles refuse to recognise the sense of my measures and see everything either through their own greedy eyes or the wastage of their sons in England.'

'Have you not completed the final arrangements for an exchange of hostages?'

'Yes,' James agreed. 'All but one of them have been released and are back in Scotland or on their way.'

'Well, that should improve your relationship with their parents, shouldn't it?'

'It should, but whether it will or not remains to be seen.'

When the exchange was completed James learnt with a thrill of dismay that the remaining prisoner in the Tower was the Master of Atholl. He wondered if the fates conspired to antagonise the old Earl further or if the English had some malicious reason for their tenacity in retaining this important hostage.

Without telling Jane he ensured in his next

Parliament that she was to be made Regent in the event of his meeting an untimely death.

A few days later James' own Herald returned from England with the news that the Earl of March had withdrawn his allegiance to James and had gone back to swear fealty to King Henry. Almost at the same moment border spies brought in the information of intensive fortifications being constructed at Roxburgh.

Without hesitation James looked to his own army and placed orders for siege weapons and some of the newfangled cannon. He did not intend to be hampered with an outdated force should the need arise.

Envoys arrived from France asking on their King's behalf when they could expect the arrival of the princess Margaret for her marriage to the Dauphin.

'I have heard much,' the French King wrote, 'of your treaties with the English and even talk of a betrothal of one of your daughters with the King of England. I trust you are not forgetting the old alliance which exists between us.'

James sent the messengers back with haste to assure Charles of his intention to fulfil his obligations and denied any intention of agreeing to a marriage of his daughter with Henry of England.

He was becoming increasingly dismayed at the necessity for duplicity which had become an integral part of his life.

If it were not for the love between Jane and himself he would have thought of the days of his captivity with something approaching nostalgia.

18

Despite this sense of failure James did not give up his schemes for the improvement of his country and its economy. Scotland had never been as prosperous before and the volume of its trade had increased even beyond his highest hopes. It infuriated him to realise that his barons could not be made to understand that if they would contribute to the national effort Scotland could become one of the leading powers of Europe.

His family continued to be his one true source of happiness and gratification and grew in intelligence and stature. They were handsome children with pleasing personalities, the girls inheriting their mother's Plantagenet colouring while James was dark.

James and Jane spent as much time at Doune as they were able to spare from their duties; riding and walking with their children.

Margaret had a special place in their affection for they could not look at her clear blue eyes and rosy cheeks without remembering that she would have to leave them and start a new life at the French Court. She was now ten years of age and the day of her departure could not be much longer delayed. James dreaded the thought of her in the strange surroundings of the Dauphin's household and had several times considered breaking off the betrothal. In less emotional moments he had realised this was impossible if he were to maintain the delicate balance of relationship between Scotland, France and England.

When he heard a French delegation wished to present themselves at his court he extended his welcome with a sinking feeling at the pit of his stomach.

He was much relieved when great storms arose and delayed the envoys' arrival for six weeks. But they could not be put off for ever and came at length with a great show of rich clothing and a huge train of followers. James received them in Edinburgh and sent Jane with Margaret to Perth. Here they could await what transpired at the meeting.

After greeting James and exchanging gifts the envoys apologised for the smallness of their escort with deprecating glances at the hoardes of men accompanying them. These, they said, were all who could be spared from the war.

They hastened to assure James that Charles was no longer anxious for the six thousand troops he had first asked from James but he would be pleased if James could see his way to renewing the hostilities on the English borders once the marriage had been solemnised.

James listened, saying very little and told the envoy he wished to consult his wife before coming to final agreement.

He left Perth and invited the French ambassadors to follow him.

He broke the news to Margaret that the time had come for her to go to France and although her eyes filled with tears she made no protest. Talking to Jane he looked in his daughter's direction and saw her lift her knuckled fist to her mouth. His heart almost failed him. She heard him stumble in his conversation and turning towards him took his hand and smiled up at him.

The next morning he agreed to send his pursuivant to France with his signature on the marriage treaty and gave his word to provision the ships Charles would send to bring his future daughter-in law to France.

It was not long before the English made strong protest at this resumption of French-Scottish friendship and sent representatives to Edinburgh.

Glad of any excuse to delay the marriage James wrote once more to Charles and told him he would send Margaret in the Autumn.

When this came it brought plague with it and a winter of extreme cold.

'It would never do my Lord,' James wrote, 'to expose our daughter to the dangers of the sea at this time. The Queen and I consider the Spring is more suitable. When, of course,' he added hastily, 'the period of Lent is over.'

So March became the appointed month.

During this time Jane had been busy with the preparation of fine garments and shifts for her daughter's trousseau. Every day she visited the sewing room where four or five seamstresses sat and cut and stitched lengths of brocade and silk into surcoats and houpelandes. The Scots women had found the fabrics difficult to handle at first but had soon learnt from the ladies-in-waiting who offered to teach them. Jane herself made some of the shifts while Margaret sat beside her slowly pushing a needle through the linen. Sometimes Jane saw her drop the work and gaze into the shadows at the end of the room as if she were watching an invisible play. Occasionally they spoke of life in the French court and what it would entail being married to the heir of the King of France.

'Father was on his way to the French when he was captured, wasn't he, Mother?' Margaret asked one day as they sat together.

'Yes,' Jane answered slowly, finding it

difficult to speak of those distant happenings now brought so poignantly close by the impending marriage.

'Why was he going to France?' Margaret continued. She looked up into her mother's face almost as if she wished to read by Jane's expression the truth of the matter.

'Scotland was in a very unsettled state,' Jane told her, picking her words carefully. 'And the King had enemies and thought it wiser to send his heir away for a time.'

'That was grandfather,' Margaret said. 'Do all kings have enemies or was he not a very good king?'

'He was an old man and had suffered with his health for many years. That prevented him from attending to his responsibilities properly.'

Jane felt as if the quiet room was closing in on her as Margaret went on as if she had not heard the last sentence.

'Do you think father has enemies?'

'No!' Jane protested. 'Of course not, he is much too wise and hard working for his people's good to make foes.'

Her pulse quickened as she tried to keep her voice calm and changed the topic of conversation to speak of the court of France as she had heard James tell her from his visit there for Catherine and Henry's wedding.

'Father said it was the most splendid marriage ceremony in Tours Cathedral with a sumptuous feast afterwards.'

'Was it as wonderful as yours?' Margaret asked.

Jane smiled, glad to have reached calmer waters after floundering in the dangerous undercurrents of the last few minutes.

Her own wedding day was an often repeated story for her daughters but they never tired of hearing of the magnificence Henry Beaufort had provided for his niece.

Now she searched in her memory for any little detail with which to divert Margaret and allay the disquiet lying at the back of her own mind.

Margaret listened apparently enthralled.

'Did father look very handsome in his cloth of gold doublet?'

'Yes,' Jane replied remembering with a contraction of her throat how fine James had been as they met in the porch of St. Mary's Church. How fortunate she had been to have married a man she loved so deeply and who had returned her love with a passionate devotion that needed not only her body but the comfort and companionship. How different it was and how cruel, for this child beside her, so like her in her glowing fairness, to be sent to France to marry a boy she had never seen.

In an uprush of emotion she bent and kissed the top of Margaret's head. The girl looked up, surprised.

'Louis will be a king one day, won't he?' she asked a little later.

'He will,' Jane agreed, thinking of the complicated agreements between the two kings if either of the children should die before the consummation of the marriage.

'Heavens!' she thought to herself. 'I am so morbid minded this morning I shall soon be weeping outright.'

She dropped her sewing and clapped her hands for Walter Stratton, her chamber page who was sitting outside the door of the room on his customary stool.

The boy came at once, a fresh faced handsome youth with a burred Scots accent.

'Some wine please Walter,' Jane said. 'Some of that the French ambassadors brought with them.'

'How can Louis become King of France when Henry of England has already been crowned in Notre Dame?' Margaret went on. 'Isabella tells me if she married him she will be Queen of France and England!'

'Where do you children hear all this talk?' Jane said in the despairing manner of parents who think they have kept their offspring apart from the gossip of the world about them.

Margaret was prevented from replying by Walter who returned at this moment with a salver and two jewelled cups. With dignity he set this on the table and poured out the wine, offering it first with a deep bow to Jane and then with a most engaging smile and a slightly smaller bow to Margaret.

Jane saw her daughter's answering look of pleasure and sipped quickly at the wine. She felt it easing her dry throat and coursing through her veins.

'We have sewn enough for this day,' she said. 'Let us go and see if there are daffodils beside the loch.'

Later, when the palace lay hushed in the stillness of night, she was sleepless, filled with anxiety not only for Margaret and her unknown future but for James also. Her daughter with her artless questioning had uncovered a dread from which she had previously shied away. Now the subject refused to return to the dark recesses of her mind where she was usually able to confine it. It was as if her suffering for her child reawoke her misgivings for her beloved husband.

She searched her mind for possible enemies of James. She disregarded the Earl of March but found her fears mounting as more and more possibilities presented themselves to her. Unredeemed hostages had been a constant source of discontent, while Sir Robert Graham and James Stewart were still believed to be harbouring traitorous thoughts against their sovereign. The Earl of Atholl and the Lord of the Isles were unknown quantities although Jane comforted herself with the knowledge that of late the young ruler of the Isles had given no further cause for suspected disloyalty. Since his pardon he had returned to Skye and carried out his duties to the best of his ability. Other Highland chieftains, lawless and mostly lacking in any education, possessed by inborn inter clan feuds gave James trouble from time to time but theirs was the rebellion of undisciplined children rather than calculated personal hatred.

Jane suddenly saw before her in the enveloping dark the arrogant face of the Earl of Atholl. She had never liked the old man and while James had been generously inclined to trust him as a half brother of his father she had never been able to agree with him. There was something about Atholl which aroused her dislike. She was reminded of the Duke of Gloucester for he had much the same manner, unctuous but with a supercilious air of condescension. Many times she had thought to speak of her animosity to James but of late she had realised there was no need for he was only too aware of the Earl's hostility since his heir still languished in the Tower.

Unable to suffer her thoughts Jane put out her arm and drew herself closer to James. He murmured her name and tightened his hold and comforted by his warmth she slept at last.

But the anxiety she felt refused to leave her waking hours.

James did not talk of his own concern for his daughter and threw himself into the preparations for the provisioning of the little fleet which was to accompany her to France.

He chose her escort with meticulous care, deciding upon the Earl of Orkney, son of the man who had been in charge of his own ill-fated expedition and who had throughout the thirteen years of his reign proved himself a loyal supporter. Under him he put Walter Ogilvy and a Bishop to act as spiritual mentor.

When the time came to depart for Dumbarton he could not bring himself to witness the leave taking between Jane and their daughter. He had been conscious of his wife's growing distress and in his own unhappiness had been unable to bring her alleviation of her misery.

Many times during the past weeks he had longed for the comparative peace of the life of

313

a small laird where he would be free to enjoy the delights of family life without the constant scheming and planning confronting him day by day. He found himself wondering more and more often if Scotland was worth the effort and sacrifice she demanded.

Margaret came out from mother's parlour pale and subdued and hardly spoke during the journey to the port.

The sight of the eleven ships drawn up at the quay or standing off from the shore with pennants streaming in the March breeze revived her interest and she clapped her hands with pleasure when she saw the quarters James had had made ready for her and the women Jane had spared from her household.

From his own experience in the Maryenknight James had ordered a small cabin to be built with bunks attached to the ship's side. Woollen hangings covered the bulwarks and canvas hid the decks. Soft mattresses made the beds more tolerable.

They ate a little of the food served to them on plate and linen especially brought from Holyrood, but neither of them were hungry and at length James pushed his platter aside almost untouched.

At last, the silence between them deepening, he rose and said he must be leaving her.

He drew the small figure towards him and told her to be of good cheer and remember what she did was for Scotland and her own future. He found himself unable to continue as the enormity of what he asked her to do struck him. Suddenly he hated Scotland with a vehemence which surprised him.

'We shall talk about you often and pray for you every day,' he managed to tell her.

At last it was she who brought the sad little interview to a close.

'Goodbye, Father,' she said keeping her eyes wide. James seeing the taut young face felt his heart contract in his chest and it was almost more than he could do to stop himself gathering her up in his arms and rushing home with her.

'You better be going now or we shall miss the tide, give my love to mo — ' she faltered.

James bent and kissed her swiftly on the forehead and rushed headlong from the cabin.

He hardly rested until he heard the fleet had put in safely at la Rochelle and Margaret had been warmly received by the French people.

Not until some months later was news brought to him of English ships which had waited to intercept her convoy and had been diverted at the moment of their possible meeting by a line of Flemish ships carrying wine. The English had been unable to resist the promise of plunder and had sheered off leaving the sea clear for the French fleet.

The marriage duly took place in the following June at Tours, the young bridegroom guided throughout the long ceremony by his tutor Bernard of Armagnac. Margaret was supported by Orkney and Ogilvy who returned immediately to Scotland leaving her with her women and Maurice Buchan her newly appointed treasurer.

James set himself the task of raising the expenses he had incurred to divert himself during this period, refusing to tax the country to this end. He had written, however, many personal letters to ecclesiastical and other bodies he had helped and had been gratified by the response he received. At the end of the exercise only a handful of local traders were owed small sums.

With this accomplished he threw himself into the arrangements for the next meeting of Parliament.

He was in the midst of these when Thomas Roulle, returning from one of his visits to London, brought news of Gloucester taking an army to support his brother Bedford in France.

'Does he so!' James shouted, banging his fist on the table. 'Then this is the moment, by heaven, to set about retrieving Roxburgh.'

Thomas looked at his master in amazement but James was still speaking.

'If Gloucester has had to go to France the English cause must be in a bad way indeed. It looks as if this Joan of Arc has been able to accomplish more than any man to unite the French armies.'

'Yes, and not only that, your Grace, but Burgundy has completely broken away from the English and thrown in his lot with the French; most people think he will not return to Bedford this time.'

'No wonder Charles did not need my troops,' James said. 'Thank God my daughter will have less difficult times to contend with than I feared. Now is the moment to show both my gratitude and support of the treaty — ' he stopped as a sudden thought struck him. 'Did you see the Earl of Northumberland when you were at Westminster?'

'He arrived very shortly after I did,' Thomas told him.

'And was he still there when you left?'

'As far as I know, my lord.'

'That's good,' James said. 'I do not want to come face to face with him should the taking of Roxburgh prove difficult.'

He quickly made known his intentions of restoring the border town to the Scottish crown and received more approval for his decision than for anything he had projected since his return to Scotland. A still small voice told him there should be a warning in this but he chose to ignore it and pressed on with his preparations, secretly pleased to be able to put into operation the skill he had acquired from Henry during their campaigns in France.

He saw personally to the equipping of his army and attended several demonstrations of the new cannons he had ordered from Flanders. Their mechanism caused much head scratching to the older warriors but he was delighted with their ingenuity and named one of them the Lion as a proof of its indomitable strength. He was convinced their power would reduce Roxburgh in a day or two at the most.

For the first time in his married life he did not tell Jane of his intentions. He had been especially tender towards her since Margaret's departure and saw no reason for adding to her distress by announcing his intention of making war against her country. He dismissed any thought of guilt he might be experiencing and if she mentioned his preoccupation with the Army he told her he was making certain of its preparedness. When the time came to set out for the English border he merely told her he had had word of possible trouble, kissed her fondly and hurried off.

It was now Autumn and in the early light of dawn the countryside was peacefully wrapped in mist. The progress of the large force James had amassed, encumbered as it was by the new engines, was slow and they crawled their way to the Border.

James was dismayed to discover when he sent scouts to reconnoitre that while it had been relatively easy to keep his intentions from Jane the English had not been so gullible.

The men who reported back to him leapt from the backs of their sweating mounts and said Roxburgh had already taken up its drawbridge and from what they heard at outlying farmsteads had stocked up with sufficient food to fill the town's granaries and storehouses. If this was not disheartening enough, other crofters to the south had told of large numbers of men marching daily to join the banner of Northumberland and the other Marcher Lords.

James cursed the ill luck which had allowed the English to become aware of his preparations but stubbornly refused to call off his army.

He made a personal round of his troops on the first night of their arrival and saw to the positioning of the guns and other large weapons. He found the men in good heart and looking forward to what he had described to them as a swift and easy victory.

He went for a short sleep confident of success. At cockscrow he ordered the attack and watched with pleasure his well trained archers and gunners stand at the ready to release their arrows and gunshot. For some reason most of these seemed to fall short of the target and he waved the bowmen forward. Now the arrows fell into the town and he gave the word for another volley of gunfire. With deep rumblings the engines belched smoke and the balls sped towards the town. James waited for the walls to crumble but nothing happened.

Neither did it on this day or the next or the day after, while deadly accurate fire from the ramparts carried off more of his men than he cared to count. His captains told him of an increasingly large amount of desertion and he was forced to admit his troops were not of the same calibre as those who had fought for Henry V in France.

At the end of a fortnight when daily

attempts to scale the walls and break into the town had been repulsed he realised his task was hopeless. He decided to return to Edinburgh.

Almost as he gave the order to strike camp it began to rain and before long the heavy waggons and cannon were axle deep in the mire of the farmyards where they had been positioned.

It took hours of digging and unloading to shift even a few of these while the rain beat down relentlessly on the soldiers. It was a miserable, bedraggled company who set out at last leaving vast quantities of equipment behind them.

James was disappointed and full of disgust for himself. He recognised his pride had suffered a severe blow and he blamed himself for his failure to push forward an effective attack. It was little comfort to realise his troops were not sufficiently well-trained to undertake the objective; this was also his fault. As had been his inability to instill those in command under him with enough authority to lead their troops properly.

He arrived at Linlithgow, where Jane had gone in his absence, tired and dispirited. She was full of concern for his weariness making him feel more guilty than ever but he allowed her to help him to bed and bring him some food. Later as he held her in his arms and the dark gave him courage he confessed what he had sought to do at Roxburgh.

She comforted him as well as she was able making no censure. She was torn between relief at his safety and sadness for his hurt pride. She knew full well it was not the time for him to suffer any reversals and hoped he would regard this episode as fulfilment of his treaty obligations to France and allow the Borders to rest in peace.

This proved to be the case and James tried to forget the matter as he became more involved with the business of the Parliament he had interrupted to make his abortive bid against Roxburgh.

However, his failure irked him more than he would have thought possible and the measures he proposed to introduce were a direct result of the effect this had upon him.

Orkney and several of his other commanders had reported that the wholesale desertions could have been prevented but that other officers were too negligent and easy going to care. This could only mean James did not have the backing of those in command. He determined to punish them by restricting their powers even further than hitherto and by taking away from them their right to try malefactors at courts of their own calling.

Jane attempted to dissuade him from being too severe but he told her he had not been able to govern successfully with the half hearted support of his magnates and he would now have to try on his own.

'They are an undisciplined lot from the castle to the croft,' he told her in a snatched hour when they went sailing on the loch in a little boat she had bought while he was at Roxburgh. 'I've done my best for them and they are too stupid and hotheaded to realise strict discipline is what a man and a country needs.'

Wondering if perhaps he was speaking to encourage himself as much as criticise his peers she told him they had not all his sense of purpose and ducked her head as he put the boat about.

When the wind had filled the sail again and the craft moved with gathering speed across the water James returned to the topic.

'Any troops who were properly commanded should have been able to save the equipment we lost at Roxburgh. The waste of those valuable guns and engines horrifies me. Alway tells me there was much drinking by the commanders and that they ordered double issue of beer for the men each time they went into action. This is what I think made them careless.'

'Did you give the authority for this?'

'No, of course not!' James retorted. 'Lee ho!'

The little boat went about and the sail filled with the crack of a whiplash as James pushed the helm over with the strength of his irritability.

'I am thinking of introducing some measure to curtail the hours of drinking in the inns and alehouses. When I set these places up as rest houses for travellers to keep strangers from seeking shelter under any lord's roof I did not intend they should become haunts where men could waste hours in drinking and gambling. Why is it Jane, that when one tries to give generously people will always take a little more than their share?'

He had cause for personal anxiety on this score for three or four of the burgesses from whom he had obtained goods for his daughter's fleet were pressing him for payment. He had had occasion in the past to grant each of them some favour and although he had been reluctant to place himself in their debt the sums had not been large and he had not anticipated them waiting long for their money. It was a measure of his shortcomings in his own estimation that these quite humble men should not be in a position to press for the return of their credit. Several times he brought himself to the brink of asking Jane to come to his rescue for she had lately been granted a small annual pension by Parliament but he drew back ashamed of his poor husbandry.

He shut his mind to his troubles and applied himself to the sheer pleasure of sending the boat swiftly across the lake. There were other things in life beside the constant search for money. It would soon be Christmas and the family would be reunited even if it were only for a short period. He made up his mind to summon the Court to Perth for this year's festivities.

19

'Perth!' Jane exclaimed when he told her of his decision 'But would you rather not be here in Linlithgow?'

'Yes,' James admitted. 'But with the conviction I have that Perth should become the capital of Scotland we must foster the idea of holding the big festivals there.'

Jane shrugged her shoulders and bent swiftly to kiss him on his cheek. Of late she had found it necessary to humour him more often and the venue for Christmas was nothing compared with the family being together. She bit her lip remembering the small daughter who would be so alone and was glad James had thought of sending Marjorie Norton to Tours to be with the child. The elderly nurse had expressed horror at crossing the channel at the worst time of the year but had gone willingly enough in the end as Jane had known she would. Since the birth of two more daughters to James and Jane the nursery had become rather beyond her with several new undernurses filling the rooms with their prattle and fluttering skirts and she was secretly pleased to be going where her word would once more be law.

In the latest despatch Buchan reported the safe arrival of the nurse, pale and a little shaky in the legs but quickly recovering from this when she saw Margaret's delight in her coming. Buchan told his master and mistress that their daughter was becoming a great favourite of the French King and hinted delicately that the marriage had not been consummated as the Dauphin was a studious boy not yet ready for the fleshy delights of marriage.

Jane went to the private chapel and gave sincere thanks for this mercy and doubled her daily prayers that the day of consummation might be long delayed. She felt as if she betrayed James while she prayed in this manner but her maternal instincts were stronger in this instance than her desire for the peaceful coexistence of France and Scotland.

Once she had learnt Perth was to be the place where they would spend Christmas she started making the preparations entailed in transporting a large household. She was midway to completing this when James came rushing into the linen room where she was supervising the sorting of sheets.

'Henry is coming for Christmas!' he shouted, brandishing a letter above his head.

'Henry?' Jane said somewhat bewildered as she had fleeting visions of the young King of England spending the festival with them.

'Yes. Northumberland and his wife are bringing some of their children.'

'Oh, that will be wonderful!' Jane cried. 'James and the girls will enjoy having other children to play with for a change and it will be pleasant to have Eleanor and Henry to talk over old times.'

'We must send word on to Perth to prepare extra chambers for them. There is a new controller of the household there, Robert Stewart — '

'Robert Stewart,' Jane echoed, slowly bringing her mind from assessing the amount of linen required for these new guests.

'Is he not one of Atholl's grandsons?'

'Yes, yes,' James agreed, walking over to the casement and looking down into the courtyard beneath. 'The old man asked me to give him the opportunity of proving he can do more than squabble with his neighbours.'

Jane said nothing but as she turned over the sheets inspecting them for holes for the darning woman a small disquiet obtruded into the task and set in motion the fears never far from her mind.

Since the last time James had not tried to conceal from her the amount of open opposition his measures had aroused. Several times he had had to send troops to put down small insurrections. These seemed nothing more than acts destined to harass James but he had taken no chances and had immediately clapped the instigators into prison. There would be several noble families not celebrating a very happy Christmas.

She shivered suddenly and pushed the rest of the linen aside; it seemed of little importance if it required mending or not.

James was still in the room. She took his hand and led him to her parlour.

'Play to me, love,' she said picking up her lute and giving it to him.

He looked at her quickly and turned her face to him. Seeing the tears filling her eyes he mistook her unhappiness for grief for her absent daughter and taking the lute up he played the opening chords of a lullaby she often sang to the children.

'Not that,' she pleaded. 'Something other.' He led her over to the window seat and drew her down beside him. More accurately assessing the cause of her distress he played the same melody he had sung when they had met for the first time in Catherine's solar.

His voice, still as melodious as on that golden evening thirteen years before, broke down her control and she began to cry. James stopped in amazement and throwing down the lute took her in his arms. She sobbed while he murmured endearments until at last his familiar nearness comforted her and she was quiet, lying limply against him.

'Dear heart,' James said with concern. 'Are you ailing? Is it not another child?' he asked suddenly.

'No,' Jane reassured him in a muffled voice. 'It's not that. Perhaps I am just a little tired and with Margaret — '

'Yes, we can't help feeling sad, but with the other children to think about we must try to be as gay as possible.'

'Yes, of course,' Jane said and sat up straightening her pleated wimple. 'Now, I expect my nose is all red.'

'No, it isn't,' James said with a little smile. He went back to the linen room and returned with a napkin.

'Dry your eyes on this and we'll have our supper sent up here and go to bed early. How would you like that?'

'Very much,' she replied in a small voice.

He made much of her during the evening sending away her waiting women and dismissing Walter Stratton and Alway. A hot fire of Durham seacoal lit the bedchamber and warmed the chill air. James carried Jane to the bed and took off her bedrobe. Her

flesh gleamed golden in the soft light.

'Aye, sweeting,' he said quietly. 'You'[re] lovely as the day we were married. Perha[ps a] little stouter with all the child bearing b[ut it] becomes you well. What would I not giv[e to] be able to leave all the troubles of our [life] here and go away to one of our lonely islan[ds] for a week, or a month or better still for ev[er.] Just the two of us and none of the myriads [of] people we seem to have collected about u[s.] Even the Bass would be acceptable with foo[d] and plenty of driftwood!'

Jane laughed and kissed him on the mouth, delighting in the strength of his arms as he pulled her close to him. She gave herself to him in passionate abandonment and was lost in the enchantment of his lovemaking. When, much later, he gently released her from his embrace he found she was already asleep, her eyelashes lying dark on the curve of her cheek. He kissed her softly and drifted into sleep.

She was much happier during the remainder of their stay in Linlithgow and set out for Edinburgh where they were to rest before continuing to Perth in good heart.

The day was cold and damp, lowering clouds obscuring the hills and forests and they were glad to come into Holyrood where food and fires had been prepared for them.

Jane went to bed praying for fine weather while they passed through the woods that lay between Edinburgh and Perth. She was not disappointed for the day was bright with a hint of frost. She was eager to make an early start for Michael Ramsay had already left Doune and had been in the royal lodgings in the Blackfriars at Perth for several days. She chaffed at the delay when some important state documents could not be found until Thomas Roulle discovered them hidden beneath a pile of linen and they were able to set out.

Once across the Firth the sky of palest blue was laced with the black branches of the hundreds of trees towering above them. As they clattered through the forest startled deer darted in and out of the boles and rabbits fled before them with scuts flashing white in the dried bracken. Streamers of old Man's beard festooned the bare bramble bushes and birds rose from the hedges on heavy wings.

Now and again they passed a charcoal burner with his back bent under a load of wood and once a troop of students gowned and hooded.

As the short day was fading into twilight they came down the last winding hill before the Tay. The river gleamed silver in the dusk and the crowd gathered at the ferry head

were dimly visible against it. They turned at the noise of the oncoming troop cantering over the frozen roadway and as some of the foremost recognised the banner of the king, drew aside to allow his party to cross over before them.

James dismounted and waved them on. He was in the genial relaxed mood of the Christmas season and he did not want to push his way past the weary men and women returning from a hard day's toil in mill or farmyard. The crowd, realising his intention retaliated with shouts of good wishes.

As James and Jane waited huddled in their mantles against the cold a man unloaded a pile of sticks he was carrying and kindled a fire.

'Come over here,' he called to the furwrapped women, 'and warm your pretty fingers.'

Laughing and pleased Jane and the others went to the fire as it spluttered into life. More sticks and twigs appeared from the onlookers and a warm glow lit the circle of waiting men and women.

James crossed to his wife's side and put his hands towards the blaze. At the same moment indistinguishable shouting was heard and a disturbance jostled the rear of the crowd.

'Where's the King? Who said the King was come?' a hoarse voice could be heard calling.

'Here! He is here!' the crowd answered and with some difficulty, for she carried two large fish baskets, an old woman elbowed her way to the front.

The light of the fire halted her for a moment and she peered round the circle. James and Jane saw a woman of medium height, her face lined and leathery with years of exposure to all weathers, dressed in hodden grey. Over her head and shoulders was a coarse woollen scarf.

Suddenly she found what she sought and was standing before them.

'Go ye to Perth?' she demanded of James, dropping her two baskets from which fish spilled in a silver shower on to the earth.

Without appearing to notice she pointed up to the sky and then straight to James. For a long minute she did not speak. Then she screamed in a high pitched cracked voice, compellingly different from before.

'Return ye whence ye come! I have dreamed of doom!'

Alway and several other gentlemen at arms recovered from their initial surprise and picking up the old woman by her elbows carried her away from the fire. Protesting violently she could be heard still screaming of doom until they were out of earshot.

Jane closed her eyes and took a deep breath. She found she was shaking from head to foot and turned to James about to suggest they turned back, so deeply had she been shocked by the awe inspiring moment.

She stopped as she saw James on his knees pushing the spilled fish back into the baskets.

'Poor old woman,' he said in his normal voice. 'She will be distracted when she finds she has lost her fish. Come Jane, the ferry has returned and if we are to be in Blackfriars this evening we had best take it.'

He hurried her along beside him giving her no opportunity to speak and when they stood close in the barge in the cover of darkness he took her hand in his. Gradually her fear subsided and by the time the ferry had grated on the pebbles of the opposite shore she was recovered enough to be looking forward once again to seeing their children.

They were waiting for her in the long stone dining room of their lodging, demure and shining with cleanliness. Before she could greet them she had to receive the formal greeting of Sir Robert Stewart and the dignitaries from the monastery and the town he had gathered to pay their respects. She spoke to them with her usual courtesy her eyes darting now and again to take in the appearance of her children. She noted in quick appraisal that they all looked in good health; but was the birthmark on James' cheek a little more prominent than before and was Joanna, the second youngest, quite as aware as the others of what was happening in the crowded room?

She accepted the blessing of the Abbot of the Blackfriars and then gestured to the pages who were hovering near to serve the wine. Seeing all the dignitaries with cups in their hands she slipped over to the line of waiting children and moved along them as they curtsied or bowed before her. The bear-like hugs and damp warm kisses would come later in the privacy of the nurseries. Now she contented herself with taking the baby Annabella from her nurse and looking at them each in turn.

She turned smiling to Michael Ramsay and the nurses who stood behind their charges.

'You have done well, sir,' she said. 'All the children look in excellent health and have surely grown.'

'Yes, mother,' the little James said proudly. 'Nurse tells me I have added another notch on the door at Doune.'

'Well done,' Jane cried. 'And Isabella you are quite a young lady and Eleanor and Mary have grown also.'

'Yes, mother and even Joanna is fatter.'

Jane looked down at her little namesake who had crept to her side and was fingering the fur edging of her long sleeve. Jane gave Annabella to her nurse and took Joanna up into her arms.

'Well, pretty?' she said gently, lifting the little rounded head to look into the child's round blue eyes. Joanna smiled and Jane hugged her to her bosom glancing up at the child's nurse as she did so, raising her eyebrows in enquiry. The woman shook her head almost imperceptibly and with a sense of dismay Jane held the baby more tightly and talked to the other children.

James, watching her from the other side of the room where he was engrossed in endless conversation with dignitaries who wished to draw his attention to their many problems, thought how beautiful she looked.

Later when at last the guests had departed they talked about their children. Jane was most anxious for Joanna, for her nurse had told her their fears for her being deaf were well founded and that this affliction would most probably lead to her being dumb as well.

'We must ensure she is helped as much as possible,' James said. 'She should not suffer so much with all the people who are about to assist her. I think she is the prettiest of all the girls.'

'Do you?' Jane said quickly.

'Yes, and the most like you!'

It was the happiest Christmas they had spent together. James spared no expense to entertain Henry and his family, Bishop Wardlaw, Orkney and the other nobles who came to Blackfriars. Food of the richest and most varied was served and entertainers had been found from France and Italy.

The Yule log burnt steadily through the twelve days of the celebration and Alexander Ogilvy acquitted himself admirably as Lord of Misrule. The wooden rafters rang with laughter and song and when all was over and his guests had made their farewells those remaining agreed James had learnt much from the English not least being the lavish hospitality with which he had marked the anniversary of the birth of the Saviour.

Henry and his family departed after Twelfth night and James rode with them for the part of the way to Edinburgh where they would stay before continuing to Alnwick. Henry and he spent several hours talking with Wardlaw, who was now an old man, racked with rheumatics and querulous with the shortcomings of the younger generation.

Both he and Henry told James that if he

did not take more exercise he would soon be as round as he was high. James laughed and promised to see what he could do about it once the next Parliament was over.

James parted from Henry, wishing him Godspeed for his journey and arranging another meeting as soon as possible.

He watched their cavalcade until a dip in the road hid the Northumberland banner from sight, then turning his horse rode back at speed to Perth. His entourage arrived at Blackfriars out of breath and protesting at his recklessness.

He laughed off their fears and called for Jane to come and drink a cup of wine with them. In good spirits they settled down at the fireside to talk over the last two weeks.

The next Parliament was to be held in Perth and James approached the task of preparing amendments and new proposals with renewed energy. Christmas and the happiness it had brought had given him a fresh impetus to tackle his problems.

'We shall find a solution to all our difficulties,' he told Jane. 'We must if we are to keep Scotland on the road to recovery. This Parliament should prove once and for all who is for me and who against.'

Jane enjoyed his optimism, listening intently as he read over the drafts of some of the proposed measures, interposing a comment here and there.

She was happier at Perth than she had dared hope and had to admit Sir Robert Stewart had put himself to endless trouble to make their residence in the Blackfriars comfortable. For the first time for years James felt able to spare the Ogilvies and Alway and had sent them on visits to their families. Walter Stratton had proved an able substitute, waiting on James with punctilious courtesy and anticipating his every need.

A few days after Twelfth Night Ramsay brought their six children to make their farewells to their parents.

Jane promised them she would come to Doune as soon as the Council was over even if James were too busy.

'When may we come to Linlithgow and sail your boat?' little James asked her.

'At Easter perhaps,' Jane told him. 'That is if the weather is settled, if not it will have to be in June. June is always a lovely month at Linlithgow.'

'Will father teach me to sail?'

'Of course, there is nothing he would like more. Now go back to Doune and learn all the lessons Mr. Ramsay sets you; and you will take care of your sisters, won't you?'

For days after they were gone Jane avoided

the rooms where the childish laughter had resounded and busied herself in the matters of the household. James took her riding with him and she walked beside him when he played golf.

They rode one morning over the moors beyond Perth, the air clear and sweet scented. James kept a tight rein on his horse so that he should not outstrip Jane's little mare. The winter landscape was majestic with its bare trees and long vistas of uninhabited emptiness. They returned to Blackfriars exhilarated and happy.

Later they relaxed in the small parlour set aside for their use during their stay in Blackfriars. James worked at some papers while Jane sat at the fireside, a piece of tapestry on her lap. Now and again she made an attempt to put in a few stitches but most of the time she sat and watched her husband, delighting in the dark, well shaped head as he bent over his work.

Walter Stratton perched apart, awaiting any signal from James.

One of Jane's women came in and asked if she were ready to go to bed but Jane smilingly dismissed her and said she would look after herself.

James did not stir and they sat in perfect domestic peace, her heart full of the love they shared. Once he looked up and their eyes met across the shadowy room; he smiled and gazed at her for a timeless moment.

'Walter,' he called softly. 'Would you fetch us some wine please.'

The boy jumped up and was gone. James stretched himself and putting down his quill came over to her side. He drew up a stool and sat beside her taking her hand. She raised it to her cheek and kissed the palm. He reached out to stroke her hair and as he did so a piercing scream shocked them to their feet.

James rushed to the table for his sword and Jane, panic making her heart race, picked up the poker.

The door of the parlour was pushed roughly open and men poured into the room, the glint of steel filling the once peaceful scene.

'The King. We want the King!'

At once seven or eight of the foremost men, who Jane recognised in a flash of horror included Sir Robert Stewart and Sir Robert Graham rushed on James with raised swords. Jane flew at them brandishing the poker but was intercepted by another man who turning quickly pierced her uplifted arm with his dagger. Jane screamed as the pain seared through her and blood poured over the velvet of her gown. Summoning all her strength she clutched the wounded arm and tried to push her way through the massed men who were surrounding James. She could only see part of him as he tried desperately to fight off those who were attacking him. His sword flashed above his head as he shielded himself from the rain of sword thrusts aimed at every section of his unarmoured body.

As she struggled to come to him one of the assailants, who looked like a burgher, pushed her roughly away and she fell. Staggering to her feet again, faint with loss of blood, she saw James fall among his attackers as sword after sword pierced him.

Mercifully she lost consciousness and heard through a haze of pain the King's household led by Sir David Dunbar burst into the chamber too late to save their master. It had all happened so quickly the men had only their bedrobes about them and they gave instant chase to the murderers who were already leaving the monastery and making good their escape.

Dunbar rushed to James but one glance at the myriad wounds told him the King was dead. He turned his attention to the Queen and shouted for assistance. The monastery was filled with confusion as soldiers came running from their quarters buckling on armour as they dashed out into the night.

Catherine Douglas, one of Jane's women came timidly to the door of the room and Dunbar supporting the queen sent her scurrying for linen and water. Jane still lived he knew but the sleeve of her dress was ripped out and an ugly wound in her upper arm was bleeding fast. Dunbar fretted as the woman seemed gone for hours but she returned and ran quickly to Jane's side. She was stripping the sleeve when one of the monks she had aroused came in with a box of herbs and a salve. He bent quickly to the wounded queen and with deft movements applied the salve and a wad of lint and showed Catherine how to continue winding the strips of linen over the injury. Jane's eyes fluttered for an instant and the monk spoke soothingly to her and she closed them again. He bade Dunbar have her carried to her bed chamber and said he would mix a potion so that if she stirred she would sleep again and have a chance to recover from the horror of what she had just witnessed.

When she was gone other monks came hurrying in to attend to James. Most of them averted their eyes from the terribly mutilated corpse and hastened to cover it and remove it to the chapel.

The household rushed to question those who had gone out into the night in a fruitless effort to find the assailants.

'Where is Robert Stewart?' Dunbar demanded.

'Not in his chamber.'

'Where is he then? How was it the doors were unbarred so that all these vile people were able to come in? Where were the watch?'

'How was it that poor child Walter Stratton was the only person awake at the time of the murder? Why was there no one at hand to intercept his murderers and prevent them coming into the King?'

All night the mournful questioning went on but it was not until one of the Queen's women came for Sir David in the late afternoon of the following day that a true picture of what had occurred could be formed.

Sir David found Jane sitting propped up against many pillows, so pale and ethereal he hardly recognised her.

'My lady,' he began. 'May I — '

'Please,' she said. 'Let us not speak of sympathy.'

Dunbar stopped, a conflict of emotion almost choking him.

'Was anyone of the murderers caught, Sir David?'

'No, my lady,' Dunbar said regretfully. 'We came too late upon the scene and although we have searched all night we have taken no one. We are hampered by not knowing who we are looking for.'

'But I know,' Jane said in a tight, hard voice. 'Sir Robert Graham, Sir Robert Stewart, burghers from Edinburgh — '

'Sir Robert Stewart!' Dunbar cried incredulously. 'So that is how they gained access and disposed of the guard.'

'There were others,' Jane said. 'Men I did not know.'

She sank back wearily against the pillow.

'Find them Sir David,' she said so low he could hardly understand her. 'Find them. They shall meet their just reward for depriving Scotland of their finest man.'

'Do not fret, your Grace. We shall not rest now we know for whom we seek.'

⋆   ⋆   ⋆

As soon as she was able she dragged herself from her bed and went to the Charterhouse where James had been laid, washed now and clothed in the doublet of gold in which he had been crowned and married. He looked peaceful and serene, his wounds hidden.

Jane sent away the attendant monks who kept watch and motioned Ogilvy and Alway, who had come hurrying back to be with her, to stand outside the door.

When they were gone she knelt beside the body. For a time she could not see for the tears blinding her but at last she forced herself to look at his face and touched his hand.

'Dear heart,' she whispered. 'Thank you for our life together and all you tried to do for Scotland. I shall see it is never forgotten.'

She knelt for a long time until the cold struck through her, numbing her, then bending swiftly, kissed James on the mouth.

An hour later, composed and rigid in her straight backed chair she sent for the Chancellor, Orkney, James' confessor, Thomas Roulle and John Lyon.

'I shall not rest,' she said, 'until this foul deed has been revenged. I shall have the heads of those who murdered the finest King Scotland has ever known!'

We do hope that you have enjoyed reading this large print book.

Did you know that all of our titles are available for purchase?

We publish a wide range of high quality large print books including:
Romances, Mysteries, Classics
General Fiction
Non Fiction and Westerns

Special interest titles available in large print are:
The Little Oxford Dictionary
Music Book
Song Book
Hymn Book
Service Book

Also available from us courtesy of Oxford University Press:
Young Readers' Dictionary
(large print edition)
Young Readers' Thesaurus
(large print edition)

For further information or a free brochure, please contact us at:
Ulverscroft Large Print Books Ltd.,
The Green, Bradgate Road, Anstey,
Leicester, LE7 7FU, England.
Tel: (00 44) 0116 236 4325
Fax: (00 44) 0116 234 0205

Other titles in the
Ulverscroft Large Print Series:

STRANGER IN THE PLACE

Anne Doughty

Elizabeth Stewart, a Belfast student and only daughter of hardline Protestant parents, sets out on a study visit to the remote west coast of Ireland. Delighted as she is by the beauty of her new surroundings and the small community which welcomes her, she soon discovers she has more to learn than the details of the old country way of life. She comes to reappraise so much that is slighted and dismissed by her family — not least in regard to herself. But it is her relationship with a much older, Catholic man, Patrick Delargy, which compels her to decide what kind of life she really wants.

IF HE LIVED

Jon Stephen Fink

Lillian is a woman who feels too much. As a psychiatric nurse, she empathizes with her patients; as a mother, she mourns for her lost, runaway daughter. Now suddenly she has a new feeling, that her house, one of the oldest in the small Massachusetts town where she lives with her husband Freddy, has been invaded, violated by some past evil. And then Lillian sees the boy . . .

MERMAID'S GROUND

Alice Marlow

It's been five years since Kate Williams' beloved husband died, leaving her with two young children to raise. Now she's built a good life in one of Wiltshire's prettiest villages, and she has her dream job, as gardener at Moxham Court. For the last year, Kate has had a lover, roguishly attractive Justin Spencer, but he won't commit to more than a night here and there. When she takes in a male lodger, Jem, Kate's secretly hoping his presence will provoke a jealous reaction in Justin. What she hasn't reckoned on is exactly how attractive Jem will turn out to be.

HOT POPPIES

Reggie Nadelson

A murder in New York's diamond district. A dead Chinese girl with a photograph in her pocket. A plastic bag of irradiated heroin in an empty apartment. A fire in a Chinatown sweatshop. The worst blizzard in New York's history. These events conspire to bring ex-cop Artie Cohen out of retirement and back into the obsessive world of murder and politics that nearly killed him. The terrifying plot uncoils first in New York — in Artie's own back yard — then in Hong Kong, where everything — and everyone — is for sale.